D

MW00648627

Don't miss these other spellbinding novels by
DONNA GRANT

DARK KING SERIES
Dark Heat
Darkest Flame
Fire Rising
Burning Desire
Hot Blooded

DARK WARRIOR SERIES
Midnight's Master
Midnight's Lover
Midnight's Seduction
Midnight's Warrior
Midnight's Kiss
Midnight's Captive
Midnight's Temptation
Midnight's Promise
Midnight's Surrender

DARK SWORD SERIES
Dangerous Highlander
Forbidden Highlander
Wicked Highlander
Untamed Highlander
Shadow Highlander
Darkest Highlander

SHIELD SERIES
A Dark Guardian
A Kind of Magic
A Dark Seduction
A Forbidden Temptation
A Warrior's Heart

DRUIDS GLEN SERIES
Highland Mist
Highland Nights
Highland Dawn
Highland Fires
Highland Magic
Dragonfyre

SISTERS OF MAGIC TRILOGY
Shadow Magic
Echoes of Magic
Dangerous Magic

Royal Chronicles Novella Series
Prince of Desire
Prince of Seduction
Prince of Love
Prince of Passion

Wicked Treasures Novella Series
Seized by Passion
Enticed by Ecstasy
Captured by Desire

**And look for more anticipated novels
from Donna Grant**

The Craving (Rogues of Scotland)
Darkest Flame (Dark Kings)
Wild Dream – (Chiasson)
Fire Rising – (Dark Kings)

coming soon!

A FORBIDDEN TEMPTATION

THE SHIELDS

DONNA GRANT

This is a work of fiction. All of the characters, organizations, and events portrayed in this novel are either products of the author's imagination or are used fictitiously.

A FORBIDDEN TEMPTATION

© 2012 by DL Grant, LLC
Excerpt from *A Warrior's Heart* copyright © 2012 by Donna Grant

Cover design © 2012 by Croco Designs

ISBN 13: 978-0988208452 (ebook)
ISBN 13: 978-0988208469 (print)

www.DonnaGrant.com

Available in ebook and print editions

CHAPTER ONE

Highlands of Scotland
Winter 1436

The icy fingers of winter had nature firmly in her grasp. The cold slammed into Valentinus Romulus's body as soon as he stepped through the time portal. As one of the youngest generals in Rome's great army, he had experienced his fair share of climates. But this one was frigid.

The Highlands, Aimery had told him.

Val blew out a breath and watched it cloud around him through the light of the full moon. The bitter temperatures had him gritting his teeth as he gripped his halberd tightly in his hand.

He wasn't here by chance. It was the magic of the Fae that had moved him through time to this very spot. When he was exactly, he had no idea. But then again, this was part of the work that he loved.

Being a Shield had its advantages. Val loved the constant danger he was in. It made him feel alive, and helped to banish the demons he couldn't shake.

The Shields were fighting mythological creatures wreaking havoc on Earth in order to reach the Chosen – women who had the power to end the evil controlling the beasts. Which is why Val had been brought here.

He scanned the darkness slowly, noting the eerie quiet that had descended upon the area. He drew in a deep breath and frowned.

Evil.

Val quickly crouched down in the thick snow. He was out in the open and the nearest grove of trees was several strides away. He would have to make a dash for it, but the heavy blanket of snow would slow him down.

Just as he was about to bolt, he heard it. The steady flap of wings. Val raised his head and spotted the great beast silhouetted against the dark sky.

"By the gods," he whispered in awe and unease. He hesitated only a heartbeat before he stood and ran to the trees.

The small grove offered little protection. With the shadows hiding him, Val took his time scouting the area. To his left, a castle stood high atop one of the smaller mountains with a village in the valley below. Massive mountains surrounded the area, making it near impossible to reach the town or castle without being seen from many leagues away.

His gaze searched the skies again, and it didn't take him long to find the creature. With no word from Gabriel, the other Shield who was supposed to meet him, Val would have to do this alone.

He missed having Roderick and Elle with him, but with the Great Evil closing in quickly, Roderick had to take Elle and the other Chosen where they could be protected.

Only one more Chosen needed to be found to end the evil. Only one more woman who bore the mark, and then all this could end.

From the brief conversation Val had with Aimery, the Fae Commander had told him that Cole, another Shield, had not only found his mate, but had also found the third Chosen. It was a cause for celebration, but the reveling would have to wait. Evil still had a tight hold on Earth.

Val was about to make his way to the village when he heard the crunch of snow, signaling someone was close. He tensed and gripped his halberd, his weapon of choice, with both hands, ready to strike at a moment's notice.

He molded his back to a tree and waited. Out of the corner of his eye, he saw a shadow against the snow. He stepped out and aimed the point of his halberd at the throat of the man just as he realized who it was.

A soft chuckle, devoid of humor, reached him. Val tried to peer into the hood of the cloaked form but saw only shadows. If he didn't recognize one of his own, he'd have taken his head.

"And here I thought I might receive a warm welcome," came the reply as he swept aside the hood of his cloak. "Especially since I'm freezing my balls off."

Val instantly lowered his weapon and grinned at Gabriel. He clasped Gabriel's forearm with a welcoming smile. "I was beginning to wonder where you were."

"I've been scouting the area," Gabriel replied. "I knew Aimery would have you arrive outside the village."

"Did you see the creature?" Val asked.

Gabriel's silver eyes met his. "I did. I was on my way to the village when you stopped me."

"Then let's go," Val said.

Without another word, the two men started toward the village. Hunting was the second thing they did well. The first was battle, and they were eager to end the beast.

They had gone only a few steps when they heard the

shrill scream.

Val exchanged a look with Gabriel before lengthening his strides to race down the mountain, Gabriel on his heels. They saw the flames of the fires lightening the sky before they reached the village.

"The creature will be after the Chosen one," Gabriel yelled over the cries of the villagers.

Val nodded grimly. "Let's hope we find her in time."

Neither spoke as they reached the village and took in the devastation. Chaos reigned as people ran about, their shrieks echoing in the night. Some held the wounded. Some held the dead.

Yet not all the village had been touched.

"He left us a trail," Val said and pointed to the line of destruction.

Gabriel smiled. "Let's not keep him waiting."

~ ~ ~

Nicole leaned against her door, her heart hammering wildly in her chest. She knew what had come for her, but she didn't have the courage to meet it head on. Instead, she hid in her small cottage while the creature wreaked havoc on the village.

Her breath shook as she inhaled. She closed her eyes, but knew no amount of hiding would change her fate. For too long, she had remained hidden in the hopes that she might have a future.

But no more.

Innocents were dying as the beast looked for her. She feared her death because she knew it would be painful, but she couldn't stand the thought of others dying because of her.

Before she lost her nerve, she turned and swung open

the door. A blast of chilly winter air hit her. With her knees shaking and her heart pounding so hard she thought it might burst from her chest, she fought against hiding once more.

The few pines around her cottage swayed ghostlike in the darkness as the full moon shed its bright beam around her. She gripped the door frame until her knuckles turned white, and she resolved to face her destiny.

Then she lifted her foot and stepped out of her cottage.

Her lungs burned with the cold air, but it was nothing compared to the icy fear in her veins. With slow, unsure steps, Nicole walked to the loch to await her death.

The beauty of the water had always held her spellbound. She had spent many hours here, and decided that it would be a nice place to die. Not many got to choose where they would die, and since she had that privilege, she was going to make the most of it.

She knew the instant the creature arrived. The air around her became heavy, and her entire body froze as the evil encased her.

With one last look over her beloved loch, Nicole turned to face her executioner. Her entire body shook, not with cold but with terror, as she stared up at the beast before her. Only in her nightmares had she seen such a fearsome creature, but the real thing before her would strike terror in the bravest of souls.

The enormous monster that stood easily three times her size had the wings, foreparts, front legs and head of an eagle. His hind paws, tail, and ears were that of a lion. And he was as dark as pitch.

Her gaze slowly traveled up until she looked into the beast's yellow eyes. "God save me," she whispered, unable to do more than pray.

She knew trying to run would only irritate the gryphon

more, prolonging her death with added pain. When his massive claw reached out, Nicole opened her mouth to scream, but it was cut off when the beast wrapped his claw around her throat.

Nicole's blood pounded in her ears as she quickly grabbed hold of the forearm of midnight fur that held her bound and began to slowly lift her from the ground.

She ceased her struggles as she looked into the eyes of the gryphon. All her life, she had feared being ripped limb from limb, when, in fact, the gryphon would only choke out her life.

Tears poured from her eyes as his claw began to tighten around her throat. She didn't want to die, especially for something that wasn't even her fault.

Her throat burned as her air was slowly cut off. Darkness crept around the edges of her vision, signaling her end was near.

Just before she succumbed to the darkness, she thought she saw remorse in the gryphon's eyes.

~ ~ ~

"By the gods," Val hissed as he and Gabriel came upon the creature. "It's a gryphon."

"A what?" Gabriel asked.

"A gryphon," Val repeated. "They aren't supposed to be evil. Never has evil touched them."

Gabriel grunted. "It has now. And he has a woman."

Val didn't stop to wonder if the woman was the Chosen or not. They had to save her. As he and Gabriel started toward the beast, the gryphon threw back his head and screeched. And to their astonishment, the creature released the woman before flying off into the night.

"Get the girl," Gabriel shouted as he followed the

gryphon.

Val's gaze had never left the woman. As he raced toward her, he saw her unmoving body slowly sink into the dark waters of the loch. When he reached the water's edge, he tossed aside his halberd and waded into the icy water before he dove under.

He caught a glimpse of what he hoped were her skirts, but he had to rise for air. Val gulped in a deep breath and dove back under the water. This time, he saw a pale hand and reached for it.

Thankfully, the woman's heavy skirts hadn't pulled her down too far, and he was able to grab her and haul her to the surface with him.

Val moved her wealth of hair out of her face to help her breathe. It took all his strength to swim back to shore and keep a hold of the woman.

As soon as his feet touched the bottom of the loch, he drew her into his arms, her thick wool skirts making things more cumbersome.

"Damned skirts," he muttered, thinking of the gauzy gowns Roman women had worn.

He glanced down to find bruises forming on her neck, but it was the pale tinge of her skin that got his feet moving faster out of the loch.

Through his own teeth chattering, Val leaned over the woman and heard her heart beating faintly in her chest. When he raised his head, he spotted Gabriel running toward him.

"She's not dead," Val said and clamped his teeth together.

"Then she must not be the Chosen, or the gryphon would have killed her. Regardless, she needs our aid, and we need to get both of you out of those wet clothes," Gabriel said as he reached down and retrieved Val's weapon.

Val shifted the woman in his arms and hurried to follow Gabriel.

"Where are we going?"

Gabriel looked over his shoulder. "Somewhere safe."

"I saw a cottage. It's close."

"Aye," Gabriel replied. "But we should wait before we make our presence known to the village."

Val knew he was right, but all he wanted was to get warm. He hadn't had any protection against the snow when he arrived, then the quick swim in the loch had only hastened his chill, even with the unique and special material he wore that helped to protect him.

He glanced down at the woman and saw her lips had turned a pale shade of blue. If Gabriel didn't find them a safe place quick, neither Val nor the woman would be much good.

"Let me have her," Gabriel said as he suddenly halted.

Val eased the woman into Gabriel's arms. He hadn't realized until then how heavy the woman had been with her wet skirts holding the water.

"Climb," Gabriel said.

Val looked at the mountain before him. Clouds covered the moon, shielding everything from sight, but Val trusted Gabriel and began to climb.

The exertion from the climb helped to warm Val. Midway up, he took the woman so Gabriel could maneuver a tricky slope. He repositioned her to get a better hold, and came in contact with the skin on her arm. She felt nearly frozen.

"We've got to hurry, Gabriel," he said.

"I'll run ahead and get a fire going. The climb is easy from here," he said before running off.

Val took a deep breath and kept climbing. Every once

in a while he would glance down at the woman. Her breath became shallower each time her chest rose. Val quickened his pace, especially when he saw the glow coming from a cave ahead of him.

By the time he walked into the cave, Gabriel had a large fire roaring, and his black bag with its contents was out waiting for them.

"Lay her here," Gabriel directed in front of him and rifled through some herbs.

Val gently set her on the blankets piled near the fire, and then he stepped away.

"What are you doing?" Gabriel snapped in agitation.

Val blinked. He was cold, hungry, and irritated and not the least bit in the mood for Gabriel's temper. "What do you want me to do?"

"Warm her," Gabriel said without looking up from his herbs.

Val went down on his left knee and reached for the dagger he kept in his right boot. He gripped the woman's soggy gown and cut it away from her. Once the gown was removed, he quickly covered her with blankets.

Gabriel reached for some water and tsked. "That'll never warm her, Val. You know that. She needs body heat. Your body heat."

Val knew it all too well. He pulled off his boots and wet clothes, and then climbed under the blanket with the woman. As soon as his skin touched hers, it was like he had fallen into the loch again.

"By Jupiter, she's freezing."

"Wrap your body around hers," Gabriel instructed. "This brew I'm making will take a little time, but it'll do no good unless she's warm."

Val moved his arm underneath the woman's neck so he pillowed her head. Next, he gently turned her onto her side and pulled her back against him. He sucked in a breath at his body's contact with her cold one. Gabriel was a master at healing, but Val couldn't hold back the concern that it might be too late for the woman.

"Why didn't the gryphon kill her?" Gabriel murmured as he ground up a few herbs together, his brows furrowed in concentration.

"I don't know. She's not one of the Chosen, but the creature killed plenty of villagers. So why not her?"

Gabriel stopped grinding the herbs and slowly raised his head. "We won't know anything until she wakes, but it does give me pause. Tell me what you know of gryphons."

"They've always been used for good, never evil. If a person saw a gryphon, it was a sign of powerful new beginnings. The gryphon is supposed to help bring the dark side of ourselves into submission, and they are powerful guardians of vigilance and vengeance."

"I'll admit that what we saw tonight was most certainly powerful, but it was a guardian of darkness – not light," Gabriel said.

Val nodded and felt the pull of sleep as the heat generated from him and the woman seeped around him. He snuggled next to her and found his face near her hair.

He inhaled deeply and smelled a hint of heather mixed with the fresh, clean scent of her. Feeling out of sorts, he cracked open an eye and stared at the inky mass of hair that spilled across his arm.

Unable to stop himself, he reached for a strand of her hair. The silky lock was thick and straight, and he couldn't stop himself from winding it around his fingers.

He loosened his hold on the strand and watched it fall onto his chest. Sleep called to him like a tempting siren, but he refused to give in. There was a chance Gabriel would need him.

When he shifted to get more comfortable and his cock brushed against her round bottom, Val found it all together too pleasurable.

And irresistible.

Val was never one to turn down pleasure when it came his way. The very feminine curves and soft body against his made desire burn low in his gut. Val wrapped his arm over the woman's narrow waist and molded himself to her. The underside of her breast grazed his hand, and he smiled.

It was too bad she wasn't awake since there were many things he knew they could do to occupy their time. Very satisfying, enjoyable things.

"You're supposed to be warming her," Gabriel said suddenly, breaking into his thoughts.

Val smiled at his fellow Shield. "Oh, I am."

A ghost of a grin played on Gabriel's lips.

CHAPTER TWO

Val opened his eyes and blinked to shake off the effects of sleep. He wasn't sure when he had fallen asleep, only that one minute he'd been thinking of how he'd like to run his hands over the woman's body, and then...nothing.

He stifled a yawn and turned his gaze to Gabriel.

"Feel better?" Gabriel asked.

"Aye. Sorry for drifting off."

"Don't be," Gabriel said as he leaned over to grab more herbs from his black leather bag. "You were in the freezing water, then warmed up quickly. It pulls most people under."

Val ran his hand down the woman's side and found her skin warm. He scooted out from beneath the covers and turned to find his clothes waiting for him.

It was one of the many benefits to being a Shield. Whatever they needed – be it clothes, weapons, food or coin – the Fae made sure they were equipped at all times.

He tugged on his pants and boots and then pulled his tunic over his head. He left his leather jerkin for the time being beside his sword, dagger, and halberd. When he once more faced Gabriel, his fellow Shield had risen from beside the woman, his frown deeper than normal.

"What's wrong?" Val asked.

"I'm missing an herb. I must find it. Get her to drink the water I mixed while I'm gone."

Val glanced at the small wooden cup and doubted he'd get much into her. He walked around the fire and added more sticks to it before he took Gabriel's place beside the woman.

"What's your name?" he asked, not that he expected her to answer, but he hated the quiet.

He scooted closer to her and gently turned her onto her back. He hissed when he saw the massive bruises on her neck. "Quite a night you've had, but with Gabriel's healing, you'll be just fine."

Val studied the woman's face. Her full lips were no longer tinged with blue but had taken on a dusky pink color. She had skin the color of cream that contrasted nicely with her raven locks. She had a small nose, high forehead, and black brows that arched regally over her eyes.

He found himself strangely curious to know what color her eyes were. He imagined them to be a bright, vivid blue. Val shook aside his musings and lifted the wooden cup.

"Gabriel wants you to drink this," he said as he moved his hand under her neck. "Let's not make this difficult. Gabriel will have my head if I don't get at least some of this down your throat."

Val lifted the woman's head and placed the cup next to her mouth, and just as he expected, she did nothing. He silently cursed his luck and lowered the cup, as well as the woman's head. For several moments, he contemplated his options.

Then, a slow smile pulled at his lips. He dipped his finger into the water and traced the woman's plump lips, allowing some of the water to drip into her mouth. Twice more he repeated the gesture, and on the third attempt, he saw her swallow.

"Aye," he whispered with a grin. "That's it. Drink for me."

The next time he moved his finger to her lips, she opened for him. So instead of tracing her lips, he let the water drip into her mouth. Next, he again lifted her head and brought the cup to her lips where he let the water slowly trickle into her mouth.

He stopped when nearly half of it was gone and sat back to regard her. Something nagged at the back of his mind, something that he should remember. The more he stared at her, the more he wondered why the gryphon hadn't killed her.

"What stopped the creature?" he murmured aloud. "Did you say something?" He shook his head. "Not possible. Not with the marks around your neck. It had to have been something else."

As soon as he said the words he realized the only thing that could control the beast were the blue stones. Only the blue stones could call up the creatures, and whoever held the blue stone controlled it.

With his heart thumping in his chest, Val pulled the blankets off the female. As much as he loved looking at a woman's body, his gaze searched for something more precious, something that could save hundreds of thousands of lives.

He lifted first one arm then the other, examining every inch of skin. He repeated the process with her legs. When he was satisfied that it wasn't on her front, he gently turned her away from him onto her side.

With one hand holding her wealth of black hair, His gaze searched her neck and then down her back to her hips. That's when he saw it, the symbol of a triangle with interlocking knotwork, encircled by a thick, dark band. He ran his hand over her round bottom and touched the symbol that rested just on the swell of one firm cheek.

"The fourth Chosen one," he whispered. He stared at the symbol a moment longer before he lowered her onto her back and covered her with the blankets.

No sooner had he lifted the cup to her mouth than Gabriel returned and shook the snow from him.

"Bloody hell, it's cold," he grumbled. "Wouldn't you know it would begin to snow as soon as I began to search."

"Did you find it?"

Gabriel nodded as Val rose and moved so Gabriel could finish his mixing. "The water I mixed will help heal her throat from the inside, but I needed this special herb," he said and held up what looked like a wilted flower, "to add to the other ingredients that will heal her bruises."

"I got half the water down her."

"Good," Gabriel said, his head bent over his herbs. Suddenly he looked up and narrowed his gaze at Val as if just realizing something was off. "What is it?"

"She's one of the Chosen."

"Are you sure?"

Val nodded. "I found the symbol myself."

"Show me."

Val knelt on the other side of the woman and turned her toward him, then pulled back the blanket so Gabriel could see the symbol. When Gabriel sat back with a sigh, Val returned her to her back.

"We need to call to Aimery so he can move her out of here," Val said.

"I agree. Let me tend to her first," Gabriel said.

Val walked to the opening of the cave and looked out over the dark, snow-covered village. "As soon as the woman leaves, we should search for the gryphon," he called over his shoulder.

"You've the right of it."

"If the Great Evil is able to locate the Chosen before the Fae, then who is to say they won't track all four women to Stone Crest?" Val asked.

He turned to face Gabriel and saw his friend regarding him silently.

"What do you propose?" Gabriel asked carefully.

"We kill the creature before Aimery takes the woman. If the evil doesn't know we have her, then that gives the other Shields more time to prepare."

Gabriel sighed and drummed his fingers on his leg. "We should send her to safety, but how do we know Stone Crest is safe?"

"Exactly," Val said as he walked back to the fire. "We only need four of the Chosen to end the evil. We now have the fourth, but if we leave now, the gryphon will follow."

"Yet, with all the Shields reunited again, we can kill it easily."

Val ran a hand down his face. "I know," he said softly. "I just have this feeling we need to battle the gryphon here. Now."

For a long moment, Gabriel stared at him before giving a curt nod. "Your instincts have never failed us before, Val. I'll follow them, but if it looks like we won't make it, promise we'll call to Aimery and have him take her."

"You have my vow."   He thought of the Fae commander, and knew they needed to update him. "Aimery," he called.

In a blink, the Fae was standing beside him. His gaze swept the cave and came to rest on the woman. "Who is she?"

"She's one of the Chosen," Val said.

Aimery's mystical blue gaze swung to him.   "You

already found her?"

"Aye," Gabriel said. "And the creature."

Aimery looked from Gabriel to Val. "Is the creature dead?"

Val shook his head. "Nay, the gryphon isn't dead."

"What?" Aimery said and stepped back in shock. "Surely you're mistaken. It couldn't have been a gryphon, they're pure creatures."

"Not this one," Gabriel said. "I saw it with my own eyes, Aimery. He was evil."

Aimery clasped his hands behind his back. "Nowhere in history has a gryphon ever become evil."

"It just means the Great Evil has grown stronger," Val said.

"It means much more than that," Aimery murmured.

Gabriel stood and crossed his arms over his chest. "What is that supposed to mean? We found the fourth Chosen. They can now defeat the Great Evil."

As soon as Val heard Aimery sigh, he knew something was wrong. He stepped closer to the Fae commander. "What is it, Aimery?"

The Fae's unusual swirling blue eyes rose to Val's. "It takes an evil of the purest form to turn a gryphon, something no evil has been able to do. And if the Great Evil was able to track the Chosen, then —"

"He'll track Mina, Elle, and Shannon to Stone Crest," Gabriel finished.

Aimery nodded. "They aren't safe there. Not yet."

"Why not?" Val demanded.

"I never expected the evil to gain such power. If he attacks Stone Crest now, all is lost."

"And how do you know he hasn't already?" Gabriel asked.

Aimery raised a brow in response. "My soldiers

would've alerted me. As it is, I'm wasting time. I must go and alert the other Shields before it's too late. You'll have to keep this woman here with you. Keep her safe," he said to Val just before he disappeared.

"Your instinct was right," Gabriel said.

Val shook his head. "Not exactly. I've not seen Aimery so worried since the Shields were first formed."

"Aye. We all thought this would be finished as soon as we found the fourth Chosen. None of us counted on the sudden growth in power from the Great Evil."

~ ~ ~

"You better have a good explanation," the voice reverberated around him.

He looked down at his claws and barely recalled a time when they had been something different. Fear should have made him answer quickly, but instead of alarm, all he felt was lost.

"Answer me," the voice bellowed.

He raised his head. His sharp eyes looked around him at the dank, dark room. Some would say he was in Hell, but only he knew the truth. He was in a place much worse than Hell.

"You called me back here," he lied to the voice.

Suddenly blood red eyes appeared in front of him, and he felt a force throw him back. Instantly, he spread his wings to help stop him before he hit the wall, but he wasn't quick enough, and slammed into the jagged stones. Pain ripped through his back.

"Do not lie to me." The words were bitten out, as if the voice was about to lose control. "You forget I know all."

Slowly he righted himself and folded his now bloodied

wings against him. "Send another creature."

"Nay," the voice whispered softly in his ear. "I want them to know just how powerful I am. You will kill the girl."

He turned away from the presence that now surrounded him. He would return immediately, and kill the girl while she was unconscious so that he wouldn't have to look into her violet eyes again.

"I'll leave now."

"No," the voice said louder. "You'll wait. Let them think you have given up."

He turned back to the presence. "You keep saying 'them'. Who are you referring to?"

"The Shields."

He had heard whispers of The Shields, noble warriors from different times and realms aided by the Fae to thwart the Great Evil. He quickly left the room before the voice could say more.

For the first time in ages, he found hope.

CHAPTER THREE

Nicole fought to stay in the darkness as long as she could. Several times she heard voices, voices of men she didn't recognize, and it frightened her. Where was she, and who was it that held her captive?

She didn't want to wake and find the gryphon staring down at her again with his evil yellow eyes. Just the thought of the beast sent a chill through her.

"She's waking."

The masculine voice was very near her. It was smooth and intoxicatingly deep, fascinatingly seductive. The voice lacked a Scottish brogue, but he wasn't English either. There was something about the voice – and the man – that tugged at her, urging her to see who such a voice belonged to.

The lure of the unknown man was too much to resist, and she opened her eyes despite the fear that settled like a ball of ice in her chest. The first thing she saw was the ceiling of what looked like a cave.

Whoever the men were, they had saved her from the icy depths of the loch. She should be grateful, but they had only prolonged her death. Still, the voice...

Nicole inhaled deeply, her body tingling from the presence beside her. For just a moment, she reveled in the swarm of thrilling, exhilarating emotions assaulting her before slowly turning her head to find a man staring at her with interested pale green eyes.

"They're violet," he murmured.

Her lips parted to ask him what he meant, when she felt another presence. She turned her head to the left and saw another man, this one with eyes the color of silver, watching her with cool intensity.

"Welcome back," he said. "How does your throat feel?"

Nicole tried to swallow and felt only a small twinge of pain. She nodded and watched him as he went back to mixing something in a bowl.

"This is for you," he said when he found her eyes on him still.

"Forgive our manners," the first man said, drawing her attention back to him. "I'm Val, and that is Gabriel. We pulled you out of the loch."

She closed her eyes as the memories of the gryphon assaulted her. The sheer power in its claws that had gripped her throat, the anger and death in its eyes.

And the evil that permeated from the creature.

"You shouldn't have," she whispered as she looked at Val.

He leaned close and peered at her with pale green eyes, his hair, a mixture of bronze and dark blond, falling over his shoulder in thick waves. "And why is that?"

"I was meant to die."

"I don't believe that."

She gave him a closer look and noted the unusual quality of his clothing. At first glance his soft leather pants, deep green tunic, and leather jerkin looked plain, common even, but they weren't the usual fabric that peasants, or even noblemen wore. His bronze hair hung loose about his face, falling just past his shoulders, accentuating his green eyes against his tanned skin.

A scar running down the right side of his face gave him an air of menace, but did nothing to distract from his good looks. If anything, it hardened his features to make him lethal, dangerous...exciting. His jaw was strong, his nose aristocratic, and his mouth wide and firm.

Those lips were tilted a fraction at the edges, but she saw a hardness about him that spoke of a warrior, a man who was used to battle.

A man who welcomed it.

A shiver raced down her spine, but she couldn't look away from him. Val intrigued her. Not because of his unusual clothes or his strange accent, but because there was much more beneath the surface than what he was showing her.

Her breath hitched when his gaze dropped for a second to her mouth. Unable to stop herself, her lips parted and she drug in a large breath, which caused her chest to rise.

When he dragged his eyes back to her, there was no denying the heat she saw there. He allowed her to see it before he blinked and it was gone.

She gave the cave a curious glance once more, but found her gaze lingering on Val's wide shoulders and muscular forearm that rested casually atop his bent knee.

The soft, worn leather of his trousers stretched tight over his thighs, molding to the rigid sinew beneath. She was beginning to think there wasn't an inch of Val that wasn't spectacularly toned and hard.

"Do you have a name?" he asked.

She swallowed and jerked her eyes back to his. "Nicole."

Val smiled showing even, white teeth. "Nice to meet you, Nicole."

"You can charm her later, Val," Gabriel interrupted brusquely. "I need to finish."

When Val rose and moved aside, Nicole found her gaze following him. Val had an easy smile, almost too easy. She'd glimpsed the hardness in him, but there was also sadness, as well.

"Can you sit up?"

Nicole cleared her throat at the sound of Gabriel's voice. She moved her arm out of the blankets to sit up and saw her bare skin. Immediately, she realized she was naked beneath the covers.

How had she not realized that sooner? Her gaze drifted to Val, and she understood all too well why.

"Don't be alarmed," Val said. "We had to get you out of your wet clothes before you froze. I give you my word we didn't touch you."

With each hand gripping the blanket to her, she slowly sat up. As soon as she did, Val wrapped another blanket around her shoulders.

The brush of his warm skin against hers made her breath catch. Nicole refused to look at him again, but she didn't need to. She seemed to know where he was at any given moment.

"When you are up to it, we have clothes for you," Gabriel said and handed her a cup of water.

She gratefully took the cup, but after one drink realized it was much more than just water. At least she had something to occupy her mind other than Val and his hard body, green eyes, and enthralling voice. "What did you put in it?"

"Herbs to help heal your throat. I also have a salve for your skin to help heal the bruises."

Her hand moved to touch her throat and frowned. An image of the gryphon flashed in her mind as his hand squeezed. He could have killed her right then, but he'd hesitated. Why? "You said you found me in the water?"

Val moved to sit on her left. "Aye, right after the gryphon nearly killed you."

"Did you frighten him away?" she asked before drinking more of the sweet water and keeping her eyes on the liquid.

"We would've," Gabriel answered. "He left on his own."

"You said earlier that you were supposed to die. What did you mean?" Val asked.

Nicole wondered how much to tell them. They didn't seem too upset at seeing a gryphon, but she didn't trust them either. She would have to be careful.

"The gryphon chose me," she finally said. "I was supposed to die."

Val knew she was lying. She was keeping something from them, just as they were keeping things from her. If they all wanted to survive this, they had to speak freely.

His gaze caught Gabriel's as his friend moved to apply the salve to Nicole's throat. Val watched as Nicole leaned her head back, exposing her slender throat discolored by ugly bruises. By tomorrow, the bruises would nearly be gone thanks to Gabriel's healing.

But it wasn't the bruises Val was looking at. He saw her pale skin, the flush that stained her cheeks as he stared at her. His fingers itched to touch her again, to feel the softness of her skin beneath his palms.

"Is anything else hurt?" Gabriel asked as he finished with the salve.

She shook her head and drank more of the water. "You aren't from around here, are you?"

Val loved the sound of her lilt, and the peculiar way she spoke her words. "Nay," he answered. "We're not."

"Where are you from?"

Val exchanged a look with Gabriel. At Gabriel's shrug, Val slowly released a breath. "We're from lands very far from here."

"Why come here? This village is small, and Laird MacNamara is on his deathbed. There's nothing here."

"Actually there is. We're searching for something," Gabriel answered. "A blue stone about the size of a child's fist. Have you seen it?"

Her brows furrowed at his words. "Nay. In a village this small, everyone knows everything. If anyone had it, I'd have heard of such a stone."

"What about the laird you spoke of?" Val asked.

She shrugged her slim shoulders, careful to keep the blankets in place. "Usually, the servants who work at the castle like to talk, so I'd imagine word would've spread by now. Is this stone valuable?"

"In a manner."

She licked her lips and set aside the now empty cup. "I'd feel more comfortable with my clothes back on, if you don't mind."

Val rose to his feet and waited for Gabriel to do the same before he said, "Of course. We had to cut away your gown. There is another behind you. We'll wait at the entrance to give you some privacy."

Once outside, Val turned to Gabriel. "She's lying about the gryphon."

"I know," Gabriel said, his lips set in a tight line. "She doesn't trust us, but then again, we've given her no reason to."

Val scratched his neck as he thought over their options. "I'm not sure we should tell her everything."

"We can't wait. You know as well as I that Aimery can't shift her through time unless she's willing."

Val knew from first hand experience, and not just regarding himself when Aimery had found him. He recalled Roderick's feeling of despair when Elle refused to go with Aimery to safety while the harpies were after them.

"In a day or so," Val said. "We're strangers, and she was nearly killed a few hours ago."

Gabriel nodded just as Nicole called out for them to return. When they walked back into the cave, Val moved to the fire to warm his hands.

"Tell me," he said casually so as to help her open up and talk, "has the gryphon come to your village before?"

He watched as she shifted from one foot to the other in anxiety, her arms folded over her waist as she gazed into the flames to avoid their gazes. "Nay."

"Drink this," Gabriel said and handed her the wooden cup again.

She peered inside and sniffed it. "What is it now?"

"It'll help to continue warming you. It's hot, so be careful."

Val shook his head in irritation and turned away. Never had he felt so helpless and frustrated. The fourth Chosen was found. They should be rejoicing and ending the Great Evil, not sitting around in the cold Highlands waiting for the gryphon to return for Nicole. For return he would.

"Val," Gabriel snapped.

He jerked to find Gabriel and Nicole staring at him. "What is it?"

"I've called your name three times."

Val shrugged off Gabriel's words. "I was lost in thought. What did you need?"

"I think we need to return Nicole to her home. This cave won't keep her warm after her swim."

"Nay," Nichole said hastily.

Val stepped toward her, his gaze narrowed on her face. "Why? Why don't you want to return home?"

"I can't return," she answered. "If I did...I just can't."

Gabriel rose to stand next to Val. "I think we're going to need more of an explanation than that."

"It's all I can give you," she said then quickly drank the last of the concoction Gabriel had given her. She held out the cup. "Thank you for helping, but maybe it's best if you two leave. I'll be fine here."

Val raised a brow at her. "Actually, this is where we're living."

"There's a small cottage near the loch. It's empty. Use it."

"You mean it's empty now because you're here," Gabriel said.

Her violet eyes grew wild as she stepped away from them. "Please. You don't understand."

"Easy," Val said as he held out his hands. "We're here to help. You've had a trying night. Maybe some sleep is what you need. Things will look different in the morning."

She shook her head. "Nay, they won't."

Out of the corner of his eye, Val saw Gabriel began to walk slowly toward Nicole. Upon closer inspection, he spotted Nicole blinking her eyes several times as if she couldn't focus. Val took the few steps separating them – just as she collapsed into his arms.

He sighed and carried her back to her pallet. "Why didn't you tell me you drugged her?"

Gabriel grinned. "There wasn't time. She needs the rest, and we need to keep her near."

"Good thinking. Did you see the way her eyes went wild. Why is it so important she dies, I wonder? And by the gryphon?" After he laid Nicole on the pallet, he covered her and stood.

Gabriel ran a hand through his hair. "We won't know until she tells us."

Val took hold of his halberd. "I'll take the first watch."

It wasn't until he was seated near the cave entrance well away from Gabriel and the fire that he allowed himself to let his weariness show.

He'd lost track of how many years he had been a part of the Shields. There was no telling where he would have ended up had Aimery not found him lying in a pool of his own blood and vomit from his constant drinking.

It hadn't been a good way to live. Each day, the liquor took a little more of his soul.

But then again, it had been the only thing to dull the pain.

CHAPTER FOUR

Nicole opened her eyes to find herself staring at Val's sleeping face across the fire. In sleep, his face was relaxed, and still just as beautiful as before.

She didn't remember agreeing to stay with them, but then again she couldn't recall attempting to leave either. The last thing she remembered was trying to talk them into taking her cottage and drinking the mixture Gabriel gave her.

Then she realized Gabriel must have put something in it to make her sleep. Anger pulsed within her until she realized she had no other place to go. Val and Gabriel were protecting her when no one else had ever tried.

It made her throat close up with emotion. She didn't want to like them, but how could she not when they had done nothing but heal and protect her? They must think she was daft or ungrateful, or worse, both.

Strange as it was, she didn't fear these men. Perhaps it was how calm they were about the gryphon, or the fact they carried themselves like warriors, but she had an inkling that her chances of staying alive were greatly improved by remaining with them.

She wasn't sure why they were helping her, but she would do what she must to keep the truth from them. If they knew about her, they wouldn't continue to help her.

There was a great debt she now owed Val and Gabriel for saving her. Whether they ran the gryphon off or not, she was alive because of them.

Her gaze raked over Val's sleeping form. He was on his side facing her with his arms crossed over his chest. The fire still blazed, which meant Gabriel was around somewhere, but it wasn't Gabriel that held her attention – it was Val.

Val. Such an unusual name. One that she had never heard before, and she was curious as to what it stood for. A smile pulled at her lips as she considered asking him, and wondering what emotion his pale green eyes would show if she did.

Neither man had given surnames, and it was obvious by their dress and speech that they didn't belong to a clan. She recalled them telling her they had come from a land far away. She had always been too curious for her own good. It's what led her to be sacrificed to the gryphon, but she wanted to know more about Val, and even Gabriel.

They were different from the men she knew but different in a good way. She couldn't think of one man from the village or castle who would have helped her with the gryphon. Not that she blamed them. The gryphon was a powerful beast, but an evil gryphon was even more powerful.

As she stared at Val's handsome face from his wide lips to the harsh brows that slashed over his eyes, she wondered how different her life could have been with someone like him in it. He had charm, strength, and most of all power, a combination that could be devastating to a woman.

Suddenly, his eyes opened, and she found herself

staring into his pale green gaze.

"Good morn," he said, his voice still thick from sleep.

"Good morn."

He yawned and rolled onto his back before sitting up and turning toward her. "Did you sleep well?"

"Aye, especially after the help from whatever herbs Gabriel put in my drink."

Val furrowed his brow. "I'm sorry, but we had to."

She nodded. "Just don't do it again."

"Good, you're both awake," Gabriel said as he walked toward them from the front of the cave.

Gabriel set aside his bow and arrow and his sword. When she turned to look at Val, she noticed his sword and halberd were leaning against the wall behind him. These men weren't travelers looking for a lost stone. They were much more than that.

"Anyone hungry?" Gabriel asked as he set down a sack.

Nicole recognized the material as having come from her cottage. "Did you find all you needed?"

His gaze snapped to hers. "I suppose I should've asked."

She smiled and shook her head. "I owe you both much more than food. Take what you need."

"Is there anything you'd like for us to retrieve?" Val asked as Gabriel handed him an oatcake.

She accepted the food and thought over her possessions. "My cloak would be nice."

"You won't need that," Gabriel said.

She raised her eyebrows wondering if they planned to keep her locked away somewhere. "And why is that?"

Val hooked a thumb over his shoulder. "There's one there."

Nicole looked to where he pointed and spotted a cloak. "Did you steal it?"

Both men shook their heads.

She looked down at the gown she wore. It wasn't one of hers because she only had the one, and it was cut in half, discarded in the corner. "And this gown? Did you steal it?"

Again both men shook their heads as they ate.

She sighed and tried again. "I know neither are mine, so can you tell me where you got them?"

"Does it matter?" Val asked. "We didn't steal them, and they fit. So wear them."

She knew the odds of them traveling with clothes that might happen to fit a woman in need along the road were slim. More secrets. As much as she'd like to keep hers tucked away, she had a gnawing suspicion they would learn her secret well before she learned theirs.

"I suppose not," she finally agreed.

Val gave her a heart-stopping smile. "Good. Now eat."

She found herself more intrigued by Val with each passing moment. Whereas Gabriel was stoic, Val was more approachable, less reserved.

Then she caught the hint of sadness in his gaze again. It was fleeting, but there was no denying it. She bit the inside of her mouth, telling herself it was none of her business what made a man such as Val so unhappy.

But he intrigued her. Each time she saw the sadness it pulled at her heart in ways she couldn't begin to understand.

"So," Val said after he had finished eating. "You won't return to your cottage, and we won't leave the cave. I suppose that means you're staying with us."

Nicole shrugged, unsure of where Val was going with his line of thinking.

"That is until we leave," Gabriel said.

Nicole swallowed her bite of food and set down the rest of her oatcake. As long as Val and Gabriel stayed, she would have food and water. She couldn't chance any of the villagers seeing her.

"What will you do?" Val asked.

"Once you leave?" she asked. At his nod, she said, "I don't know."

"Tell us why you can't return to your cottage," Val urged.

For so long she'd lived with her secret. No one would get close to her for fear that the curse would rub off on them. It was hard living without friends and people barely speaking to her because of their fear.

"As I said last night, I was supposed to have died. Everyone expected it."

"Did everyone also expect the gryphon to attack the village?" Gabriel asked.

"I don't think so."

Val leaned on one hand and bent the other so that his arm could rest on his knee. "Did you know what was coming for you?"

She shuddered. "Nay."

"But you knew *something* was?" Gabriel asked.

"Aye. It had been predestined."

"Nothing is predestined," Val said.

Gabriel nodded. "He's right."

"We each believe in life in our own way," she said softly.

Val rose and began to pace. "What will happen if the villagers see you?"

"It'll come for me again."

"How do you know it won't anyway?"

Her heart skidded to a halt as she raised her gaze to Val. "I just assumed that he let me go because he didn't want me dead yet."

Val came down on his haunches beside her. "I hate to be the one to tell you this, Nicole, but the gryphon will return whether the villagers see you or not."

"Why?" she whispered.

"Because it wants you."

Nicole jumped to her feet and paced the spacious cave just as Val had done moments before. "That can't be right. I was told that, with my death, the villagers would be satisfied and not call up the creature again."

"What?" Val and Gabriel said in unison.

She looked at the two men now standing side by side. "It was the villagers who called up the gryphon. They want payment in blood. My blood."

CHAPTER FIVE

Val could only blink at Nicole. "Who told you this?"

She shrugged and continued pacing as she wrung her hands. "It doesn't matter. I've known since I was a little girl that I would die."

"They gave you an exact date?"

"Oh, aye," she nodded. "They wanted me to know just how long I had to live."

"Who did?" Gabriel asked.

She stopped and gawked at him. "Haven't you been listening? The villagers."

Val's voice lowered. "But who told you all of this?"

"Margda," she said as her gaze swung to him. "She was the only one who dared to raise me. I often wondered why she did it, but she said it was her punishment for past deeds."

Val stepped closer to her and looked deeply into her violet eyes. "We can't help you unless you tell us everything."

"I've told you all I know."

Val glanced at Gabriel to see his fellow Shield deep in thought. "What are you thinking?"

"It can't be the entire village," Gabriel said. "There is only one that controls the creatures, except with Hugh and Mina."

"That's right. You said both the brother and sister tried to control it."

Gabriel nodded. "It was disastrous for them, but fortunately, worked to our advantage."

"What are you two talking about?" Nicole asked.

"I agree," Val said to Gabriel, ignoring Nicole. "It can't be the entire village."

"Yet it was," she argued. "I know what they told me."

Val looked at Nicole and then turned to Gabriel. "I think it's time she knew the truth."

With a loud sigh, Gabriel lowered himself to the ground. "I think you're right. Nicole, you might want to sit."

Val couldn't help but remember when he and Roderick had told Elle what she was and who, exactly, they were. Elle had been from the future and took the discovery rather well. But would Nicole?

He glanced at Gabriel, but it was clear he was going to let Val begin. After he licked his lips, Val waited for Nicole to sit but she remained as she was.

"Gabriel's right. You should sit."

She shook her head. "I'd rather stay as I am."

"All right," he said and took a deep breath. "Nicole, we did come here looking for the blue stone, but that isn't the only reason we came. We came for you."

"Me?" she asked. "Why? I'm no one of importance."

"Actually, you're much more than that," Gabriel said.

Nicole looked from one to the other before turning to Val. "How did you know who I was? I've never seen either of you before."

"We didn't know it was you, exactly. In order to find

who we sought, we needed to find a mark on your body."

"What?" she asked softly, wariness creeping into her voice.

"It's a special mark," Gabriel said.

Val watched as she visibly swallowed. He didn't wish to frighten her, but it seemed there was no way around it. "The mark is a symbol, a symbol that helps us identify the women we seek."

"So you go looking for us...them?"

"Aye. It's very important we find all of you before the creatures do." When she didn't respond, Val continued. "The symbol is small, and barely visible. It has three points with interlocking knots and a thick ring encircling it."

"And you think I have that symbol on my body?"

Gabriel was the one who answered. "We know you do. We saw it."

"You know it, too. Don't you?" Val asked when her gaze flicked away for a moment.

Slowly Nicole nodded her head and lowered herself to the ground. Val followed, unsure of what to tell her next. Thankfully, Gabriel continued for him.

"The symbol marks you as one of the Chosen we were sent to find and keep safe until it was time for the Great Evil to end."

Her brow furrowed at his words. "How many others are there?"

"In total, there were twelve infants sent to Earth," Val said. "Most are dead, but you're the fourth we've found."

"Sent?" she repeated and turned her eyes to him. "What do you mean sent?"

Gabriel cleared his throat. "You're from another realm."

"There's no such thing," she said with a half-hearted chuckle. "Are you both daft?"

"You nearly had an evil gryphon kill you last night, and you ask us if we're daft?" Val questioned. "We are far from daft, Nicole. What we speak is the truth."

She hugged her knees to her chest. "If you're to be believed, then I and these other three women are from another realm sent here to end a Great Evil. What evil?"

"The evil that the gryphon sprang from," Gabriel said. "We've been fighting creatures like it for years."

Her violet eyes widened. "What are you exactly?"

"Shields," Val answered. "We help to keep the evil from destroying Earth as it has many other realms. Your realm was destroyed, but before the evil could finish it, there was a plan to send twelve infants to Earth to keep the information alive on how to kill the evil."

"Why didn't my realm do it if they had the information?"

Val shrugged. "That I can't answer, but I can attest to the destruction that just one creature can accomplish in a night. You haven't seen what the gryphon has done to your village in his attempt to find you."

Her face paled at his words. "Were many injured?"

Val found himself admiring her for her forgiving nature. Not many people would worry about a village that wanted her dead. "A few died, but for the most part, the village was spared."

"Thank the saints," she whispered as she lowered her eyes. Then, her gaze jerked to his. "So tell me, exactly where are you from?"

This is the part Val had wanted to postpone. "Rome."

"Why do you hesitate in telling me?"

"Because I'm not from this time."

"When exactly?" she asked when he didn't say more.

Val studied her carefully. "39 A.D."

She gasped as her eyes widened. "How?"

"Because we have help from the Fae," Gabriel answered.

Her gaze swung to him. "The Fae? They really exist?"

"Aye, they do. I'm sure you'll meet Aimery soon."

Val watched as she worried her lower lip between her teeth as she took in all they had said.

"Where are you from?" she asked Gabriel.

Val winced and looked at his friend. When he spoke, Gabriel's face was devoid of emotion.

"I don't know," he answered. "The Fae found me alone and wounded."

Nicole's face softened. "You've no memories then?"

Gabriel gave a swift jerk of his head in answer.

"We would've left with you last night for Stone Crest," Val said to change the subject, "but we worried the Great Evil would follow before we had a chance to prepare."

"So what do we do now?" Nicole asked.

"We wait and keep you safe. It might be wise for you to remain hidden here until we find the blue stone."

Her eyes were troubled as she shook her head. "I still don't understand what the blue stone has to do with all of this."

"The blue stone is what controls the creature," Gabriel said. "If we destroy the blue stone, we destroy the creature."

Nicole thought back to the gryphon. There had been something in his yellow eyes, something she didn't know how to put into words.

"So you think someone in the village has the stone?" she asked.

Val nodded. "The creatures have been showing up just where the Chosen are, and it's usually someone nearby that has the stone."

"As I told you last night, in such a small village,

something as unusual as a big, blue stone would have spread quickly."

"I know," Val said and scratched his cheek. "Which is a puzzle. If we could find where the gryphon flew to, it might help us find who controls him."

She swallowed and tried to wrap her mind around everything she had been told. "Whoever controls this creature, can they make it do whatever they want?"

"Aye," Val answered. "Why?"

"Did they stop the gryphon from killing me?"

Val shrugged one massive shoulder. "It could be, but why? If they've taunted you all these years, why not go through with it?"

"Good question," she said and rested her chin on her knees.

For long moments, none of them said anything, each lost in thought.

Finally, Gabriel spoke. "I'll head into the village and see what I can find. Maybe someone will be willing to talk."

"Good idea," Val said.

She stood when both men did, and walked with them to the entrance of the cave. She put her hand on Gabriel's arm just as he was about to leave. "Don't mention me," she warned him. "As soon as you do, any hope of discovering information will be gone. The villagers fear me, and all who have contact with me."

"Thank you," he said before walking away.

She turned back to Val. "What do we do?"

He smiled. "We wait until Gabriel returns."

Nicole stayed at the entrance as Val turned and walked back to the fire. She was amazed the bitter cold stayed out of the back of the cave. As she looked over the landscape, she could see several small trails of smoke that disappeared into the low-lying gray sky.

The smoke was too large to be coming from chimneys, so there must have been a fire. Then she recalled Gabriel telling her the gryphon had gone through the village looking for her. Her first thought was of the children and animals. She prayed none had strayed near the gryphon's path as he went through the village.

Her gaze shifted higher to the castle atop the mountain overlooking the village. At one time, the castle had seen many visitors, but as Laird MacNamara grew older, he declined to see anyone.

Nicole crossed her arms over her chest and thought how different her life might have been had she been born a nobleman's daughter. Or even if she'd had a family, someone she could trust to help her through life.

Instead, she discovered she wasn't even from Earth, but from another realm. She still didn't quite know whether to believe Val and Gabriel or not. It did help make sense of her life though.

"Another realm," she whispered.

She had been found as an infant, that much she knew for certain, but why everyone would fear her, she had never understood. Who would fear a babe? Surely none of the villagers could have known where she had come from.

Or had they?

Her head began to ache the longer she thought about it. She looked toward the loch. She could just barely make out the top of her cottage. Despite living alone, she had always loved her cottage and being so near the loch. The beauty had been undeniable, even in winter where the snow blanketed the ground thickly as it did now.

The nearby trees drooped from the weight of the snow on their branches. The wind whistled softly as it added to the freezing temperatures.

No light from the sun penetrated the thick clouds, nor would it for several days most likely. The only certainty was more snow.

There was a loud crack as a limb broke from the weight of the snow and ice. It made no sound as it was cushioned in the mounds of snow below the tree.

Would that be her life? Would there be no sound when she died? She rubbed her hands up and down her arms.

She didn't know what would happen now. Val and Gabriel claimed to kill creatures such as the gryphon, which she found difficult to believe. Ordinary men killing extraordinary creatures? Not very likely.

But then she remembered their weapons. Val's halberd looked normal at first, but if they were affiliated with the Fae as they claimed, then the Fae must aid them somehow.

"Everything all right?"

She jerked around to find Val behind her. His pale green eyes held a hint of worry. "I'm just trying to go through everything I've been told. I don't know whether to believe it or not."

He held out his hand. Nicole took it and he led her back to the fire and pulled her down beside him.

"I can't imagine what you must think of us, but all I ask is that you trust us for now until you come to understand what we've told you is the truth. We'll keep you safe from the gryphon. Of that, I can assure you."

She stared into his eyes, and found herself wanting to believe him. It could be because it was nice to have a friend with her, but then again, she worried that it might be because she found herself attracted to him.

Something she could not allow to continue.

CHAPTER SIX

Gabriel walked into the village to see people standing and watching their homes burn, while others sifted through the rubble that was once their house.

He sighed. They all looked devastated, but he knew that if the gryphon returned that night, there would be few left standing the next morning.

As he walked, he saw a dog sitting beside a man lying on his side, obviously dead. The dog looked lost and alone. Much like Gabriel felt every day. He walked to the dog and patted its head.

"He's gone," he murmured to the dog who licked his hand. "If you stay here, you're liable to starve to death." Though Gabriel knew he shouldn't, he couldn't leave the dog. "Come, boy," he said as he stood and started to walk away.

He looked back and found the dog staring after him. "Come on," he tried again and whistled.

This time the dog stood up, then turned and looked at his dead master.

Gabriel sighed and waited. The dog looked from his dead master to Gabriel. He couldn't leave the wolfhound.

Gabriel whistled again. This time the dog slowly walked toward him. He rubbed the dog's big gray head.

"I'll keep you safe," he promised and turned to continue through the village.

He didn't bother to look down to see if the dog followed, because the poor beast kept his head right under Gabriel's hand the entire time.

Despite the years he had spent with the Shields, and how he thought of them as family, there was something about the look in the dog's dark brown eyes that pulled at Gabriel's soul. He had felt dead for so long, that he wondered if he would ever again feel anything.

As he walked through the village, few looked him in the eye, and the ones that did, hastily turned away. He thought he would return to the cave empty handed when he saw an old man sitting on the ground next to his burned cottage.

Gabriel stopped beside him and gave him a nod of greeting. "Is there anything I can do?"

The old man shook his balding head and raised his wrinkled face to Gabriel. "I lost me wife," he said. "She was sick, and I couldna get her out in time."

Gabriel took a deep breath, unsure of what to say. "A terrible loss," he murmured.

"Such is life, aye," the man said and wiped at his eyes with the back of his hand. "At least she isna hurtin' any longer. I sure will miss my Maud."

Gabriel couldn't help but wonder what it was like to love someone so much that you were lost without them. He had studied the way Cole looked at Shannon, but had gleaned nothing. What was it that pulled two people together?

Aimery, the Fae commander, would say it was their destiny, mates reunited again. But Gabriel didn't believe it. There had to be something more, something deeper.

He lifted his coin purse and dug inside before bending down and placing the coins in the old man's weathered hand. "I'll be around. If you need anything, let me know."

The old man's lips pulled back into a smile showing a few missing teeth. "Doona worry, lad. I'll see my Maud soon enough." He narrowed his faded blue eyes on Gabriel. "Ye are no' from here?"

Gabriel shook his head. "I was passing through and saw the devastation. What happened?"

"Evil," the old man said. "The purest form of evil."

Gabriel went down on his haunches beside the man. No sooner had he done that, then the dog sat and leaned his massive weight against Gabriel. He reached over and absently scratched the dog behind his ears.

"Tell me what kind of evil," Gabriel asked.

The old man squeezed his eyes shut and shook his head. "I wasna quick enough ta see it, but I warned them that the more they delved into the evil, the greater our punishment would be. No one listened."

"Who?" Gabriel asked, his heart beginning to pound.

The old man lifted his hand and pointed behind him. "The village."

"Everyone?" Gabriel was beginning to wonder if the old man had gone daft.

He turned and looked at Gabriel. "Of course I mean everyone. And now, wee Nicole is gone. All because of their hatred and greed."

"Nicole?" Gabriel asked, hoping the old man would tell him more.

The old man stuffed the coins Gabriel had given him into a small bag he had attached to the waist of his trousers. "Aye, Nicole. Poor thing has lived alone ever since the old witch that took her in died. Nicole was a good lass, always pleasant, even when they threw rocks or spit at her. She didna deserve the fate they gave her."

"And what fate was that?"

"Her death," the old man said, once again staring at what was left of his cottage. "Me and me wife wanted ta take her in and raise her ourselves, but the rest wouldna let us. I did try ta make sure she had enough food since na one would sell her much."

Gabriel couldn't believe what he was hearing. How could an entire village want to kill one lone girl? And for what?

"What was the reason the villagers gave for wanting her dead?"

"Her penance," he answered. "When she was brought here-"

"What?" Gabriel interrupted. "Brought here?"

The old man looked at him and nodded. "Aye, brought here. The man who brought her left her on the shore of the loch, no' far from Nicole's cottage. Every one of us knew the man was evil."

"What did the man say?"

The old man shook his head and closed his eyes. "It doesna matter. I shouldna be talkin' aboot it anyways."

Gabriel knew he would get no more out of the man this day. Maybe in a day or so he would come back and ask a few more questions. For now, he had more information than he had hoped for.

He stood and began the walk back to the cave, the dog still beside him with his head beneath Gabriel's hand. He hoped Val and Nicole didn't mind the animal joining them.

~ ~ ~

He waited and watched. He could hear the wails from the village as they buried their dead and sifted through the rubble of their homes. He cringed inwardly because he had ravaged the village all in the name of evil.

How many centuries had he killed innocents? He had lost count after the second century. Now, he was being ordered to kill her – Nicole.

Of all the things he had done, this one was the one thing he had prayed never to have to do. Yet, he had no choice.

She had to die.

He felt the Great Evil's presence. He was being watched. Anger simmered just beneath the surface. After all the years of dedicated service, the Great Evil had begun to question his loyalty. He nearly laughed aloud. As if he had the option to turn his loyalty. That had ended the day he had accepted the evil.

A day he vividly remembered, half a millennium later.

~ ~ ~

At the sound of approaching footsteps, Val jumped to his feet and grabbed his halberd before racing to the entrance of the cave. He expected to see Gabriel, but what he didn't expect to see was a large gray dog running up the mountain next to him.

Val braced one hand against the wall of the cave while the other held his halberd as he waited for Gabriel. When his fellow Shield reached the cave entrance, Val raised a questioning brow at the dog.

Gabriel glanced down at the dog that now stared up adoringly at him and shrugged. "Don't ask," he said as he continued into the cave.

Val could only stare in wonder. He had never seen Gabriel become close to anything, let alone an animal. There were many things the Shields didn't know about

Gabriel, but to be fair, Gabriel didn't know a lot about himself.

Val followed Gabriel and the dog deeper into the cave until they reached the fire where Nicole sat. She let out a little yelp and clapped her hands together, and the dog rushed to her side.

"Oh, Laird, I wondered what had become of you," she said as she scratched the dog behind his ears. She raised her gaze to Gabriel. "Where is Fergus?"

"Fergus?" Gabriel asked.

"Aye," she said as the dog lay down beside her. "He's Laird's master."

"He's dead."

Val cringed at Gabriel's harsh tone, but when he glanced at Nicole, all she did was shake her head.

"I knew it had to be something as bad as that for Laird to leave him," she said and patted the dog's massive head. "This wolfhound has to be the most loyal dog I've ever known."

Suddenly, Laird rose and padded over to Gabriel, who absently rubbed the dog's head. Val wondered if Gabriel knew just how telling his actions were.

"Did you learn anything?" Val asked him.

Gabriel sighed and sank to the ground. "I did, and none of it good."

"Tell me," Val said as he sat.

Gabriel licked his lips and stared into the fire. "I came upon an old man who sat beside his burned cottage. He was the only one who would talk to me. I didn't expect to discover much, but it seems I got lucky since he knew quite a lot about Nicole."

"Interesting," Val said and glanced at Nicole who watched Gabriel with fascination.

"Hmm. Very," Gabriel said. "It was indeed the entire

village who summoned the gryphon."

Val jerked and shook his head as if he hadn't heard Gabriel right. "That isn't possible."

Gabriel's gaze rose to his. "It hasn't happened before, but I think we're looking at something completely different here."

Val scratched his head. "Go on."

"Nicole was brought to the village and left on the shores of the loch. The old man said a witch took her in despite him and his wife offering to raise Nicole themselves."

"Margda," Nicole whispered as her gaze slowly moved to Val. "She's the witch who raised me."

"And the couple who wanted you?" he asked.

A small smile pulled at her lips. "Donald and Maude. They were a kind, older couple who never had children of their own. Donald would come by at least once a week and check on me, despite Margda threatening to turn him into a frog."

Val turned back to Gabriel. "Anything else?"

"Oh, aye," he said and ran a hand down his tired face. "Though I couldn't get much out of Donald, I did discover that they thought it was Nicole's penance to die. Supposedly, they think it has something to do with the evil that brought her."

Val thought over Gabriel's words and couldn't help wondering if the evil Donald spoke of was the same evil that they were trying to destroy.

"I still don't understand why the evil brought Nicole here, to this small village in the middle of the Highlands," Val said.

Gabriel nodded. "I've been thinking much the same thing. If he knew what she was, why not kill her then?"

"Good question," Val said. He slid a glance at Nicole

and found her staring at the ground near her feet seemingly lost in thought.

Val and Gabriel exchanged a look. They needed to speak with Aimery. Immediately.

.

CHAPTER SEVEN

Nicole watched her two saviors and Laird walk from the cave. She tried to pretend that Gabriel's words didn't bother her, but the truth was they did. Even after knowing how the village felt about her, it was difficult to hear it from another person.

She had often prayed that Donald and Maude would be able to take her in, but Margda had gone to great lengths to ensure that didn't happen. Each time Nicole questioned Margda about it, the witch would only say that Donald and Maude would interfere, and prevent Fate from dealing her hand.

Nicole hadn't understood then, but she did now. Margda had known that if Donald and Maude had taken Nicole in, they would have left, leaving the village to reap their own greed and sins without Nicole there to be the sacrifice.

She wiped at the sudden tears that sprang to her eyes. She had managed to live out her life with as much happiness as she could muster. Granted, there had been times she had wanted to run away and start over, but she hadn't dared. Margda's threats still rang in her ears, which is why she had stayed in the village even after Margda had died.

With a loud sigh, she rose to her feet and thought about her future. Val was right. The gryphon would return for her and continue to return until she was dead.

But I don't want to die!

"You don't have to."

Nicole whirled around to see a man behind her. He was unlike anything she had ever seen. So blindingly handsome that it was nearly impossible to look at him, yet it was impossible to look away. His long, flaxen hair hung straight down his back, while many tiny braids held his hair away from his face.

He was tall and clothed in royal blue and white. His face was perfection right down to his lips. He exuded power and seduction as easily as breathing, and Nicole's heart raced just being near him. But it was his eyes that swirled different shades of blue that held her attention.

She swallowed and blinked, unsure she was really looking at a man or had conjured him from her imagination. "Who are you?"

"Aimery, the commander of the Fae army. Val and Gabriel have called for me, but I sensed your distress and thought I would see you first."

"Fae?" she repeated and took a step back. "Are you real? Val and Gabriel told me about the Fae, I just didn't imagine I'd ever get to meet one."

He smiled kindly. "Indeed I am real. The Fae have a strong link to this realm, a link that many humans don't know about or refuse to believe."

"Maybe it's for the best."

His smile grew. "That it is, Nicole. How are Val and Gabriel treating you?"

"Like gentlemen."

"Good." He turned to walk out of the cave, then stopped and turned back to her. "Nicole, don't worry about the gryphon. Val and Gabriel will protect you with their lives."

His words calmed her as nothing else could, and as she watched him walk from the cave, she found herself anxious to leave and start a new life.

~ ~ ~

Val stared over the still waters of the loch, the water lapping at his feet. He had to admit, the Highlands were quite lovely, even in the middle of winter. He found himself wondering what it would look like in the summer.

"Do you miss it?" Gabriel asked.

"What?"

"Rome."

Val sighed. "Sometimes. Rome was unique and powerful and majestic, but destined to fall. Had I not joined the Shields, I don't know what would've become of me."

"You were a powerful general. You held a place of honor."

Val nearly snorted. "If there was one thing you could count on in Rome, it was for someone to try and kill you either politically or literally. I was quite glad to be out of the viper's nest."

He turned when he saw Gabriel face him. Gabriel's gaze held a hint of envy and remorse.

"Do you regret leaving your family?"

Val closed his eyes and breathed deeply. He could still remember seeing his father for the last time. The man he had looked up to for years wouldn't even look him in the face.

Slowly Val opened his eyes. "It was for the best."

"That's not what I asked," Gabriel said.

"Aye," he said and turned back to the loch. "I miss my family."

For long moments, neither man said anything, as each was lost in their thoughts. Val didn't like thinking of his family and the hatred his father had for him, or how he let his sisters down in the worst possible way.

With each breath that left his body, he felt the vise around his heart start to constrict as it had before he joined the Shields and Aimery had given him something to focus on. Now, it seemed that the farther he tried to push his past away, the closer it came.

"Easy," Aimery said as he laid a hand on Val's shoulder.

Instantly, his anxiety subsided. Val looked over at Aimery who now stood between him and Gabriel. Aimery had done exactly the same thing when he had first found Val, drunk in an alley and beaten to a pulp.

He silently nodded his thanks to Aimery and turned his attention to Nicole and their present problem.

"Aimery," Gabriel said. "I was beginning to think you didn't hear our call."

"I heard you," Aimery said and clasped his hands behind his back. "I wanted to see Nicole first. She was anxious about tonight and the gryphon's arrival, so I went to calm her."

Val looked to the cave and saw Nicole at the entrance. Her black hair, loose and hanging around her, blew in the gentle breeze as she watched them.

"Whose dog is this?" Aimery asked.

Gabriel laid a hand on the tall beast. "Mine."

For long moments, Aimery simply regarded Gabriel. "I've no news," Aimery finally said. "I've been to Stone Crest and Hugh, Roderick, and Cole are fortifying the castle as we speak."

Gabriel fingered the hilt of his sword. "I don't like this, Aimery. We're taking a huge chance."

"We don't have any other way. I have my soldiers surrounding Stone Crest."

Val nodded. "Even if we were able to reach Stone Crest, based on what you told me today, I think it's imperative we kill the gryphon here."

"What did you learn?" Aimery asked sharply, his Fae eyes riveted on Gabriel.

Val paced the shoreline as Gabriel told Aimery of his findings and Nicole's reaction.

When Gabriel was finished, Val turned to Aimery. "There is something different here. No one has heard of the blue stone."

"That doesn't mean it isn't here," Aimery said. "You just need to look for it."

Val shook his head. "I don't think so. An evil brought Nicole here. Why do you think that is? For her entire life, the village has made sure she stayed here," he said pointing to her cottage. "She was left on the shores of this loch, Aimery."

"He's right," Gabriel said. "The village has gone to a lot of trouble to keep her here. I doubt they would let her leave easily."

Aimery turned to the cave and waved Nicole toward him. "Let's find out, shall we?"

"What is it?" Nicole asked when she reached them.

Val looked deep into her beautiful, violet eyes. "If you could leave right now, would you?"

She nodded eagerly. "Aye."

"Then, let's try," Aimery said and reached for her hands.

Val waited for Aimery to disappear with Nicole, but nothing happened. "What is it?" he asked Aimery.

The Fae commander released Nicole's hands and blew out a frustrated breath. "Whoever brought her here has also anchored her to this place."

Val hated that he was right, but at least now they knew what they were up against. In order for them to take the fourth Chosen back to Stone Crest, they had to kill the gryphon.

"What is it?" Nicole asked. "Are you saying I cannot leave?"

Aimery shook his head. "You were right, Val. There is something much more going on here than the stone and the creature. I must speak with Theron and Rufina."

In a blink, Aimery was gone. Val turned to Nicole whose eyes had gone round with fear. "Nay, you can't leave. Not yet at least."

"I'm doomed then," she said and wrapped her arms around herself.

Val removed his fur-lined cloak and wrapped it around her. "You shouldn't have come out here without your cloak. You'll freeze to death."

When she raised her face to him, he saw the desolation in her eyes. "It would be better than being ripped apart by the gryphon."

"We won't let that happen," Gabriel said.

Val wrapped his hands around Nicole's arms until she faced him. "I vow that I won't let the gryphon harm you. Do you hear me?"

She nodded and lowered her eyes. "I appreciate what you are both doing, but it's useless. I've known it my entire life, but I allowed myself to hope for the first time last night. Having that hope ripped from me is worse than never having any at all."

Val let her go when she stepped out of his arms and turned to walk to the cave. He dropped his head and raked a hand through his hair.

"What's going on with you?" Gabriel asked.

Val shook his head and turned away from his friend. There was no way he could tell Gabriel the truth. "She depends on me. I won't let her down. I can't let her down."

He didn't wait to see if Gabriel would respond but quickly walked away, needing time alone with his thoughts and a past that forever haunted him.

~ ~ ~

Gabriel watched his friend walk away. There was no doubt that something bothered Val. Usually Val was calm and stoic. Nothing much affected him. Odd that since they had met Nicole he seemed on edge.

Very odd.

Gabriel glanced at the cave, then at Val's retreating back. Only four of the Chosen were needed, and three found their mates in the Shields. Could Nicole find her mate in Val?

He hoped so, because Val deserved happiness. Gabriel refused to think about being the only one who didn't find his mate, but then again, men without a past didn't deserve much of anything.

CHAPTER EIGHT

Regardless of how far or fast Val walked, he couldn't leave his past behind. He thought because he hadn't been plagued with the nightmares for a while that they had left him. They might be gone in his sleep, but he could still hear his sisters' screams as they begged for his help.

When he came to a fallen log, he brushed off the snow and sat because he didn't know how much longer his trembling legs could hold him. The memories, when they came, always struck hard and ruthlessly.

The only thing he was thankful for was that none of his Shield brethren could see him now. He made sure they only saw the staid, calm Val.

For so long, his concentration had been on killing the creatures, and then on locating the Chosen. Now, he found himself in a situation he had prayed never to be in again - and like a fool, he had given a vow. At least this time, it was a vow he knew he could keep. He wasn't the naïve young man that he once was.

Time and evil had seen to that.

He raised his gaze from the calm waters of the loch to the sky and found the sun above him. Though he wasn't ready to return to the cave, he knew Gabriel and Nicole would be waiting on him.

Somehow, he reined in his memories and tamped them down into a dark corner of his mind. He'd done it countless times before, and each time he prayed the memories would stay hidden.

When he was back in control, he rose and began the trek back to the cave. He refused to think about the past, and instead, looked at the beautiful scenery blanketed in white. The only sound was the crunch of his boots on the snow.

Right before he got a whiff of evil, the hairs on the back of his neck rose, alerting him that someone was watching - someone evil.

Instead of walking to the cave, he changed directions and stood at the loch where just hours before he and Gabriel had talked with Aimery. He crossed his arms over his chest to warm his hands in case he needed to use his sword. As he pretended to admire the loch, his eyes scanned the mountain and groves of trees around him.

Nothing moved. Nothing made a sound.

But something was definitely out there.

Behind him, he heard footfalls and rocks sliding down the mountain. Val didn't need to turn around to know it was Gabriel. Each of the Shields knew each other's habits, voice and walk, and could pick each other out of a crowd blindfolded.

"What is it?" Gabriel whispered as he came to stand beside him.

"Evil."

Gabriel took a deep breath. "Ah, the stench. Do you think it's the gryphon?"

"Nay. Something worse."

Gabriel swore under his breath. "My bow and arrows are in the cave."

"It's all right," Val said and turned to Gabriel with smile

that told his friend he was looking forward to the fight. "You protect Nicole. I'll face whatever is out here."

"Not alone," Gabriel argued. "You may have a gift of mastering any weapon, but I refuse to allow you to face this unknown evil alone."

Val knew arguing was futile. "Fine. We'll both return to the cave."

"It's a better defense anyway," Gabriel said as he turned and started toward the cave. "Give me a moment to get in and my bow notched."

Val gave a quick nod while he tried to locate which direction the evil came from. A short time later he heard Gabriel give a three-toned whistle. Val took one more glance around before he turned and started up the mountain.

When he stepped inside, Nicole stood several paces behind Gabriel twisting her hands nervously while Laird sat at her feet, his dark gaze looking out, waiting.

"What is it?" she asked. "Is it the gryphon?"

"I don't know," Val answered and reached for his halberd. "Just stay at the back of the cave if something happens."

She nodded and moved away with Laird following her. Val didn't know how long he and Gabriel sat in the shadows waiting for something to attack, but nothing did.

"Whatever it was is gone," Val said as he stood.

Gabriel nodded after he took a deep breath. "I hate the stink of evil."

Val stretched the kinks from his back. "This has me worried. If they saw Nicole come from the cave earlier, then they know she's here."

"I didn't smell the evil then, and Aimery surely would've noted the evil."

"True, but just in case, let's make sure Nicole stays in

the cave until all of this is over."

"I agree," Gabriel said. "Now come, let's eat."

Val's stomach rumbled as soon as he reached Nicole and the fire. She gave him a relieved smile and handed him a large piece of bread and cheese.

"I don't have much in my cottage, but we should get it while we can," she said as she handed Gabriel food after he had lowered himself to the ground.

Gabriel nodded as he took a bite, and Laird moved closer to him.

"I'll go down later and get what you need," Val said around his food.

They ate in silence, each lost in thought. Several times, Val caught Nicole glancing apprehensively toward the entrance.

"You're safe," he said.

"I know."

But he didn't believe her. She was frightened, and with what was coming for her, he would be scared too. He looked over his shoulder and saw the light fading quickly.

"We've lost most of the day. Going to your cottage may have to wait until morn," he said.

"There's nothing I need."

With the entrance a good fifty strides away, Val moved near Nicole, turning so he could see if anyone dared to come into their cave. Where Gabriel had built the fire was hidden by a large formation that jutted from the cave wall, so anyone walking into the cave wouldn't automatically see the light.

It was a perfect defense. Val just wished the rest of the Shields were with him. All five of them could easily take the gryphon.

He sighed and rubbed his eyes with his thumb and forefinger as he yawned.

"What was your childhood like?" Nicole asked.

Val turned to find her staring at him. "Mine?"

She nodded with a grin. "I am looking at you."

"It was a typical childhood of any Roman senator's son."

She laughed, the sound delightful in the somber atmosphere. "Since I know nothing of your Rome, you'll have to be a little more detailed."

He glanced over and saw Gabriel watching him. Val rarely spoke about his time in Rome, and he knew Gabriel was curious. Just as he was curious about Gabriel's past.

"There isn't much to tell, really," Val said with a shrug even as the sights, sounds, and smell of Rome filled his senses until, for just a moment, he thought he was once more in Rome.

"My father, as a senator, was immersed in politics. Everything our family did was a reflection on him and of him. We dressed a certain way, acted a certain way, and said the right things at all times. Without question."

He thought back to his mother and smiled. She'd always had a warm smile, her hands always gentle as she smoothed his hair from his forehead and urged him to be patient with his father. From the time he was a young lad until he became an adult, it had been the same. His mother had never seen the ugly side of her husband.

"My mother hated the time he was gone from us. Father was always with the senators debating some issue or another, and the higher my father rose in the political arena, the less we saw of him. She tried to make his absence less noticeable by keeping me and my sisters occupied."

"She sounds like a good mother," Nicole said.

Val looked at her and smiled. "She was. Oh, she had her faults like everyone, but she was a wonderful woman. And beautiful, too. She had the most amazing dark blonde hair that curled into ringlets that I would wind around my finger."

He didn't know why he was telling them all of this. Maybe it was because they were good memories, and he didn't mind sharing those. Or maybe it was because he knew Nicole hadn't had a childhood and she wanted to have a peek into his.

Nicole's eyes went distant. "Sounds lovely. And your sisters?"

"They were mischievous little vixens that were constantly in trouble," Val admitted with a smile as he recalled how they badgered him endlessly. "It was my duty, as their elder brother, to get them out of whatever trouble they got into. We were all very close for a time."

"What happened?" Gabriel asked.

Val picked up a stick to stir the fire. "I came of age. My father thought it was time I received the proper training of a senator's son."

Nicole leaned forward. "Which meant what?"

"Learning of course," he said. "I hated him for taking me away from my mother and sisters, but I quickly found a group of boys who became my friends. From them, I learned of the debauchery and excess my mother had kept hidden from me."

He didn't wish to say more, regardless that he had already said too much and Gabriel and Nicole would want to know the rest. He stayed silent, hoping they would drop it.

He should've known better.

"So what happened?" Nicole asked softly.

"To my disgrace, I became the very thing my mother had wanted to keep me from. I became a true Roman in every sense of the word. Just as my father was. It wasn't until I joined the army that I learned she was ill. I was away in battle when she died."

Nicole's hand came to rest on top of his. "I'm so sorry."

He shrugged, but the hurt would never diminish. The one person who had wanted to protect him and love him he had left behind. How could he ever forgive himself for that? "By the time I was granted leave and returned home, it had been three months since her death. My sisters had grown up in my absence and married. They had my mother's beauty and my father's adventurous spirit. Not a good combination."

Before Nicole or Gabriel could ask more, Val rose up on his knee and reached for the waterskin. If he started talking about his sisters' husbands, he was likely to lose it. "Tell us more about Margda, Nicole."

Nicole wasn't fooled. She knew Val changed the subject because there was something he didn't wish for them to know. She glanced at Gabriel to see the worry that lined his face as he watched Val with hooded eyes.

"There isn't much to say," Nicole finally answered. "She was a witch, in every sense of the word."

"She practiced black magic?" Gabriel asked.

Nicole shrugged. "I don't know. I never saw anything, but there were times she would disappear and not return until morning."

"Do you think she was seeing a man?" Val asked.

Nicole snorted and shook her head. "Nay, I don't think she was seeing anyone romantically. Margda was the ugliest woman I've ever seen."

Gabriel leaned back against the cave wall and asked, "How long did you live with her?"

"Until I was ten and four. She caught a fever at the beginning of spring and never recovered."

"So, you stayed in the cottage?" Val asked.

Nicole recalled the day she had started to pack so she could leave, only to find the villagers had other ideas. "Before Margda was even buried, the village elders came to say that the cottage was mine."

"Why didn't you leave?"

"Where was I to go?" she asked. "I had no coin and no family. Starving didn't really appeal to me."

Gabriel hid his smile with a cough at her sarcasm and scratched Laird's neck. "They didn't allow you to leave, did they?"

She shook her head. "At the time, I thought it the right thing. I was finally alone, to do as I pleased without Margda standing over me. I thought I was free."

The longer Val sat beside her, the more Nicole found it difficult to think. His mere presence was so large, so powerful with the heat radiating from him. It was distracting.

She had never been around many men, and the ones she had were usually the village elders. The men of the village tended to stay far away from her.

Oh, there were the few who would venture near her cottage to see if they could catch a look at her to see if she really were as crazed or evil as the villagers claimed her to be.

But Val was different.

Not only was he as handsome as sin, but he also had an easy way about him that immediately put her at ease. She couldn't describe exactly what it was. Only that she found herself looking at him, trying to decipher who he was.

And to make matters more complicated, she couldn't understand that while Gabriel was a handsome man, he didn't make her stomach flutter as Val did.

She found her gaze on Val's lips, wondering what it would be like to be kissed by him. Since she had never been kissed, she had no idea if he would taste as good as he looked.

Suddenly, his lips curved into a small smile, and she jerked her gaze to his and saw a flicker of something cross his eyes. Her breath caught in her throat as his gaze slowly lowered to her mouth.

Gabriel saved her from making a fool of herself when he cleared his throat and said, "So, you thought you were free. I take it the villagers made sure you knew otherwise."

"Aye," Nicole said and hastily looked away from Val. He was more tempting than the freedom she sought so desperately, and having never found herself attracted to a man, the emotions were heady indeed.

"How?" Val asked.

She shrugged and tugged at her skirts. "It was little things at first. The elders would bring me food and other items. It wasn't until later that I realized they did it to keep me out of town."

Gabriel's brow furrowed. "Did you not go into the village with Margda?"

"Nay. Margda rarely went by herself, so I never thought anything of it. It was only after I told the elders that I could get the food myself that they made it clear they would bring it to me. Or I could starve."

"How long did this last?"

Nicole turned to Val at his question. "Another three months at the most. Then, they stopped coming at all. I knew where Margda stashed the coins, so I gathered them and went into town when I ran out of food."

She remembered that day vividly. She had been so excited to finally see the village and meet someone her own age, someone that could be a friend. But it wasn't meant to be. She suppressed a shudder as she recalled the force in which the first rock hit her.

CHAPTER NINE

"What happened?" Gabriel asked softly.

Nicole swallowed and looked at her hands in her lap. "It wasn't what I expected. No one would sell me any food."

"What did they expect you to do? Starve?" Val asked.

"Nay. They just didn't want to supply me with food anymore. It wasn't long after that when Donald began to bring me food and material for clothes, as well as showing me how to hunt for my own food. I always paid him for his troubles because I knew what the villagers would do to him if they ever found out."

Val sighed. "So Donald and his wife supplied you with food all these years?"

"Donald taught me how to use a slingshot to fell the smaller animals, while Maude showed me what plants could be used as herbs for healing or to season a meal."

"Amazing," Gabriel murmured.

Nicole pulled the blankets over her feet. Just thinking about her past put a chill over her soul.

Val reached over and placed his hand atop hers. A bolt of awareness shivered across her skin and she slowly raised her gaze to his. It was as if something had well and surely connected them.

She saw it in his green eyes, knew he had felt it, as well.

"It's over now, Nicole. The village can't hurt you anymore."

She nodded, not trusting her voice with her heart hammering in her chest. Her gaze was locked with his, the heat of his skin on hers made breathing difficult.

"I'm going hunting," Gabriel said as he rose to his feet. Laird quickly stood and waited.

Val looked away and Nicole took the time to calm her racing heart and get herself under control. She inwardly winced, hoping they didn't realize how naïve she was about everything. She might not have had a man touch her, but she'd seen animals and humans couple. She knew what it was all about.

"For what?" Val asked, jerking her out of her thoughts.

Gabriel chuckled as he picked up his bow and arrow. "Food."

"Be careful."

"Laird will be with me. If something happens, I'll send him to you."

Val watched as Gabriel and his dog walked from the cave. With his cock hard with need, the last thing Val needed was to be alone with Nicole. He had seen the hunger in her eyes when she had stared at his mouth.

And when her pink tongue had darted out and she licked her full lips, it had nearly been the death of him.

His body ached to feel her against him. He yearned to run his hands over her skin once more and kiss her sweet mouth. There was a chance he could deny the attraction he felt if only Nicole would stop looking at him with such stark desire in her violet depths.

He wished he could say he wanted her because it had

been awhile since his body had found release, but it would be a lie. Maybe it was her innocence that he found alluring, but whatever it was, he knew he couldn't act on it.

Not if he wanted to keep Nicole alive.

"Val?"

He nearly groaned at the husky sound of her voice. Slowly, he turned his head toward her. The uncertainty and nervousness in her eyes alerted him that she was about to ask something he wouldn't like.

"What is it...what I mean to say is, would you kiss me?"

Val jumped to his feet and backed away, his balls tightening when he looked at her lips. When he saw the sorrow flicker across her beautiful eyes before she lowered them, he could have kicked himself.

"I shouldn't be the one to kiss you."

She played with the edge of the blanket and asked, "Why?"

"My duty is to keep you safe."

"I know." Her gaze rose to his then. "I've never kissed anyone. I heard some of the village girls talking about it once. They said it made them feel weak in the knees."

Val closed his eyes and groaned. He could well imagine what her full lips would taste like as he nipped and licked them until they parted. Then, he would sweep his tongue inside her mouth and let it mate with hers.

"Is that what every kiss feels like?" she asked.

Val opened his eyes to find her watching him intently. The fire cast a red-orange glow over her as she sat innocently, waiting for him to answer.

"Nay," he finally answered. "Some kisses are chaste, some sweet, while others make you burn."

"Burn," she repeated and sighed wistfully. "I'd like to receive a kiss that makes me burn."

By the gods!

Val gripped the stone wall of the cave and forced himself to stand still and not lay her back on the blankets and give her a kiss that would make them both go up in flames.

"Have you ever received a kiss that made you burn?" she asked.

His breathing increased and his cock strained painfully against his pants, but he refused to move even a hair's breadth.

"A few times," he said through clenched teeth. "Those kisses are few and far between."

"Why?"

"Sometimes you think you've found someone who will give you a kiss to make you burn, and although you enjoy the kiss, it isn't everything you thought it would be."

"Ah," she said and turned to study the fire.

Val used the opportunity to turn his back to her and adjust his aching rod. Despite the scar on his face, Val had always had an easy time finding women to share his bed. He didn't have women coming to him in droves, but he rarely had one turn him down.

He looked over his shoulder and studied Nicole's profile. She was an innocent in so many ways, and he knew she was curious about the world and men. Having been kept away from human contact for the most part, she craved it desperately.

Just as he craved her.

He clenched his jaw and fisted his hands at his side. He would not give in to temptation and fail Nicole. His duty was to keep her safe - even from himself.

When a small hand touched his arm, he jerked around to find Nicole behind him.

"You seem angry," she said. "Is everything all right?"

"It's fine," he replied.

His gaze lowered to find her licking her lips again. It was everything Val could do not to lean down and pull her tongue into his mouth.

"Do you find me unattractive? Is that why you won't kiss me?"

His eyes snapped to her face. "Nay."

"Then please kiss me. Just one kiss and I won't ask for anything else."

She had no idea what she was asking for, Val realized. "I can't."

"All right," she said and moved past him.

"Where are you going?"

"To find Gabriel and see if he'll kiss me."

Val took hold of her arm and dragged her back until she stood in front of him. "You want a kiss? I'll give you a kiss," he said and cupped either side of her face with his hands.

Her dark, silky hair flowed between his fingers as her violet eyes widened in surprise. Val lowered his head and placed his lips over hers.

He intended to give her a chaste kiss, but once his lips touched hers, he was lost.

Leisurely, his lips moved over hers, kissing and tasting as he nipped and licked. When her mouth opened on a gasp, he slanted his mouth over hers and let his tongue explore her.

When she groaned and molded her body to his, as her arms slid around his neck, Val knew he was lost. The kiss had gone far beyond what he had planned, but no matter what he told himself, he couldn't end it.

Though she was an innocent in the art of kissing, she quickly learned and copied everything he did until Val found himself breathless with need.

His hands moved from her face, over her shoulders and

down her back to pull her hard against him. Her soft curves fit him nicely, and her moans drove him onward, enticing him in a way he never expected.

He lost himself in the kiss, forgot everything and everyone around them. As the kiss lengthened, his desire grew until only one thing remained - Nicole.

Just as he was about to lower her to the ground, something nudged his leg. It was then he became aware of his surroundings and that they were no longer alone.

Val ended the kiss and opened his eyes to see Laird standing beside him. He dropped his hands as Nicole stepped back and touched her lips with shaky fingers.

"Is this what it feels like to burn?" she asked, her eyes ablaze with desire.

As much as Val wanted to tell her the truth, he knew in order to keep her alive, he would have to lie. "It was your first kiss. Most everyone burns after their first kiss."

"Mine didn't...make you burn?"

With the fire behind her and her face hidden in shadows, he couldn't see her expression, but he heard the hurt in her voice.

"I prefer more experienced women," he said and hastily moved to the entrance of the cave.

As he breathed in the cold night air, he looked around for Gabriel and berated himself for kissing Nicole in the first place.

"Why did you lie?"

Val spun around to find Gabriel behind him. He didn't know how much Gabriel had seen, but it was more than he would have liked. "I had to."

For a long moment, Gabriel stared at him before turning on his heel and walking into the cave.

~ ~ ~

Realm of the Fae

Aimery waited patiently for his king and queen to respond to the news he had just given them.

"Are you sure?" Theron asked.

Aimery nodded solemnly. "No amount of my Fae power could move her from that place."

"We must do something," Rufina said. "She's the fourth Chosen one."

Aimery looked to his queen. "I have complete faith in Val and Gabriel."

"As do I," Rufina said. "I didn't mean to suggest otherwise, but even you had reservations about splitting the Shields up before. Now, three of them are at Stone Crest keeping three of the Chosen safe, while two more battle an evil stronger than we've ever encountered."

Aimery sighed deeply and stared at the floor with its beautiful blue tiles. "We've faced this evil before."

"What?" Theron thundered. "You can't mean...."

"I do," Aimery said and lifted his head. "It's the Great Evil. Somehow, he found Nicole as an infant just after she was brought to Earth. He's had a hold on her ever since."

He watched as Rufina took Theron's hand and they looked into each other's eyes. No one had to tell Aimery that the collective silence of his sovereigns meant the doom they had tried, thus far, to avoid was nearly upon them.

"I haven't given up," Aimery said.

Theron shook his head and helped Rufina from her throne. He bent and placed a kiss on Rufina's protruding belly. "Go rest and take care of our babe, my love."

For once, Rufina didn't question him. She kissed him before making her way out of the throne room.

Aimery turned to Theron when the door closed behind the queen. "What are your plans?"

"I wish it were that simple," Theron replied as he clasped his hands behind his back and walked across the large throne room to the opened balcony overlooking *Caer Rhoemyr*. "If I weren't king, my answer would be to keep my wife and unborn child safe. But I am king. I have an entire realm that is counting on me to keep them alive."

"It's not over yet," Aimery reminded him. "Val is master of any weapon that he palms, and Gabriel with his bow is like having a dozen men at your back. Give them a chance, Theron."

Theron's Fae blue eyes held sadness as he turned to Aimery. "The fates of two realms are in their hands, Aimery. There is nothing more we can do but wait and pray."

"I can move the other three Chosen here."

Theron shook his head. "You know better than I that we cannot. It's too risky a chance."

"How do you know the Great Evil doesn't already know where the three Chosen are?"

"Because," Theron said as he looked over the City of Kings, "if he did, they would already be dead. We're cloaking them now, but it will only be a matter of time before he finds them."

Aimery sighed and watched the sun sink below the mountain. He knew Theron was right, but he also knew the Great Evil was counting on killing Nicole, thereby ending any chance of the Fae or Shields killing him.

"There's one more," Aimery blurted out. He turned to Theron as his king watched him. "There were five Chosen left. We've found four."

CHAPTER TEN

Despite the warmth of his fur-lined cloak, Val couldn't find the heat he so desperately sought. He had taken the first watch since he needed to free his mind of Nicole.

Even now, hours later, he could still taste her kiss, a kiss that had burned him all the way to his soul. She would probably hate him now, but it was for the best. If he were distracted, he couldn't keep her safe. It was a mistake he had made in the past, and he refused to make it again.

His eyes scanned the mountainside and the loch as he heard Gabriel walking toward him.

"Anything?" Gabriel asked as he sat on the other side of the entrance.

Val shook his head. "Nothing but the occasional animal."

"I expect him around midnight."

"Most likely. They don't call it the witching hour for nothing," Val said sarcastically.

He could feel Gabriel's gaze on him. "I've never seen you like this, Val. What makes this assignment so different? And don't tell me it's Nicole, because I've seen you with women."

"If I remember correctly, you've had your share of women, too."

"But we aren't talking about me," Gabriel pointed out.

Val shifted and looked away from his friend.

But Gabriel wasn't about to give up. "Does this have something to do with your family?"

"What gives you that idea?"

"All the years the Shields have been together we learn something of each other along the way. Pretty soon, it isn't hard to put the pieces together."

Val took a deep breath before he blew it out and turned to look at Gabriel. "I once gave a promise to keep someone safe, but I failed in that promise. I won't do it again."

"We've given promises to many people that we've saved from the creatures. You should've earned your redemption by now."

Val shook his head. "I never made anyone a promise before today."

Gabriel finally understood. He watched Val carefully but didn't say more. Whatever ate away at Val went deep, very deep. And wounds like that usually never healed.

He looked over his shoulder to see Nicole moving around near the fire as Laird sat and watched her. The kiss she and Val had shared had been as passionate as any he had seen, and despite what Val wanted to believe, Gabriel knew the kiss had lit a fire inside his friend.

He knew that no matter how hard Val tried to run, he wouldn't be able to outrun his past. He would have to face it, but Gabriel knew better than to tell him that now.

Ever since they arrived in Scotland, Val had been different. Nay. That wasn't right. Ever since they had found Nicole, Val had been different.

It all came back to Nicole. Yet, no matter how hard

Gabriel tried, he couldn't imagine how one lonely girl could get to Val as no other had been able to do.

His gaze slid past Val as he looked at the valley below. If he leaned out far enough, Gabriel could just make out the top of Nicole's cottage. As it had been the night before, the mountain and loch were silent.

Too silent.

Gabriel ran his hand over his bow, marveling as he always did at the beauty of it and the intricate work the Fae had done to carve the symbols into the magic wood.

He pulled back on the string to test the bow, then reached over and pulled an arrow from his quiver. He glanced at the double-headed arrow before he notched it and sighted down his arm.

With his arrow still notched, he swung his arm slowly from the left to the right. Then just before he released the arrow, he raised his arms slightly.

A slight "bing" sounded when he released the arrow. He and Val watched as it sailed silently through the night to land in a grove of trees near Nicole's cottage.

Gabriel wasn't surprised to hear the wounded howl of an animal.

Val rose to his feet. "The gryphon."

"Aye."

"How did you know?"

Gabriel shrugged. "I smelled him."

"Good. Stay here with Nicole," Val said and started out of the cave.

Gabriel quickly caught his arm and yanked him back. "I'm not letting you go down there alone."

"He needs to be destroyed," Val stated.

"I'm not arguing that, but rushing down there alone to get yourself killed isn't the answer."

Val brushed a hand through his hair. He knew Gabriel

was right. It wasn't like him to act without thinking. At least it hadn't been before Nicole. Now, all he could think about was keeping her safe at all costs.

"You're right," he said. "Our best defense is here."

"There's the old Val I knew," Gabriel said with a smile. "Welcome back."

"Kiss my arse."

Gabriel wrinkled his nose. "Not for all the magic of the Fae."

Despite his mood, Val chuckled. Gabriel wasn't known for his jokes, but he always seemed to know when one of them was in need of something or other.

"Thanks."

Gabriel waved away his words. "Thank me by staying alive. I've no desire to fight this creature alone."

They sat for hours, but the gryphon didn't attack. Sometime in the early morning hours, Val left Gabriel to keep watch and moved to the back of the cave.

The fire had begun to die down, so he piled more wood onto the embers and coaxed them back into flames. Satisfied that the fire would burn for an hour or more, he turned to see Nicole huddled in a little ball.

He pulled another blanket over her and lay on his pallet that was next to hers. Laird was lying on Gabriel's blankets softly snoring.

Val couldn't help but smile at the picture they made. He stretched and winced as he felt a stone under his pallet. After removing the stone, he lay down and thought of a soft feather mattress.

Although he was used to sleeping on the ground, Nicole was not, and deserved to be in her own bed. He inwardly groaned as he thought of Nicole again. She was constantly in his thoughts and he didn't like it.

He closed his eyes and told himself to forget her and

sleep. Though he tried to sleep, he was only able to doze for a few moments at a time. Every time she moved, he would come awake.

It was nearly dawn when he rolled onto his side and found himself facing her. As he gazed at her beautiful face, he couldn't help but recall their kiss, a kiss that he wanted desperately to repeat.

A kiss that hadn't just made him burn – it had scorched him.

Before he knew what he was doing, he found himself scooting between his pallet and hers. He gently rolled her onto her back and watched as she slowly came awake.

"Nicole," he whispered, before he leaned down and lost his battle with temptation.

She didn't resist him as his lips moved over hers. When she sighed and ran her hands up his chest, he wound his hands in her blanket to keep from molding them to her breasts.

When she opened for him, Val slanted his mouth over hers and drank from her sweet nectar. And with each taste, he found his need grew.

With the last shreds of his control slipping away, Val ended the kiss and raised his head to look at her. Before he could explain the kiss, Nicole's eyes closed and she fell back asleep. He ran a hand down the smooth skin of her face and gave her one last kiss before he stood.

After adding more wood to the fire, he walked to the entrance. Gabriel turned to him as he approached.

"Quiet?" he asked.

Gabriel nodded. "Not a peep or smell of anything. He's long gone."

"Good. Go catch some sleep while you can."

Gabriel yawned as he stood and stretched. "You didn't sleep long."

"I find it hard to sleep with evil so close."

"I know what you mean," he said with a frown. "I just knew he would attack tonight."

"I know. It doesn't make sense."

"Unless they're playing with Nicole."

Val didn't like that idea. "Then we need to end this little game."

~ ~ ~

"What's your excuse this time?"

He was really beginning to hate the voice. A faceless voice that followed him wherever he went.

"The Shields are not to be taken lightly," he said.

The voice barked with laughter. "She can't leave. I've bound her to the village. No amount of Fae magic will release her."

"The Shields aren't Fae, and if you haven't forgotten, they've killed the creatures you've sent out."

The silence was deafening, and he knew he had gone too far. But he refused to retreat.

"I've forgotten nothing. It's you who have forgotten just how strong my powers are," the voice said menacingly.

He unfurled his left wing as his wound began to throb. He still wasn't sure how the Shields had known he was near. Though his powers were limited, he had cloaked himself so he could observe them and see just how close an eye they were keeping on Nicole.

His wound would heal, but if it did nothing else, it proved to him that he couldn't take the Shields for granted.

Something brushed against his tail and he swished it to the side and turned his head to look around him. He might not be able to see a body, but he knew the Great One was all around him.

"I've served you well," he said. Loyalty to the Great One had gotten him far, and he wasn't about to let him forget it.

The voice chuckled. "I've never doubted your loyalty, but what I am beginning to doubt is your ability to obey a command. Maybe it's time I bring back the stone."

He froze as dread iced his veins. He had been the first to have the stone removed, and had proven himself an apt soldier for the Great One. For the Great One to even hint at the stone let him know he couldn't wait any longer.

"Ah, I thought that might get your attention," the Great One said. "I want her dead. Immediately."

He looked down and drummed his claws on the ground. "I went to observe last night. They have her inside a cave."

"Is that how you received your wound?"

He quickly folded his wing and nodded.

"Then you didn't hide yourself very well. Tell me more. How many are there?"

"Two," he answered. "Aimery paid them a visit, as well."

The air crackled with anger. "You should've killed her when you had the chance! I want the deed done tonight or the stone goes back on."

He didn't wait for the Great One to say more. Enough had been said. He knew what he had to do.

CHAPTER ELEVEN

As soon as dawn arrived, Val left Gabriel to guard the cave as he made his way down the mountain to Nicole's cottage. Snow crunched under his boots and his breath billowed around him as large snowflakes began to fall.

The wind chapped at his skin, but he ignored all of it as he trudged through the snow while keeping his senses on high alert. Waiting, searching for anything out of the normal.

His hand gripped his sword beneath his cloak while he let his gaze roam the land for any adversaries that might show themselves. To his surprise, he arrived at Nicole's cottage without encountering so much as a wild animal.

As he approached the cottage, his steps slowed and he removed his sword from its scabbard. When he reached the cottage, he flattened himself against the outside and listened. He could hear no signs from within, so he crept toward the door and reached for the handle.

Holding his sword with one hand, he pushed opened the door and again flattened himself against the cottage. When nothing came barreling out of the house, and he still didn't hear any sounds from within, he turned and stood in the doorway.

The cottage was dark inside, so he sheathed his sword and opened the shutters to let in the light. The structure was small, but Nicole kept it clean and tidy. His gaze slowly took in her home, and though it hadn't started out hers, she had made it her own.

A small pile of wood was stacked next to the fireplace where a black pot hung suspended over the now dead coals. A table with two chairs stood near the fire. He could well imagine her eating her meals alone with no one to talk to.

He sighed and looked at her array of herbs drying as they hung from the ceiling. A small table with a stool sat near one of the windows, showing how lonely her existence was.

He turned and saw her bed against the far wall near the hearth. Across the bed was a stunning tartan with a bold red and bright blue.

Despite the fact Aimery had given them more blankets than they would need, Val took the tartan and folded it. He set it on the table and moved about the cottage taking items he thought she might want.

After the tartan, he found a brush, another gown, and her tattered cloak. Once the tartan was tied around those items, he hurriedly gathered up what food he could and wrapped it in another piece of cloth.

He closed the shutters, gathered the two sacks, and took one last look around before he walked out and shut the door behind him.

The snow had begun to fall in thick, blinding sheets as Val made his way back to the cave. With the two heavy bundles he was carrying and the slippery slope of the iced mountain, it wasn't long before he found himself losing ground.

His breath burned his lungs as he struggled up the mountain. Gusts of wind battered his body and kept him constantly off balance. He had gotten half way up when he felt something at his thigh. He looked down to see Laird pushing at him from behind.

As soon as he thought he had a foothold with Laird helping keep him upright, his boot slipped on a patch of ice. No sooner had his feet came out from underneath him than someone took hold of his arm.

He looked up and spotted Gabriel through the blizzard. "About time."

"Stop grumbling and get your arse inside," Gabriel yelled over the howling wind.

When Val had gotten his feet underneath him again, Gabriel took one of the bags. Val was able to make the rest of the climb up, but his affection for Laird grew as the dog never wavered from his side. It wasn't until Val was inside the cave and Laird had shaken off the snow on his coat that Val reached down and patted the dog's head.

"Good lad," he said and he could have sworn the giant wolfhound smiled.

He looked up to find Gabriel's brow raised. Val shrugged and brushed the snow from his hair and cloak. "What's that look for?"

"I didn't think you liked him," Gabriel said.

Val's brow furrowed. "Whatever gave you that idea?"

"Just the way you acted toward him."

"He's a well trained dog, Gabriel. I just have to wonder what's going to happen to him when we're done here. It's one of the reasons I try not to get attached to anything."

"I'm not leaving him."

It was the vehemence in Gabriel's tone that brought Val up short. He gazed at his friend and saw that in the short time he had acquired the dog, Gabriel had become more than attached.

"It's not up to me whether you keep the dog."

"I know," Gabriel said and turned to the back of the cave.

Val shook his head as he followed him to Nicole. He found her sitting near the fire, staring into the flames. She looked bored, but he had just the cure for that.

As soon as she saw him and what they held in their arms, her eyes lit up. "You went to my cottage?"

"Aye," Val answered. "No one has been there. I didn't know what to bring. If there is something missing, I'll return for it."

"Nay," she said as she took the bag from Gabriel. "This will be fine."

He watched as she unknotted the cloth and opened it to find the food. She nodded in satisfaction and began to put it away for later. Then she looked up and saw the bag he held.

She gasped and reached for the tartan. Her eyes met his as she gently lowered it to the ground. "How did you know?"

He shrugged, not expecting such a reaction from her. "I saw it on your bed and realized it might mean something to you."

She smiled as she ran her hand over tartan and gently untied the knot. "This is the only present I've ever received. Donald and Maude gave it to me a couple of years ago. It's the tartan of his clan," she explained.

Val felt rather pleased with himself as she opened the bag and looked through its contents. Each item she picked up she would smile and then set it aside. It was the same with everything from her brush to her gown, until she found the embroidery kit.

She jerked her gaze to his and Val shifted, suddenly

uncomfortable. He licked his lips. "I thought you might be bored sitting here day after day."

"Thank you," she whispered and turned her back to them as she began to put stuff away.

Val didn't look at Gabriel as he turned and walked toward the entrance.

"Did you see anything?"

Val shook his head. "All seemed normal. No footsteps in the snow, no foul stench of evil, nothing."

"Odd, don't you think?"

"Very. He was here yesterday, and I can nearly guarantee you it was him that spied on me after Aimery left."

"I'm sure it was," Gabriel said and crossed his arms over his chest.

"I don't like the waiting." Val would rather have the gryphon attack now so they could get the battle over with.

Gabriel grunted. "Reminds me of the minotaur Cole and I fought. For weeks, we had no idea what creature we were looking for. The baron's men would bring villagers to the castle to be fed to the minotaur."

"I still don't understand that," Val said. "Before, the creatures always attacked the villages, killing all that they could."

Gabriel nodded. "But with each creature we've slain, they've become smarter, stronger...deadlier." He turned to Val. "I don't think anyone from the village is controlling this gryphon."

"I don't like this," Val mumbled. "I hope Aimery returns with good news. First, we discover the creature has arrived before us and is about to kill Nicole, then we learn Nicole has been bound to this land, and now we think the gryphon isn't being controlled by the blue stone."

"Which means," Gabriel said slowly, "that the Great

Evil is controlling it personally."

Val sighed and leaned against the cave. "We need the rest of the Shields."

"What we need is a miracle."

~ ~ ~

Nicole gazed down at the tartan as she ran her hands over it once more before she folded it and put it away. She hadn't realized how much her things had meant to her until she'd had to leave them behind.

Now she found herself missing her small cottage.

The one thing she found she didn't miss was the loneliness. Donald may have come by occasionally, but he had never stayed more than a few moments. She never begrudged him though. He was afraid for his wife's life and she understood that.

"What has you so deep in thought?" Val's deep voice intruded on her thoughts.

She looked up and gave him a small smile. "I was thinking how you take so much for granted until you don't have it anymore."

"Your home?"

"Aye. It might be small and sparse, but it was mine."

"It's a lovely cottage," he said as he lowered himself to the ground and sat opposite her, the fire between them.

She listened for a moment. "Is that the wind I hear?"

He chuckled. "Aye. A blizzard blew in just as I was leaving the cottage. It looks like we're all trapped in here."

"You sound disappointed."

"I am," he admitted. "Gabriel and I are both ready to face the gryphon and get the first battle out of the way. That way we can size up our opponent and see exactly what we're up against."

"Wish I could be of help," she said and fiddled with the hem of her skirt.

"The best thing you can do now is stay alive."

She raised her gaze to his. The fire cast a warm glow over his golden brown hair and tanned skin. She found herself thinking of the kiss they had shared yesterday. It had lingered in her mind so heavily that she had even awoken this morning with the taste of it on her lips. She wanted another kiss, to feel the burning inside her and the thumping of her heart at his touch.

"As soon as we kill the gryphon," he continued, "you'll be taken to Stone Crest where the other three Chosen are waiting."

She made herself look away from his tempting mouth. "Have you met these other three?"

"Aye," he said with a warm smile. "Mina, Elle, and Shannon are very nice. You'll get along with them well."

"And you say we're all from the same...realm?"

He nodded. "Once the other three met, it was like a bond none had ever noticed was suddenly visible. Mina was the only one that had been raised with a family, though they had never included her."

"So, all three were alone like me?"

He scrunched up his face and thought over her words. "Not exactly like you, but aye, in a way, they each had grown up alone."

"Are they all from Scotland?"

Val laughed and scratched his chin as he shifted to his right. He leaned on his right hand and bent his left leg so that he could rest his arm atop it.

"Nay," he said. "Mina is from England in the year 1123."

Nicole gasped and shook her head. "And the others?"

"Well, both Elle and Shannon are from the future."

"How far into the future?"

"Several centuries. I was there in 2012."

"By the saints," she said. "What was England like at that time?"

"I don't know," he answered. "We weren't in England. We were in a place called America."

"I've never heard of it," she said, wondering if he was jesting with her.

"You wouldn't have. Even then, the country was only two hundred and some-odd years old."

She smiled because she knew he was jesting with her for sure. "Stop. Tell me the truth."

"I am," he said as the smile dropped from his face. "The place is loud, dirty, hot, and completely uncivilized. It reminded me of Rome," he said with a bright smile.

She laughed. "Neither this America nor Rome sound like places I'd like to visit."

"I think you might like certain aspects of Rome. The people can be highly entertaining."

"How so?"

"That was one of our great pleasures. We enjoyed ourselves with food, plays, tournaments, and the like."

"What was the one great pleasure of Rome?" she asked.

"You mean besides conquering?"

She nodded eagerly.

"Sex."

CHAPTER TWELVE

Val knew he had shocked her, but he hadn't been able to help himself. Plus, it was the truth. Romans loved sex.

"Really?" Nicole asked, a small frown marring her forehead.

"Really."

"Did you have lots of sex?"

He was surprised at her forthright question, and impressed that she had asked it. "As I told you, I was a true Roman in every sense of the word."

"So you know all there is to know about lovemaking?"

He knew exactly where this was going, and he wanted no part of it. "Don't ask me to have sex with you."

She waved away his words. "Nay, I wasn't. I know you didn't like my kiss. I was hoping you could teach Gabriel so he could have sex with me."

Had Val been drinking something, he knew he would have spewed it all over her. "What?" he asked when he finally found his voice.

"I'm being realistic," she said solemnly. "My chances of getting out of this situation alive are slim. I've been alone for so long, and missed out on so much that I'd like to make up for it."

"I'm not sure this is the way," he answered while trying to buy himself some time to think.

"Maybe not, but most women my age have already been married with children."

He stopped and really looked at her then. There was no denying the loneliness in her violet depths, nor the sadness. She *had* missed so much.

"Nicole, don't rush this. I know you want to experience the world, but if you don't find the right person to share things with, it won't mean near as much."

She became quiet, and he was foolish enough to think that his words had halted her wild thoughts. He should have known better.

"Do you have someone special?"

Val sighed and sat up straight. "I'm a Shield, which doesn't leave me much time for things like that."

"So, you're as lonely as I am."

Her observation hit him like a catapult in the stomach. "In some ways, aye, I am."

Suddenly, her gaze moved over him and he heard her ask, "Are you lonely, too?"

Val turned and saw Gabriel standing behind him. He raised a brow and waited for Gabriel to answer.

Gabriel pushed off the wall and walked to his pallet and sat. "Everyone is lonely at times, Nicole. Some people don't mind being alone, while others need the company of several just to feel safe. It all depends on the person."

"You didn't answer my question."

Val couldn't help but smile as he watched Nicole's attention turn from him to Gabriel. It was about time Gabriel answered some of her questions.

"Nay," Gabriel answered. "I enjoy my solitude. I've never been one who likes to be in one place too long."

Val learned something new about Gabriel. He found it

hard to believe that Gabriel didn't get lonely at times, for Val had seen him staring off into nothing deep in thought.

He could only imagine Gabriel was still trying to figure out his past and just where he came from. Though Gabriel hid it well, all the Shields knew it was something that troubled him greatly.

At least with Cole, he'd had a few memories of his parents and life, memories of a child, but still memories. Gabriel had nothing.

No memories to help answer his questions. The only thing they all knew was that the Fae had found him alone and nearly dead. When Gabriel had woken, he remembered nothing. It was only because the name Gabriel had been stitched into the back of his shirt that they knew a name.

"The blizzard doesn't seem to be letting up," Gabriel said into the silence.

Nicole nodded. "I suspect it'll continue most of the morning and maybe past noon."

Val looked over his shoulder at the entrance and contemplated their choices.

"What are you thinking?" Gabriel asked.

Val look at Gabriel. "After yesterday, I'd say our chances of an attack are imminent."

"What happened yesterday?" Nicole asked.

Gabriel shrugged. "I smelled the evil and shot an arrow toward a stand of trees. The gryphon had been sitting there observing us."

"He was here?" she asked, her voice low and fearful as her eyes darted about.

"He never got close," Val hastened to assure her. "He never attacked."

Nicole got to her feet and paced the distance of the cave. "I can't stand the waiting. If he's coming, then let him come and get it over with."

"Exactly," Val said as he gained his feet and stood in front of her so she would stop pacing. "He's waiting for us to make a wrong move. You're protected in this cave. The only way in is through the entrance, and we're guarding that."

"So," Gabriel said, "as long as you stay in here you'll be safe."

She looked from one to the other and then faced Val. "Why are you doing this?"

He frowned. "What? Guarding you? Because it's my duty."

"Nay. Why are you jeopardizing your life for the Shields? Why is it so important to you?"

A myriad of answers ran through Val's head, but he understood what Nicole really wanted to know. She wanted him to admit his true motive, something he hadn't even done to Aimery.

"I'm a soldier. I've fought something or someone my entire life, and fighting the evil that threatens this realm and the Fae is a more noble fight than trying to take over a country."

She shook her head sadly then turned to Gabriel. "And you? Why do you fight for the Shields?"

Gabriel scratched his chin before he got to his feet. As soon as he stood, Laird came bounding over to him. "I do it because, like Val said, it's a noble fight. To sit idly by while an evil destroys realms isn't something I could have done."

"Cole, a fellow Shield's, realm was destroyed by the evil," Val said. "Roderick's is on the verge of ruin, as well. Even your own realm was destroyed by this evil."

"And yet, that evil saved me," she said.

Val blinked and took a step back. "How can you say

that?"

"Isn't he the one that brought me here?"

"And ordered your death. He's trying to kill you now."

"So you say," she argued. "The gryphon didn't kill me."

Gabriel grunted. "The way I saw it, it was nearly a done deed, Nicole."

She flipped her long black hair over her shoulder and crossed her arms over her chest. "I'm tired of being afraid. I'm tired of hiding from the world. I want a life, maybe even a husband and children."

Val could hear the anger as her voice shook and her violet eyes blazed in the firelight. "Then let us keep you safe."

"I just want to know why the man that saved me suddenly wants me dead."

Val looked to Gabriel to answer, but Gabriel shook his head, leaving it to him. Val licked his lips and studied Nicole as he struggled to find the right words.

"We know that twelve infants were sent from your realm just before it was destroyed. All the infants came to Earth to different times and places. The Fae discovered your presence too late to keep all of you alive."

"Can't they travel through time?" she asked. "Let the Fae go back and save all of them."

Gabriel let out a long breath. "They can't alter history."

"Isn't that what they are doing now?"

"Nay," Val answered. "The evil is the one altering history. The Fae have sent us to keep it from doing more harm."

Nicole shifted her feet. "Go on."

He cleared his throat. "When the Fae discovered that all six of the males sent from your realm were dead, they immediately started looking for the females."

"And you identify us by the mark, right?"

He nodded.

"Do you go around asking to look at every woman you meet?" she asked, the sarcasm dripping from her voice.

Val tried to hold his temper. He could only imagine what she was feeling now and how frustrated and fearful she was. So, he kept that in mind. "At first we thought we might have to. Your people didn't put the mark for the world to see in case the evil discovered their plot."

"So they hid them to help keep us hidden," she finished.

"Exactly. Roderick and I were sent to the future before Gabriel, Cole, and Hugh discovered that Mina was one of the Chosen."

"So how did you find out about...what was the other's name?"

"Elle," he supplied. "Only because she had the blue stone and the creatures came after her. Roderick told her of the mark and asked her if she had it."

"What then?"

Val grimaced. "She refused to leave with Aimery. It was because she didn't destroy the blue stone when given the chance that she felt like she needed to aid us in finding it and killing the creatures."

"Which you did."

He nodded, and then her attention turned to Gabriel. "And you? Did you go looking at every woman?"

Gabriel's mouth lifted in a wry grin. "There wasn't a need. After we found Mina's mark, the Fae realized that the evil was sending creatures to where the Chosen were. We simply followed the creatures, but then it was a matter of finding which woman was the Chosen."

"And this was Shannon?" she asked.

"Aye."

Nicole sighed and rubbed her neck. "I'm sorry," she said and walked past Val.

Val turned and followed her as she went near the entrance of the cave. She stared pensively out into the blizzard. He reached for her cloak and wrapped it around her shoulders.

"Thank you," she mumbled and looked at the ground.

"What were your dreams when you were little? What did you want your life to be like?"

When she raised her face, she had a small smile. "On occasion, Margda would let me wander near the loch by myself for hours. I would pretend I had a mother and father who loved me dearly, several brothers and sisters to play with, and a grandmother who doted on me."

"A lovely dream."

She lifted one shoulder in a shrug. "It was one I often played."

"And for your future? Did you wish to be a lady of the castle?"

She laughed and cut her eyes to him briefly. "Nothing so grand as that. I was content in my cottage by my beautiful loch and the mountains. It's quiet and peaceful."

"That it is."

Her gaze met his. "I dreamed of marrying a nice, handsome lad. One who would grow old with me and give me many children. I wanted love and laughter."

"There's no reason you can't still have it once this is over."

She turned and looked out of the cave. "Really? Where? I cannot stay here. I don't belong at this Stone Crest in England. I'm Scottish, Val. I may not have been born here, but Scotland is in my blood."

He found himself wishing to give her all that she desired after such a painful childhood. He took her shoulders and turned her to face him. "Then I promise you, once this is over, I'll return you here or anywhere else you wish to live."

"Really?"

"I give you my word."

"And if something happens to you?"

"Then I'll make sure Aimery knows to carry out my vow. Don't lose hope, Nicole. It's all we have to hold on to."

CHAPTER THIRTEEN

Aimery arrived at the cave to hear Val's declaration. He nodded to Val to let him know that he would most certainly carry out his promise.

Besides, Aimery knew Val well enough to know the Roman didn't make vows lightly. Whatever made Val feel the need to pledge such words meant that something had transpired between him and Nicole.

Aimery used his magic to search Val's mind, and was surprised to find the Roman doing his best to keep Nicole at arm's length. He had seen Val with women on numerous occasions. Val usually always got the woman he wanted, so Aimery was more than a little perplexed to find Val trying hard to stay away from Nicole.

And that's when it hit Aimery. It had to do with Val's past, a past he hadn't shared with Aimery. But then again, he hadn't needed to. Aimery had seen it all, and understood why Val kept it to himself.

"Aimery," Val said as he stepped back from Nicole.

"Val," Aimery said and nodded to Nicole when she turned toward him. "I see you're weathering the storm well."

"It's warmer here than in my cottage," Nicole said. "I would never have guessed that."

Aimery smiled before he looked to Val. "Let's find Gabriel. There is something I need to tell you."

He followed Val and Nicole as they returned to the fire where Gabriel lounged back with his feet toward the fire and Laird dozing across his legs.

Aimery couldn't help but smile. If anyone had told him Gabriel would take a pet, he would have called them a liar, but then again, his Shields constantly surprised him.

"You look right at home," Aimery said to Gabriel.

Gabriel showed one of his rare smiles and said, "Who knew all it took for me to be content was a cave and a dog."

Aimery joined in Val's laughter. He was grateful that his Shields had always been able to laugh and jest in the most difficult of times. His smile quickly faltered when he remembered why he had come.

"What is it?" Gabriel asked.

"As I said yesterday, you and Val made an excellent decision to stay in the cave instead of the cottage where I know it would have been more comfortable."

"But?" Val urged.

Aimery inwardly sighed. His Shields were perceptive. It was one of the many reasons he had recruited them. "It isn't enough. I've come as quickly as I could to help."

Gabriel's brow furrowed as he slowly sat up. "Come for what?"

"To use my powers. Just as the evil bound Nicole to this land, I must protect the cave so that under no circumstances will evil be able to enter."

"Thank you," Nicole said.

Aimery turned and found her gaze troubled and anxious. She wasn't yet aware of how precarious her position was, and he'd rather she never know. "You have two of the best Shields protecting you, Nicole. I have no doubt they will succeed."

Her smile was forced, and he didn't miss her glance that darted to Val. It would take the tiniest of thoughts to discover her feelings for Val, but he didn't have time for that now. He must protect the cave before it was too late.

"I'll come with you," Gabriel suddenly said.

Aimery knew it wasn't because he wanted to speak to him, Gabriel was leaving to give Val and Nicole a chance to be alone. Aimery turned on his heel and walked to the entrance of the cave before he spoke.

"Why is Val pushing Nicole away?"

Gabriel blew out a loud breath. "I don't know. I came upon them kissing yesterday. I've seen him with a lot of women, but he's different around her."

"Different how?"

"The same kind of different that Roderick was with Elle and Hugh was with Mina."

"Ah, so you think they are mates?"

Gabriel shrugged. "I don't know. I just know that being with Nicole has made him edgy, moody. You haven't looked for yourself?"

"I know that Val is pushing her away, but I didn't look further."

"All that power and you don't know more than that?" Gabriel asked with a grin.

Aimery chuckled. "Ah, but that is one thing all Fae must remember never to do."

"What's that?"

"Abuse our powers. In our realm, we know how to block other Fae from seeing into our thoughts. Humans don't have that kind of power."

"But you taught us."

"True," he admitted. "For some, like you and Cole, once that block is in place, it never moves. For others, if they're focused on something else the block shifts."

"So Val has to work to keep his up?"

Aimery nodded as he looked around him. "For the most part, Val has offered for me to search his memories if I needed to. I only search if I fear that one of you may be in jeopardy."

"I didn't realize my block was still there. Besides, I have no memories. You've already tried to look. Many times."

"Aye, I have. But it may be that you had erected that block before we found you."

"But I wanted you to search my memories. I wanted to know my past."

Aimery clasped Gabriel's shoulder and gave him a calming touch. "Give it time."

"You've said that for how many centuries now?" he asked with a sneer. "I don't think I'll ever remember, and maybe it's better that I don't. What if I wasn't a good man?"

"If you had any evil in you, any of the Fae would have felt it," Aimery reminded him. "Be easy, Gabriel. Once the Great Evil is gone, I'll take you back to my realm and we will break down your mental barriers and find your lost memories."

When Gabriel nodded and turned away, Aimery stepped into the snow and closed his eyes. He wanted to speak with Gabriel more, but there wasn't time. It would have to wait, like everything else, until the evil was destroyed.

Aimery began to chant the spell as he lifted his arms above his head, his palms toward the cave.

~ ~ ~

Nicole took off her cloak and draped it over one of the large boulders as Val and Aimery walked away. She couldn't shake the feeling that no matter what Val or the others promised, she was going to die.

Try as she might, she couldn't keep her gaze from Val. He stood stoically near the fire. With his arms crossed over his chest and his brow lined with worry, it was obvious he was lost in thought.

The flicker of the firelight caught on his scar, and she found herself curious about it. It didn't seem to bother him, nor did it detract from his handsomeness. In fact, it seemed to make him more appealing, more tempting.

She wanted to run her finger down the scar before she delved her fingers into the cool locks of his hair. Her body began to warm as she recalled how he had taken her in his arms for her first kiss. It had been the most glorious experience she'd ever had, and though he may not have liked it, it was all she could think about.

"May I ask you something?"

His gaze jerked to hers as if just now realizing she were still there. "Of course."

"Your scar. How did you come by it?"

His hand rose and his finger traced the scar that ran from his temple to his jaw. "Ah, my scar. I forget about it sometimes."

"Is it painful?"

"Not anymore. Aimery offered to heal it so that it was completely gone, but it reminds me of my past."

"A good reminder?"

He smiled a heart-stopping smile. "Aye. It was before I earned the general's position. We were fighting the Germanic people. They defended their land aggressively."

"In other words, you were nearly killed." She didn't like how his pale green eyes twinkled as he recalled that long ago day.

"That's one way of putting it. My horse had been struck from underneath me. I kicked free of the stirrups and managed to get free, but before I could gain my feet I was surrounded."

"Surrounded?" she repeated, wishing she hadn't asked now.

"It was a fine battle. There were four of them that fought valiantly. I didn't expect to come out of the battle alive at that point, so I decided to give it my all. I had taken down two of them before a sword struck me in the leg. I crumpled and went down."

Nicole swallowed as if she could see the scene playing before her eyes with Val bloodied and near death.

"I was on my knees, when one of the men took my arms from behind to hold me still. The other was about to cut off my head when one of my comrades happened to see me. He fired off his bow and killed the man behind me. I wasn't able to move my arm in time to stop the other before he struck me, but all he managed was the cut to my face before I killed him."

She never understood why some men loved war, and she had hoped Val wouldn't be one of those. "So, you love to fight?"

He shook his head. "I like to kill evil, Nicole. There's a difference."

"Are you saying the Germanic people you killed were evil?"

"Not at all. At that time, I was a soldier doing as I was told. We all were. It was kill or be killed, and it was our way of life."

It made sense, and she had never thought of it that way

before.

"War is, unfortunately, a way of life. I foolishly thought as a youth in Rome, that once Rome conquered the world, there wouldn't be a need for wars. I was terribly wrong."

She studied his handsome face, scar and all. "You wanted to keep the scar because it proved that you survived when most would have died."

A slow smile spread over his face. "Aye."

She took a step toward him. "Every time I think I know what kind of man you are, you surprise me."

"And what kind of man do you think I am?"

"A noble one."

The smile vanished, and a strange light came into his eyes. He took a step toward her and her heart began to pound. All she could think about was feeling his lips on her again, to taste his exotic flavor and feel his hard body.

"Nicole," he whispered as he lowered his head and placed his lips on hers.

It wasn't the passionate kiss of yesterday, but it was more poignant, more intense. She couldn't stop her hands from moving to his chest. She pushed aside his leather jerkin to feel the unique texture of his tunic and the heat beneath her hands.

When his arms came around her and pulled her close, she didn't try to stop the moan of pleasure that escaped her. Once she was tight against him, his tongue licked her lips, seeking entry.

And she didn't deny him.

Her lips parted, and his tongue plundered her mouth leaving her breathless and wanting more. And then the most unusual thing happened. Her body came alive. Her breasts grew heavy and her nipples hardened. An intense need began to throb between her legs, and she found herself wanting to rub against Val. When it grew to be too much, she broke the kiss and stepped out of his arms.

They stared at each other, their breathing labored as they both struggled to regain some composure before Gabriel or Aimery returned.

"What have you done to me?" she whispered.

He lowered his gaze and swallowed as if he were in pain. "I've awakened your desires."

"Why? Why if I didn't make you burn yesterday with my kiss?" And that's when she realized what he had done. "You lied yesterday."

He didn't bother raising his eyes to her as he nodded. "I have my reasons."

"I want to know this passion you've awoken. I want you to teach me."

His head snapped up and his eyes glittered dangerously. "Nay." His voice was low and deadly. "Forget about everything but staying alive. You can delve into anything you want once this is over."

"But I might never see you again."

"That will be for the best," he said as he turned to leave.

"For who?" she whispered to his retreating back.

CHAPTER FOURTEEN

Aimery finished his chanting and walked to Gabriel. "It is done."

"Good," he said and couldn't help but breathe a sigh of relief. There had never been a need for Aimery to use his magic like this before, which made Gabriel realize just how dangerous their mission was.

"Make sure Nicole stays inside no matter what," Aimery said just before disappearing.

Gabriel turned and began the walk back to the fire. Midway there he saw Val coming toward him. The angry look on his face let Gabriel know that something had happened between him and Nicole.

"What's wrong?" he asked when Val reached him.

Val looked over his shoulder at Nicole and continued walking. Gabriel hurried to catch up and stopped Val at the entrance.

"Val?"

He growled and ran a hand down his face. "Did you know that she asked me to kiss her yesterday? Actually asked me. Then, later informed me that she wanted to experience sex, but since I didn't find her kisses enjoyable, she wanted me to make sure you knew everything about sex so she could ask you."

Gabriel didn't know what to be more shocked about, that Nicole wanted to have sex with him, or that Val was about ready to beat him to a pulp because of it.

"She's asking you," Gabriel said carefully, "because she's attracted to you. She doesn't know that's what she's feeling since she's been excluded from people."

Val sighed and raked a hand through his long hair. "I know."

"Then what's the problem?"

"She's the problem," Val said between clenched teeth. "I can't be around her without thinking of bedding her."

"Go into the village and find a willing woman then."

Val propped an elbow against the cave wall and leaned his head into his hand. "That's the crux of the matter, Gabriel. I want her too desperately for someone else to do."

"You want her but you won't take her. Is that it?" Gabriel asked. At Val's nod, Gabriel snorted and crossed his arms over his chest. "You've never held back from taking a willing woman. Why now?"

"Because she reminds me of my sisters."

It was a huge admission for Val, one that Gabriel wasn't going to press. If Val wanted to share more he would. Asking wouldn't help matters.

"I have no words to guide you."

Val's sad eyes rose to his. "I know. I don't expect anyone to. I've made a vow to keep her safe, and that's what I'll do."

Gabriel silently wished his friend all the luck he was going to need in his endeavor to stay away from Nicole, because Gabriel had seen their passion. There was only one thing that could keep passion like that from being fulfilled

– death.

Val jerked and turned toward the entrance. He peered through the blizzard that still held the land in its grip.

"Has it come?" Gabriel asked.

"Aye," Val said and turned to find his sword and halberd. Once his sword was strapped on, he reached for the array of daggers Gabriel always kept with him and chose two, one for inside his boot and one for the back. After everything had been secured, he reached for his halberd.

Gabriel finished checking the daggers he had on him and began to inspect his bow and quiver of arrows. He smiled when he reached for a particularly dangerous arrow that had a ball with tiny spikes.

"Ready?" Val asked.

"Since we arrived."

Val turned to find Nicole watching them. "No matter what, don't leave this cave. If something happens to us, call out Aimery's name. He'll hear you and come."

She opened her mouth to respond, then closed it and stared at him a moment. "Be careful."

"Always," Val said with a wink.

He didn't want her to know just how crucial killing this creature was. She had enough to worry about, there was no need to add more. Besides, he and Gabriel were more than capable of handling the gryphon.

Just don't fail her.

Val gave her one last look, then turned to Gabriel. At his nod, Val walked into the blizzard. He had left his cloak so he could move easier and reach his weapons.

The snow stuck to his eyelashes and pelted his face. He ignored the biting cold and slowly worked his way down the mountain. The plan was for him to coax the gryphon out, and then Gabriel would kill it with his arrows. Somehow, Val knew their plan would never come to fruition because of the weather, but it had worked in the past, so they were willing to try it again.

A distant sound reached Gabriel over the snow. He looked to the right and then the left, but found nothing. It wasn't until he looked straight ahead over the loch that he saw the dark shape that was moving closer at an incredible speed.

He heard Gabriel shout, "gryphon!" the same time he realized what it was. Instinct alone had him diving to the ground as the gryphon reached him. The snow cushioned his fall, but he still felt the rocks dig into his stomach and thighs.

Val looked up and saw the gryphon circling back around for another attack. Thankfully, the snowfall began to lessen so that it wasn't stinging Val's face like tiny swords.

He gripped his halberd and rose to his feet, ready to strike the gryphon when he approached. Instead, the creature stared down at him and smiled.

"You can't win, Shield."

Val didn't even bother to wonder how the gryphon knew what he was. "I can, and will."

"We'll see about that," the gryphon said before he dove straight at Val.

Val tried to jump out of the way again, but the gryphon was faster. His talons snagged Val's leather jerkin and tossed him into the air. Val saw the ground approach quickly. He knew there was going to be pain upon the landing, so he tried to roll with the impact.

Instead, he felt a deep pain in his right side. He tried to rise to his feet despite the stinging in his side and saw that somehow he had dropped his halberd. There was no time to look for the weapon though as he heard the beating of the gryphon's wings as he advanced again.

This time when the gryphon went to attack him, Val heard his scream and knew Gabriel had let loose one of his arrows. Val got to his feet and chanced a look over his shoulder as he hurriedly made his way down the mountain and saw the gryphon pull an arrow out of his hind leg.

Val silently thanked Gabriel for giving him some time to reach the bottom of the mountain. He unsheathed his sword once his feet hit the ground and turned to find the gryphon flying toward the cave entrance.

As soon as the gryphon reached it, it was as if he ran into an invisible shield. He was thrown backward and tumbled down the mountain in an ugly array of feathers and fur.

Out of the corner of his eye, Val saw Gabriel leave the cave and move to the side of the entrance. Val would keep the gryphon occupied while Gabriel let loose a volley of arrows, and with the snowfall nearly stopping, it would be easier for Gabriel to see.

Val turned back to the gryphon and watched it stagger to its feet. The creature was massive in height and brawn, and he knew it was going to take cunning to kill it.

"Did the snow break your fall?" Val taunted.

The gryphon shook off the snow and turned his eagle head to Val. "You both will pay for that."

"Come and get me," Val said as he planted his feet and evened out his weight for the attack.

The gryphon launched himself at Val, and Val raised his sword and sliced open part of the gryphon's wing as he pivoted to the side. He didn't get clear in time though, and felt the gryphon's talons rake across his back, tearing open his clothes.

Val cursed as pain blinded him. His side still ached

from the landing, and with his back now throbbing with new agony, he knew he was going to have a difficult time deflecting the creature's attacks.

An evil chuckle reached him then. Val slowly turned to find the gryphon standing ten paces away regarding him silently.

"Something amusing?" Val asked.

"I thought all Shields were immortal, but by my guess, you're very much mortal."

"What does that matter?"

The gryphon clicked his beak. "It means I cannot toy with you as long as I'd like."

Val renewed his grip on the sword. "Give it your best then."

The gryphon shook his head. "I think I'll take him instead. For now."

Val looked over his shoulder and saw Gabriel making his way down the mountain. When he turned back around, the gryphon was gone. Val tried to get his feet to move faster as he raced up the mountain shouting Gabriel's name.

"Look out," he warned just before the gryphon dove at him.

~ ~ ~

Nicole's heart plunged to her feet when she saw the gryphon toss Val about as if he were a sack of flour. Then, when the gryphon turned to attack Gabriel, she tried to shout out a warning but it was already too late as the creature used its claws on Gabriel.

The gryphon turned in midair and made to attack again, even as Gabriel notched an arrow. Out of the corner of her eye she saw a gray blur race past her and realized too late that it was Laird.

"Laird, nay!" she screamed, but the wolfhound cared only about protecting Gabriel.

Val was climbing up the mountain as fast as his injured body could manage, and Gabriel was lodged between the snow and two boulders, sealing off any chance at dodging the gryphon who attacked without mercy.

The once blinding white snow was now soaked with blood from both men, and it seemed the gryphon wasn't going to stop until both Val and Gabriel were dead.

There was a savage scream as the gryphon lodged its talons in Gabriel and lifted him before slamming him into a boulder. Gabriel's body slid to the ground, his eyes closed. The creature gave another scream and started to dive toward Gabriel again.

With her heart pounding maddeningly in her chest and her blood running cold in her veins, she watched helplessly as Laird propelled himself from a boulder and clamped down on one of the gryphon's hind legs just before he was about to rip Gabriel to shreds.

Tears streamed down Nicole's face as she watched the wolfhound fighting to keep the gryphon from both Val and Gabriel. The huge dog fought valiantly as he hung on with his massive jaws while the gryphon used his long talons to slice at Laird. The gryphon's screams of pain reverberating off the mountain.

But through the cries of pain, Laird never relinquished his hold on the gryphon's hind leg. Until the gryphon slammed the wolfhound against the side of the mountain.

The many cuts combined with the vicious knock were too much for Laird and he fell with a small yelp of pain. Val released a bellow.

She looked to the sound in time to see the gryphon tuck its wings and dive at Val. They rolled a ways down the mountain before the gryphon jumped into the air with a screech. Then there was silence.

Nicole slowly pulled her eyes from Val's still form to see the gryphon turn and fly into the night. She dashed from the cave and ran to Gabriel since he was the closest.

His breathing was shallow and blood was everywhere. Nicole had never felt so helpless in her life as she tried to figure a way to drag Gabriel into the cave before the gryphon returned. Fear kept her from rational thinking as she moved to Gabriel's head and lifted his arms as she pulled back.

Her hands slipped from the blood on his arms as she tried to drag him, and she fell hard on her bottom. She wiped away the tears with the back of her hand and then used her skirts to try and get some of the blood from Gabriel's arm before she tried to drag him again.

Inch by agonizing inch, she pulled Gabriel toward the cave. In the distance, she could hear the gryphon screaming in anger. She chanced a look and saw him destroying her cottage, the only home she had ever known.

Anger gave her the extra strength to move Gabriel up the steep slope. She glanced at Val and saw him stirring. She wanted to call out to him but didn't want to draw the gryphon's attention yet.

The harder it became to pull Gabriel up the mountain, the more she cursed her weakness and helplessness. But she refused to give up. Val and Gabriel had protected her, the least she could do was try to save them.

To her relief, she discovered she had nearly pulled Gabriel into the cave. With one last pull, she tugged his torso into the entrance and then raced around to push his legs inside. And though she wanted to tend to his wounds, they would have to wait until after Val as safely inside the cave.

Nicole picked up her skirts and raced down the slope. She passed Laird and wanted to check on the wolfhound, but she knew there wouldn't be time now. After she got Val inside the cave, then she would return for Laird.

She slid on some icy rocks and her feet came out from under her, landing her on her behind as she slid the remainder of the way down the mountain. She ignored the cuts and scrapes to her leg as she jumped to her feet and raced to Val.

He moved his arms as she knelt beside him. "Val? Val, can you hear me?"

She glanced at her cottage when she realized she could no longer hear the gryphon's mighty roars as he unleashed his anger.

"Val, please," she begged. She knew the gryphon was most likely circling the air, and she wanted back in the safety of the cave.

"Leave me," he choked out.

She shook her head and pushed her long hair out of her face. "Never. Now get to your feet, general," she said in her most stern voice. "It's time to get moving."

When his pale green eyes opened to look at her, she felt her heart break at the pain she saw.

"Leave me. I'm not going to make it and you need to get to safety."

"Save your strength, because we're going to need it to get you up that mountain. I used most of mine to pull Gabriel inside. I don't think I can pull you up that steep slope."

"Nicole-"

"Stop," she demanded and wiped at another tear. "You gave me your word."

His hand suddenly reached over and took hers. "All right," he said after a tense moment of silence.

Nicole silently said a prayer to God and helped Val first sit up then gain his feet. She staggered under his heavy weight once he leaned on her, but she refused to give up.

"We have to hurry," she urged him.

"Where is the creature?"

She took a quick glance around. "I don't know."

"Damn," he muttered and tried to move faster.

Nicole clenched her teeth and urged her legs to move quicker under the weight. They were nearly half way there when Val spotted Laird.

"Laird?"

"I'll tell you everything once we're inside the cave."

"How bad is Gabriel?"

Nicole tripped over the hem of her skirts and barely stopped them from falling to the ground. "He's bad, but not nearly as bad as we're going to be."

He pulled his weight off her and fell to his knees. She was about to argue with him to get up when she saw his hand clamp around something, and then he lifted his halberd.

She took his arm and brought it back around her shoulders as they once again started up the slope.

And then they heard it. The flap of the gryphon's massive wings.

CHAPTER FIFTEEN

Val felt Nicole stiffen and realized something was terribly wrong. He sifted through the fog of pain and looked over his shoulder to see the gryphon fast approaching them.

Using what little strength he had left, Val pushed Nicole toward the cave and yelled at her to run then he turned and faced the gryphon. Just before the gryphon reached him, Val lifted his halberd and threw it with all his might as he had done with the javelins when he was a boy in Rome.

The pain in his side doubled, and he wrapped his arms around his torso as he fell to his knees. He knew the halberd couldn't kill the gryphon, but he wanted to give Nicole all the time he could for her to reach the safety of the cave.

He raised his head and saw his halberd sticking from the creature's chest as it screamed in pain. A small smile pulled at Val's lips before he fell to his side as the pain became too much to bear. He knew he had lost a lot of blood. Too much blood.

His vision began to darken, but he was able to see the

gryphon turn and fly away. Val let his lids fall closed. He had fulfilled his promise and kept Nicole safe.

"You bloody well haven't," a sweet voice whispered in his ear.

He cracked open an eye and saw Nicole kneeling over him. It was difficult for him to speak, but he had to make her understand that she needed to be in the cave.

"Nay," she stopped him. "You can't give up. You vowed to keep me alive. I need you."

Her violet eyes were filled with doubt and fear, but her determination brought a smile to his lips.

"We're almost there," she urged. "Get to your feet so I can help."

Val shook his head. His blood poured from him with every beat of his heart, and he was becoming weaker by the moment. There was no way Nicole could get him into the cave, not by herself.

He licked his lips before he said, "Tend to Gabriel. He'll kill the gryphon."

To his surprise, she leaned her head close and placed her lips on his for a soft kiss. "I'll tend to Gabriel but not before I get you inside."

He watched as she reached for her skirts and tore a long strip. Then, she helped him sit up as she wrapped it tightly around him to help staunch the flow of blood.

"We're almost to the cave," she said as she looked deep into his eyes. "Can you make it?"

There was no way Val was going to give up after everything she had done, so he nodded, and with her help and several tries, got to his feet.

The climb to the cave brought even more pain and was made more difficult because he was so weak. He didn't like how vulnerable Nicole made herself by trying to help him, but it was also because she exposed herself to the gryphon that he simply refused to give up before he reached the cave.

When they finally stepped into the entrance, he let out a deep breath and wanted to sink to the ground.

"Not yet," she stopped him. "I need to get you to the fire."

Val turned his head and saw Gabriel's still form just inside the entrance. "Gabriel?" he called, but as he expected his fellow Shield didn't answer.

"He's bad off, Val," she told him. "I'll get you settled and then come back for him."

But Val knew by then it might be too late. As much as he hated to do it, he silently called out to Aimery. He wasn't sure how strong his call was, and tried to call out again just to be sure as Nicole helped lower him to his pallet. But he couldn't keep the blackness from closing in on him, and his last thought before he passed out was that at least Nicole was safe.

~ ~ ~

Nicole breathed a sigh of relief and quickly added more wood to the fire so she could boil the water. Their supply of wood wouldn't last the night, but she didn't know if she could chance leaving the cave again.

She put that worry out of her mind and rushed to Gabriel. His complexion was pale and his skin cool to the touch. It could be because he had lain in the snow for so long, but Nicole couldn't chance it. She lifted his arms again and pulled him further into the cave.

Her muscles screamed in protest, but the trail of blood he left to the fire was enough to keep her moving.

She wasn't able to get him to his pallet, so she moved the blankets to him. The first thing she did was take one of his daggers and slice open his tunic. Then she rolled him onto his side and cut both his jerkin and the tunic down the back. She was then able to remove both easily.

When she saw the extensive wounds on his chest and sides, she knew it would take a blessing to keep him alive. She got to her feet and dashed to Gabriel's things to find his black bag of herbs. She took a quick look at Val and found his breathing erratic and slow.

She realized then that she could very well lose both men. Her mind scrambled to find a way to tend to both of them. With a quick shake to clear her mind, she unrolled Gabriel's black bag and stared at the herbs - none of which she recognized.

Vial after vial she picked up and examined, and there were only two of several dozen that she recognized. She sat back on her feet and blinked back her tears.

"What am I going to do?" she whispered.

Time was of the essence and she couldn't afford to sit and wallow in self-doubt when two men's lifeblood drained slowly from their beaten bodies.

She quickly yanked off more of her underskirt and hastily tied it around Gabriel's torso to help staunch the flow of blood. Then, she jumped to her feet and brought a cup of water to Val.

"Drink," she whispered near his ear as she held his head and the cup to his lips. To her great delight, he parted his lips and took some of the cool water.

Once he had his fill and she checked his wounds, she hurried back to Gabriel and his black bag. She looked at the vials again and wished she knew what to do.

A soft touch near her hand made her gaze jerk toward Gabriel where she found his eyes cracked open. He licked his lips and she brought him some water. He drank and then sighed with pain.

"How bad is it?" he asked.

Nicole swallowed and licked her lips. "Bad."

"I feel like hell, so that explains it." He tried to take a deep breath and stiffened with pain. "Where is Val?"

Nicole glanced at Val's still form. "Near the fire." When she returned her gaze to Gabriel it was to find him watching her intently.

"Is he hurt?"

Nicole nodded. "He's unconscious. I brought your bag, but I don't recognize any of the herbs."

"You wouldn't," Gabriel said softly. "Did you call for Aimery?"

In all the excitement and worry she had completely forgotten about the Fae commander. "Nay, I didn't."

Gabriel clenched his teeth and tried to roll to his side. "I'll call for him. Take the vial of red leaves and remove two."

Nicole hurried to do as Gabriel bade. Once she replaced the vial, he was instructing her to gather other ingredients. When she had all that he had told her, she turned and waited.

"Put them all in the bowl and grind them until they're a fine powder. When you've done that, add two spoonfuls of boiling water and then sprinkle a pinch of the yellow powder from one of the vials. It will make a paste that you need to spread on Val's wounds."

"Yours as well," she said as she set about grinding the ingredients. When she looked up, Gabriel was gone. She jumped to her feet and raced to the cave entrance to see him limping down the mountain.

Her gaze scanned the sky praying the gryphon had retreated to whatever Hell he had come from. She was about to call out to Gabriel when she saw him stop and kneel down. When he stood, he had Laird in his arms.

Nicole turned on her heel and made a place for Gabriel to lay Laird when he returned. She picked up the bowl and continued to grind the herbs as she waited. By the time she added the water and the yellow powder, she began to worry about Gabriel.

A curse and some stumbling alerted her that he had made it back to the cave. She rose to her feet to try and help him, but he shook his head.

"Tend to Val."

"I need to tend to you, as well," she argued.

But he shook his head again. "I'll see to Laird while you tend Val. Once that is done, I will look at my wounds."

"You'll bleed to death by then."

His silver gaze narrowed on hers. "If you allow Val to die, I'll never forgive you."

Nicole knew arguing more wouldn't help, so she knelt beside Val and closed her eyes. She thought long and hard about Aimery and then silently called his name.

She opened her eyes, expecting to see him standing before her. When he wasn't, she began to think she had done something wrong, but there was no more time to think about it. She touched Val's skin and found it feverish.

Her breath lodged in her throat as she cut away his bandage and his tunic and jerkin just as she had with Gabriel's. The blood did not flow as easily as before, but neither had it stopped.

"If the wounds turn green, you must let me know."

"Green?" she repeated and glanced over her shoulder to see Gabriel tending Laird.

"Aye. It'll mean there was dark magic used."

"Perfect," Nicole murmured. "Something else to worry about."

Before she applied the paste, Nicole carefully wiped the dried blood from Val's chest. With each wipe, she saw the scars that crisscrossed his chest and shoulders.

When the dried blood had been removed, she dipped her fingers into the yellowish paste and began to gently spread it over Val's wounds. With the wounds on his chest and shoulders taken care of, Nicole moved so that she could roll Val to his side and clean up his back.

By the time she had finished and wrapped new bandages around him, she knew only a miracle could save him. His blood loss was great and his breathing shallow. But she refused to give up. She reached for some water and cradled his head in her arms.

"Val? You need to drink for me," she said and lifted the cup to his lips. This time, however, he didn't drink.

She licked her dry lips and tried again. "Drink, Val."

Still nothing. She dipped her finger into the water and ran it over his lips, silently praying he took the liquid. Then she had an idea.

"Drink, soldier. That's an order," she said in her sternest voice.

To her surprise Val's lips parted and she was able to get some of the liquid down his throat.

"By all that is magical, what is going on?" Aimery's voice boomed around them.

Nicole raised her gaze to him after she slowly lowered Val's head. "What happened?" she repeated as she climbed to her feet. "The gryphon happened."

Aimery's unusual blue eyes took in the scene around him. "Why didn't someone call me?"

"They were unconscious," Nicole answered, "and I'm not used to the idea of calling to a Fae for help."

She watched as Gabriel slowly climbed to his feet with the aid of the wall. Blood had begun to soak the bandages she had applied and she took a step toward him when he raised his hand to stop her.

"Stay with Val," he said, his voice low and filled with pain.

"Quit being stubborn, Gabriel. Let me see to your wounds."

His head jerked around to her. "I ask only one thing from you...keep Val alive."

Nicole turned to Aimery to see the Fae commander regarding Gabriel peculiarly.

"What happened?" Aimery finally asked.

Nicole waited for Gabriel to speak, and when he didn't, she took a deep breath and began to tell Aimery about the attack.

By the time she was done Aimery rubbed his eyes and shook his head. "One of you should've called to me."

Nicole looked at Aimery expectantly. "Aren't you going to heal them?"

His calm demeanor once more in place, he simply shook his head. "The Fae cannot interfere."

The last of her control snapped. "Interfere? Wasn't it the Fae who interfered and sent the Shields here to begin with? You supply them with weapons and clothes and coin when needed, but you can't aid them when they are wounded."

"That's what I am for," Gabriel said weakly.

She turned to Gabriel. "I suppose none of you thought about what would happen if you were injured or dead, did they?"

Gabriel chuckled then clutched his side. "It doesn't matter now."

"It does," she said and went to him. She wrapped her arm around him to help him stand. "I'm scared, Gabriel. I can't keep Val alive on my own. If you don't let me tend to you now, it may be too late."

With a bone weary sigh, he said, "All right."

But when she unwrapped the bandages, she got the surprise of her life. Gabriel's wounds still bled, but they had begun to close up.

CHAPTER SIXTEEN

Nicole could only gape at the healing wounds. She raised her gaze to Gabriel to find him staring over her head at Aimery.

"Does this mean...?"

Aimery shrugged. "I think it does."

Nicole looked from one to the other. "Mean what? What are you talking about?"

"Never mind," Gabriel said. "Get the paste."

Nicole felt as if she walked in a dream world where nothing was as it should be. She retrieved the paste and walked back to Gabriel. After she applied the paste and wrapped more bandages around him, she went back to Val.

She shivered and pulled an extra blanket over her legs. Now that most of her underskirt had been used for bandages, there wasn't much protection for her legs from the cold besides her wool stockings. She felt Aimery's gaze on her and lifted her eyes to him.

"Next time something like this happens, you need to call out to me," he said.

Why? So you can sit back and watch since you can't interfere?

Aimery's gaze narrowed, but before he could react, she

said, "Of course."

It seemed to placate him because he turned to Gabriel. "How is the pain?"

"Minimal," Gabriel said as he ran his hand down Laird's coat.

"I'll be back," Aimery said then was gone.

Nicole let out a sigh and turned to Gabriel. "How is Laird?"

"I'm not sure."

The raw emotion in Gabriel's silver eyes made her heart ache. "If anyone can save him, it's you."

He gave her a weak smile and she turned back to Val. Sweat beaded his brow and chest. Nicole dipped a piece of her underskirt in water and wiped him down.

While Gabriel got better, Val got worse.

~ ~ ~

Aimery raked a hand down his face and paced his chamber at the palace. He could still feel Val and Gabriel's pain. If only he weren't bound by the rules set in place ages ago. He could have healed both Gabriel and Val in a matter of moments.

Instead, he would have to wait and watch Val battle the blood loss and massive wounds. Thankfully Gabriel was there with his herbs.

Gabriel.

To say that he was surprised to discover Gabriel was immortal would be putting it mildly. For years, they had wondered about Gabriel's mortality and had never known until now.

"Is it true?" Theron asked as he poked his head around the door.

Aimery waved him in. "It's true."

"And Gabriel was surprised?"

"More surprised than I was, I think," Aimery answered. "He didn't heal as fast as Cole does, but he is healing."

"Interesting," Theron said.

Aimery nodded. "Very."

"But he still didn't remember anything of his past?"

"If he did, he kept it to himself, but in all honesty, I still think his mind has closed off his past."

Theron sighed. "Something will trigger the memories eventually."

"Let's just hope it's once we've finished the Great Evil."

Theron and Aimery stared at each other.

"You don't think-" Aimery said, unable to finish.

Theron nodded and leaned against the wall. "I most certainly do think the evil knows about Gabriel."

Aimery sank into a chair and dropped his head into his hands. "With Val close to death, there is no one to watch Gabriel's back."

"Then send one of the other Shields. You know Hugh, Roderick, or Cole would go in an instant."

"True," Aimery said and raised his head. "I'll send one of them immediately."

Theron put out a hand and stopped him. "Are you going to tell Gabriel?"

"What? That the evil will target him and tell him things that might or might not be true?" Aimery shook his head and blew out a breath. "These men are more than just warriors to me. They are my family, and I'll protect them with my life if I have to."

"But you can't," Theron reminded him. "Gabriel has long sought his answers. Maybe it's time he receives them."

"And if it's something we aren't expecting?"

Theron inhaled deeply and crossed his arms over his chest. "Then we pray that the time he spent with the Shields will influence him."

"That's counting on a lot."

"It's all we have," Theron said sadly.

It was all they had, but that didn't mean Aimery couldn't do something about it. He nodded to Theron then closed his eyes and thought of Stone Crest.

In an instant, he stood in Hugh's chamber. He cleared his throat when he spotted Hugh and Mina in a passionate kiss.

"Bloody hell, Aimery," Hugh said and stepped away from Mina to face him. "You could at least knock."

"My apologies," Aimery said as he nodded to first Hugh then Mina.

Mina laughed, her turquoise eyes crinkled at the corners as she smoothed her hands down her gown. "No need. We know you only appear if it's important."

"A man shouldn't have to worry about being interrupted in his own chamber," Hugh grumbled.

Aimery couldn't help but grin. He watched the couple as Mina intertwined her hand with Hugh's. It had pleased him immensely when Hugh and Mina had fallen in love.

"What brings you here?" Hugh asked.

Aimery's smile vanished. "Gabriel."

"I'll get the others," Hugh said and walked from the chamber.

"Is he all right?" Mina asked.

"For now, but we're not sure what tomorrow will bring."

It was only moments later that Hugh returned with Roderick and Cole.

"What has happened?" Cole asked.

Aimery walked to the narrow window and looked out

over Stone Crest. "The creature Val and Gabriel battle is a gryphon."

"Impossible," Roderick said.   "They   are   pure creatures."

Aimery looked over his shoulder. "Not this one."

"And the blue stone?" Hugh asked. "Have they found it?"

"Nay," Aimery said and turned to face his men. "The gryphon isn't ruled by the blue stone as the others have been."

"By the gods," Cole said. "The evil controls it."

"Exactly. Val and Gabriel arrived in Scotland to find the gryphon about to kill a young woman."

"Is she...one of us?" Mina asked softly.

Aimery nodded. "She is, and they have kept her safe thus far."

"Then what are you waiting for?" Hugh asked. "Send them here so we can end the evil."

"I wish it were that simple." Aimery leaned back against the wall. "The evil has bounded Nicole to the land. I cannot shift her through time."

Roderick raked a hand through his golden hair. "The gryphon is too powerful for Val and Gabriel, isn't it?"

"Aye," Aimery answered. "It attacked them today. Val hangs onto life by a thread."

"Why isn't Gabriel healing him?" Hugh demanded.

This is the part Aimery had dreaded. "He couldn't at first. His wounds were as extensive as Val's. Nicole alone took care of both men. When Gabriel became conscious, he told her what herbs to mix to heal Val."

Cole sat in a vacant chair and leaned forward so that his elbows rested on his knees. "And his own wounds? Did this Nicole not tend his?"

Aimery wasn't fooled by Cole's cool tone. He could

feel Cole's worry and fear for both Gabriel and Val. "Gabriel refused at first. It wasn't until she finished with Val that he allowed her to tend to him."

"What do you need of us?" Roderick asked. "I'm ready to leave right now. Obviously Val and Gabriel need us."

"More than you realize," Aimery said. He looked at each Shield before he said, "Gabriel discovered something of his past."

Cole was the first to realize what Aimery hinted at. "He's immortal."

Aimery nodded. "Aye, though he doesn't heal as fast as you. I worry that the Great Evil knows more about Gabriel than we do, and could very well use it against him."

"Shift us," Hugh said. "We cannot waste any more time."

"I can't shift all of you," Aimery said. "The Chosen need to be guarded."

"Let me go," Hugh said.

Cole jumped to his feet. "Nay. Stone Crest needs her lord. I'll go."

Aimery nodded. "I'll give you a moment to say farewell to Shannon."

"No need," Shannon said as she walked into the chamber. She went to Cole and wrapped her arms around his neck as she kissed him long and hard. "Be safe and bring them all back soon."

"I will," he said and ran a hand down her cheek. "I love you."

She smiled. "I love you, too."

Cole turned to Aimery. "I'm ready."

Aimery laid a hand on Cole's shoulder and thought of Val and Gabriel. He felt the time shift around him and just when they reached the cave, they were jerked back to Stone Crest.

"What the devil?" Roderick thundered.

Aimery looked from Cole's bewildered face to Hugh then Roderick. "It seems the Great Evil has more power than we realized. He has prevented me from moving you to aid Gabriel and Val."

"What are you going to do?" Hugh asked.

"Find a way around it," Aimery promised and then promptly vanished.

CHAPTER SEVENTEEN

Nicole woke to find Val had kicked off the blankets covering him and was shivering. She wiped her eyes and berated herself for falling asleep. Once she pulled the blankets up to cover Val and felt how chilled he was, she glanced at the now dwindling fire.

Gabriel was nowhere to be found, so she rose and started for the cave entrance. She had nearly gotten to the entrance when Gabriel's deep voice stopped her.

"Where are you going?"

She jerked to a stop and looked around for him. He stepped out of the shadows, his silver eyes troubled. "We need more firewood."

"I'll get it," he said.

"You are still wounded."

He shook his head and moved farther into the light so she could see his bare chest. Where long, deep slashes from the gryphon's talons had once marked his chest, there weren't even scars to show of his wounds.

She took a step toward him. "It's so hard to believe."

"Val has a fever," he said as he walked back to the fire to retrieve a new tunic.

"I'll stay with him."

Gabriel nodded. "I'll get the firewood, then make a tonic to spread over his wounds that will help battle the fever. For now, keep him warm," he said as he walked to her. He stopped and looked her in the eye. "By any means necessary."

Nicole watched him walk out of the cave and down the mountain. She glanced at the overcast sky, unable to determine what time of day it was, but by the hunger in her belly, she knew they had missed lunch.

But there was no time to worry over food, not when Val's life hung in the balance. She rushed back to him and scooted under the covers with him. To better help him, she had to get as close to him as she could, but it was nearly impossible with his wounds.

She lifted her face to his and said, "I'm sorry if I hurt you, but I must get you warm." Then she pressed herself to his side and gently laid her hand across his stomach.

As she lay next to Val, all she could think about were his passionate kisses and how she had watched him nearly be killed by the gryphon.

He and Gabriel had boasted as to how they had killed the other creatures, but now she knew the gryphon was different, much different, than the others. Now she realized just how tenuously her life hung in the balance.

This Great Evil Val kept speaking of wanted her dead. She couldn't understand why the evil that had saved her and brought her to the village now wanted to end her life. It just didn't make sense.

She jerked when she heard Val murmur, and carefully lifted her head to look at his face. His forehead was creased and his mouth pinched, but she couldn't make out his words. She began to worry that if he thrashed around he would reopen his wounds.

"Shhh, Val," she said softly. "Sleep and heal."

Over and over she repeated her words until the lines on his forehead smoothed away. She closed her eyes and laid her head next to his. Dimly, she heard Gabriel enter the cave and begin stacking wood. She knew she needed to rise and fix them something to eat, but she wanted to rest her eyes for just a moment.

~ ~ ~

"What happened?" Hugh asked after Aimery had left the chamber.

Cole took Shannon's hand as she came to stand beside him and shook his head. "Nothing. We began to shift through time, and I was beginning to see what looked like a cave, when all of a sudden we were jerked back here."

"Strange," Roderick said.

Hugh grunted. "This doesn't bode well for Gabriel and Val."

Cole had never felt so frustrated. "There isn't anything we can do but wait and hope."

"And pray," Shannon said.

He looked at his mate and smiled. "And pray," he added.

"There must be something we can do," Mina said as Hugh pulled her onto his lap.

Roderick ran a hand down his face and sighed as Elle wrapped her arms around him from behind. "There's nothing, Mina. They may be on the same continent, but they are three hundred years in the future."

"I understand that," she said patiently. "However, the Fae magic is supposed to be the strongest magic there is. How is it that one evil is thwarting their magic?"

"Good question, my love," Hugh said. "But there is no

answer. By Aimery's face, he is as stumped as we are. My fear isn't losing Val. Gabriel is there, and he will make sure Val recovers."

"It's Gabriel," Roderick said.   "A   man   without memories of his past can be a tricky thing."

"Aye," Hugh said.

"But Gabriel isn't evil," Shannon said from beside Cole. "He's a good man who has fought alongside each of you for years."

"We know," Hugh replied. "Which is what makes this all the harder. Once Gabriel discovers whatever it is his mind has shut off, it could change the outcome of the future. No one, not even the Fae, know what Gabriel has locked in the deep recesses of his mind."

"We're so close to ending it all," Mina said.

Roderick sighed. "And Gabriel and Val have to do it alone. No one can help them."

"God help us," Elle whispered.

~ ~ ~

Gabriel fed more wood into the fire before he turned back to Laird. He was more worried about the wolfhound than about discovering he was immortal.

The wolfhound hadn't moved since Gabriel had brought him into the cave and began to tend to his wounds, and he feared Laird wouldn't heal. Gabriel removed the bandages and looked at the wounds, which had begun to heal nicely.

He ran his hand across Laird's fur to his head. He had known as soon as he had seen the wolfhound that he needed to walk the other way, but there had been something about the dog that called to him. In a few short days, the wolfhound had come to mean more to him than he had allowed himself to feel in a very long time.

Laird was his, his responsibility, and he had let him down. He had never questioned his healing abilities, but now he cursed them for not knowing how to heal Laird.

The wolfhound's breathing was even and deep, as if he slept, and his wounds didn't fester with dark magic, so Gabriel was at a loss as to what to do.

He glanced over his shoulder at Nicole and Val. They slept peacefully, but Gabriel could see Val shudder every now and again. As quietly as possible, Gabriel set about making another paste for Val's wounds, this one to rid his body of any infection.

When he was finished, he stepped around the fire and knelt beside Nicole. He gently laid his hand on her shoulder and saw her eyes flutter open and then turn to him.

"For Val's fever," he whispered and held out the bowl.

Nicole yawned then scooted out of the blanket and took the bowl. "Thank you."

"Spread it as you did the first paste, then rewrap the bandages. By morning, he should be well."

Her violet eyes gazed at him a moment, then she softly laid a hand atop his. "I will take good care of Val. Stay with Laird."

He knew she wanted to say more, but she held back and sent him a reassuring smile. Gabriel gave her a quick nod before he went back to Laird. He leaned back against the cave wall and watched as Nicole pulled back the blankets and removed the bandages. Then she tenderly wiped the dried blood and the previous paste off with a damp cloth before she applied the new paste.

Gabriel had seen many people care for the sick or wounded, and something he had taken note of was that when someone cared deeply for another, their touch was the softest, gentlest of anyone's. It was that way with Nicole. She had known them but a few days, but even a blind man would have seen the passion between Val and Nicole, a passion that Val was fighting hard against.

Gabriel nearly snorted. All the Shields hid something of their past, knowingly or not, and whatever Val hid was what had prompted him to join the Shields. Gabriel just hoped it wouldn't blind him to what stood willing in front of him. Nicole was not only beautiful and kind, but had a good spirit despite the fact she had been surrounded by evil since the day she arrived on Earth. Not many could have withstood such evil.

He blinked and strained to hear the melody that she hummed as she worked the paste into Val's wounds. Gabriel watched as Val turned his face toward her voice as if he sought her out even as he slept.

Then and there he decided to help Nicole seduce Val. It wouldn't be difficult since Val was already attracted to her. It would just take a little convincing to nudge Val into accepting the fact that there was something between him and Nicole.

Gabriel sighed wearily and glanced at Laird. He hated the fact that he wished he had someone just as the rest of the Shields did.

But then he remembered his newly found immortality. What else lay hidden in his mind? Was it something that could destroy him or the Shields? Or could it be something less wicked, something inane that had nothing to do with the Great Evil?

Yet, no matter how hard Gabriel tried to discern his past, all he found was nothing – just as it had been for the past several years. He prayed that whatever his past held, it wouldn't hinder the Shields in destroying the Great Evil.

Because if it did...he would never forgive himself.

~ ~ ~

"What?" bellowed the voice as it echoed around him until his ears rang with it.

He had the strongest desire to shred the voice's soul with his beak until nothing was left, but he knew no matter how powerful he was, the Great Evil was more powerful.

"Aimery bespelled the cave. No evil can enter it," he said for the second time."

"Impossible," the Great Evil murmured, his shadowy form only seen as he flitted between candelabras.

He watched as the Great Evil tried to mold his soul into a form. But no matter how many times he tried, he couldn't manage it.

"He must have tried to leave with the woman," he said.

A loud hissing noise surrounded him, and he knew the Great Evil was consumed with rage.

"Aimery is too smart for his own good, but he'll never figure a way to stop you," the Great Evil said. "By now, he's already tried to shift another Shield into this time. And failed."

"Then it's just a matter of time before I kill them."

Suddenly he was pushed back and pinned to the wall. "Tell me again why you didn't kill the Shields when you had the chance?" the Great Evil whispered into his ear. "Both Val and Gabriel were there for the taking."

He knew better than to fight the Great Evil, but being held bound as he was tested the limits of his patience. He fisted his talons as he fought the urge to push the Great Evil off him. "I knew wounding both of them would make the woman vulnerable."

"Did you also know that Gabriel is immortal?"

He jerked and wished he could look into the Great Evil's eyes as he used to. "How is it that I didn't know that?"

"You didn't need to know it until now. As I told you at the start of your mission, kill the woman and kill Val, but do not touch Gabriel."

At one time, he was the Great Evil's right hand, meeting out punishments and delivering death sentences. Now the Great Evil kept things from him, but that was all right. There was something he had kept from the Great Evil since he had been made.

"Why do you want Gabriel?"

"You just worry about not killing him," the Great Evil threatened. "Finish Nicole. I want my body back. I'm tired of existing as I am," he said and released him.

He rolled his shoulders and tucked his wings against him. "I haven't let you down yet." He turned to leave when the Great Evil's voice stopped him.

"You won't let me down now either."

He jerked as he felt the blue stone against his chest over his heart. He had worked many centuries to earn the trust from the Great Evil to have the hated stone removed. And now it was back. Now he was controlled once again.

"Why?" he asked.

"To ensure that I survive.

CHAPTER EIGHTEEN

Nicole woke and immediately reached over and felt Val's forehead. No longer did his flesh burn. She sat up and looked to where Gabriel had sat beside Laird all night, but he too was gone. Laird still hadn't moved, and she knew Gabriel was upset by not being able to heal the wolfhound.

She put her hand over Val's heart to find it beating strong and steady. She breathed a sigh of relief and pushed down the blankets to check his wounds. As she untied the bandages she noted that there were no signs of fresh blood, which proved how good Gabriel's herbs were.

It wasn't until she removed a bandage from his chest that she saw how the wounds had healed drastically overnight. They weren't gone as Gabriel's had been, but already they had nearly closed up and the skin around them was pink. Unable to stop herself, she moved her hand to a wound on his side near his hip and gently moved her fingers over the skin.

She heard a quick intake of breath and then felt a hand atop hers. Her gaze jerked to Val's face to find his eyes open and a smile pulling at his lips.

"That tickles," he said after licking his lips.

Nicole smiled and lifted her hand away from him. "How do you feel?"

He chuckled and then winced. "As if I had been attacked by a gryphon."

As she looked into his pale green eyes, Nicole realized how scared she had been for Val. "You frightened ten years off my life."

"I know," he said, the smile now gone. "It's what I do, Nicole. Every time we battle one of these ancient creatures, we face death."

"Knowing it and witnessing it are two different things," she argued.

Something moved in his light green eyes that pulled at her heart. It was as if he knew exactly what she was talking about, and she found herself wanting to comfort him, to touch him...to feel his hard body against hers.

Her head lowered until their lips were breaths apart. Then she felt his hand cup the back of her head and gently pull her toward him.

When his warm lips met hers, she couldn't stop the sigh that escaped. She willingly opened for him when his tongue ran along her lips. His tongue plunged inside her mouth and took her in a kiss made to curl her toes.

With her heart hammering against her chest and her breasts full and aching, Nicole ended the kiss and pulled back to see his arm shaking.

"You don't have the strength for this," she admonished him as she turned to get him water.

"It's a good thing, too. I'd have taken you, I want you so desperately."

Nicole nearly spilled the water she was so shocked to hear his words. She sought his gaze and saw the truth of it shining in his eyes. "I thought you didn't want me."

"I've wanted you from the first moment I saw you, but that doesn't make it right. You're a temptation that is forbidden to me. I need you to understand that."

"Tell me why I'm forbidden," she urged.

He shook his head and reached for the water with a shaking hand. She pushed away his hand and helped him raise his head so he could drink. When he had drunk his fill, she lowered his head back onto the blankets.

"I noticed how well Gabriel's herbs work. It's amazing."

"Hmm," Val said. "Speaking of Gabriel, how are his wounds? I gather he woke long enough to tell you what to mix?"

She wasn't sure she should be the one to tell him of Gabriel's new development. "He's doing better."

Val's eyes narrowed and his voice lowered. "What aren't you telling me?"

"Gabriel's wounds were just as extensive as yours. He was unconscious for hours, and I had no idea how to use his herbs. Just when I thought I would lose you both, he woke long enough to tell me what to mix."

Val's eyes closed as he nodded his head. "Good. None of us ever thought about what would happen if Gabriel weren't around with his herbs and knowledge."

Nicole picked at her skirts, praying Val wouldn't ask more until Gabriel returned.

"Nicole," Val murmured and opened his eyes. "Where is Gabriel?"

She glanced over her shoulder toward the entrance of the cave and debated on what to tell him.

"Is he...dead?"

"Nay," she hastily assured him. "Gabriel is very much alive."

"Then where is he?" Val's voice had gone cold, his

need to know where his comrade was evident by his clenched jaw and fisted hands.

"I don't know. I awoke to find him gone."

"You're holding something back. What is it?"

"That I'm immortal," Gabriel's voice said from behind her.

Nicole turned to find Gabriel standing with his arms crossed over his chest. She threw Val a quick glance to see his reaction. If he was surprised, he hid it well.

Val felt as if he had been run over by a chariot. "How are you taking the news?" he asked Gabriel. As long as they had been Shields, they all knew that Gabriel searched for answers that had eluded him.

"I don't know," he replied. "It answered one question, but spawned hundreds more."

Val longed to rise and offer Gabriel whatever solace he could. "Does Aimery know?"

"Aye," Nicole replied. "He was here when we discovered it."

Val looked from Gabriel's tortured silver gaze to Nicole's worried one. "And Aimery's reaction?"

Gabriel shrugged. "There wasn't much he could say. He did try to hide how much it concerned him."

"Are *you* concerned?"

For the first time in a very long time, Gabriel let Val see how anxious he was. "Aye," he admitted softly. "Don't you think it odd that of all the times I've been wounded, I now discover I'm immortal?"

"It is a rather odd time."

"I don't understand," Nicole said. "What does it matter when you find out?"

"It matters," Gabriel said, "because we battle an evil that has powers strong enough to withstand the Fae. That doesn't happen, Nicole."

"If you're trying to frighten me, you've succeeded."

Val could have run Gabriel through. Instead, he slowly sat up and reached for Nicole's hand that hung limply by her side. "Sit," he told her before turning to Gabriel. "She knows what she faces. We don't need to make it worse."

"I'd rather know everything," Nicole said.

Gabriel shook his head. "Nay, you don't. I was wrong to say what I did. Forgive me."

She nodded and Val sighed. "So, what all did Aimery have to say?"

"He refused to aid in your healing," Nicole stated, her words heavy with anger.

Val looked at her and smiled. "We've always known that. There are rules the Fae must follow. They are bending many as it is by shifting us through time, clothing and arming us, and supplying us with coin for necessities."

"It seems to me he bends the rules that he wants." Though her words were harsh, her tone wasn't quite as ruthless as before.

Before Val could answer, Gabriel spoke up. "Many see us as a means to an end for the Fae. But to us, we know just how much we mean to Aimery. We are more than his soldiers. We are part of his family."

Val stared at Gabriel. Never would he have contemplated that Gabriel knew how Aimery thought of them. He was discovering much about his fellow Shield, and the fact that Gabriel was so open showed him just how vulnerable Gabriel felt.

Which wasn't a good sign.

"I retrieved our weapons," Gabriel said as he walked to his side of the fire and sat down.

Val saw him pet something gray and noticed it was Laird. "How is he?"

"Slowly getting better. I thought for a moment last

night that I had lost him, but he improves with each hour."

"And the gryphon?"

"Nowhere in sight," Gabriel spat. "I'm ready to finish him."

Val nodded. "I'm with you, brother, but we learned a valuable lesson. He's twice as strong as any creature we've battled so far."

"Aye," Gabriel agreed. "Our weapons do no more than anger him."

"And without the blue stone, we can't kill him that way."

For long moments, they stared into the fire, each lost in thought. While Val was sure Gabriel thought of the gryphon, all he could think of was Nicole's lush body and how badly he wanted to bury himself inside of her.

This was exactly why he hadn't wanted to kiss or touch her. Now she was a temptation that was hard to resist, and if she wanted to remain alive, she needed to stay away from him.

He glanced at her and found her staring at him, the hunger burning bright in her violet eyes. He cursed and closed his eyes.

"I think it's time I head back into the village," Gabriel said. "Maybe I'll even visit the castle."

"Nay," Val said. "I'll go."

Gabriel leaned forward and wrapped his arms loosely around his legs. "I'm not arguing with you, Val. Besides, you still aren't fully healed."

"I will be by tomorrow."

"Aye, but I'm going today. And you need to stretch your muscles so you'll be prepared for another battle."

Val knew by Gabriel's determined look that he could argue until the stars ceased to exist, but Gabriel wasn't going to change his mind.

"All right," Val conceded. "But you must be back before nightfall."

Gabriel shrugged. "The gryphon attacked in broad daylight yesterday. I don't think that is going to bother him."

"And by the way he destroyed my cottage, I don't think he cares who stumbles upon him," Nicole said.

Val turned his head toward her. "He destroyed your cottage?"

"There isn't anything left standing. He even knocked over the stone hearth."

"Odd," Val said and looked at Gabriel. "Don't you think?"

Gabriel nodded, his brows raised. "The mark of anger and frustration."

"I think I see an advantage for us."

A slow smile pulled at Gabriel's face. "I knew you would."

~ ~ ~

Nicole walked to the entrance of the cave to stretch her legs and found the sky dawning a vivid pink and orange through the thick clouds. There would most likely be more snow before nightfall.

"Will you be all right?" Gabriel asked as he came to stand beside her.

She nodded. "After yesterday, I think I can face almost anything."

He smiled. "You're a strong woman, Nicole. Look what you've survived your entire life."

"True," she said and regarded his chiseled face now hidden partly by a beard. Since their arrival, neither he nor Val had shaved. She licked her lips, wondering if she should ask him the question that had burned through her mind all morning.

"Go on," he urged as he casually leaned against the wall as if he had all the time in the world.

She didn't bother to ask how he knew she had a question, just accepted it. "How does a woman seduce a man?"

His smile grew. "I hoped you would ask that. One thing you have to understand about Val, he's fighting hard to stay away from you."

"I know. Why?"

Gabriel shrugged. "That I can't answer, but I do know that it won't take much to push him over that proverbial edge."

CHAPTER NINETEEN

It didn't take Val long to become restless. He needed to feel a weapon in his hand and stand on his feet again. With Gabriel leaving, he refused to drink any of his drugged water knowing it would only put him to sleep, and sleep was the last thing he needed to be doing when he was supposed to be guarding Nicole.

Nay, the last thing I need to be doing is bedding her. But, oh what a tempting morsel she is.

Gaining strength with every breath, Val pulled himself to his feet with the help of the cave wall. Once he stood, he leaned against the wall to slow his breathing. When he didn't feel as though he had run from Rome and back, he pushed off the wall and started toward the entrance.

He passed one of the large boulders protruding from the cave wall and saw Gabriel and Nicole standing close together with their heads almost touching. An unusual emotion spiked through him--jealousy.

It wasn't an emotion he had felt before, so it took him a moment to realize what it was. Then, he chastised himself for it since he had no claim to Nicole, and in fact, had pushed her away.

Still, it irked him to see her so close to Gabriel. Maybe more so since discovering Gabriel was immortal and could protect her better than he could. It was the first time in many years that Val felt unworthy, the last time being when his sisters and their families died.

He tried to shake off the feeling, but it sunk its claws into him, and he knew the only way to rid himself of it was to keep Nicole alive at all costs. It was something he knew he could easily do. Dying to keep the evil from invading his and the Fae realms was an easy choice.

But no matter how much he had changed, he still heard his sisters' screams. He swallowed and had the sudden urge to find some wine.

"Everything all right?" Gabriel asked.

Val nodded. "Do you happen to have any wine?"

Gabriel's silver eyes narrowed and he shook his head. "You know I don't. Why?"

"I've a thirst for it."

"Is it the receding pain?" Gabriel asked. "If you'll drink the herbal water, it will finish the healing process."

Val wished now he hadn't asked. "It's not the pain."

"It has been a long time since you've sought wine."

Val knew exactly how long, for when Aimery had found him, Val had been so drunk he couldn't stand. Once he had gotten sober and pledged himself to the Shields, he hadn't touched alcohol again.

"Forget it," he said. His eyes came to rest on his halberd and sword that rested against the wall. He reached for his weapons, needing something to occupy his mind.

"Val," Gabriel whispered as he moved closer.

He looked over Gabriel's shoulder to find Nicole regarding him intently. "I'm fine. Really."

"I'll stay. I can visit the town and the castle tomorrow.

Val shook his head, hating that Gabriel had seen how

far he had fallen. "Nay. We need all the information we can gather so we can get Nicole to safety."

He waited as Gabriel studied him for long moments. Finally, Gabriel gave a quick nod and turned and went to Nicole.

"Remember what I told you," he said to her.

Val strained to hear her reply, wondering what they could have been talking about, but Nicole's response was mumbled. The look they exchanged proved that they had shared something between them, something that didn't include him.

"If I'm not back by nightfall, don't worry. I may stay in the village tonight," Gabriel called as he reached for his bow and slung his quiver of arrows over his shoulder.

"Be careful," Val warned as he watched him walk from the cave. He hurried to the entrance and looked to the sky to make sure the gryphon didn't suddenly attack.

He and Nicole watched as Gabriel slowly made his way down the mountain. Val felt something near his hand and he looked down to see Laird standing beside him. Laird let out a bark, which made Gabriel turn around.

"Stay," Gabriel said to the wolfhound then continued down the mountain.

Val patted the wolfhound's head. "Go rest," he told Laird and was amazed when the wolfhound slowly walked back to his spot by the fire and gingerly lay down.

He turned to Nicole then and stared as her eyes followed Gabriel. "He'll be fine."

Her violet eyes moved to him and she gave him a smile. "I've no doubt. Being immortal puts a new perspective on things."

His need to find wine grew. "Aye, but not all of us can be immortal."

"I'm not sure I'd want to be immortal," she said, tilting

her head to the side to regard him. "Do you?"

He shrugged, not willing to give her his real answer. "At times."

"Aimery said there were other Shields who were immortal."

"Cole and Roderick."

"Only two of your five?"

"Three now," he reminded her.

Her brows rose at his statement. "Yet you and Hugh have managed to survive as mere mortals. In my opinion, that takes more cunning."

Her words were like a salve to his wounded pride. He had never been jealous of Roderick or Cole for their immortality, but for some reason the discovery of Gabriel's had opened a wound he hadn't realized he had.

"It bothers you, doesn't it?" she asked quietly.

"What?" he asked, pretending he didn't know what she referred to.

She licked her lips and leaned back against the wall. "Gabriel being immortal."

Val turned his head away from her and caught a glimpse of Gabriel before he disappeared around the mountain on the trail to the village. His first thought was to lie to her, but he found he didn't want that.

"A little," he finally confessed.

She made a clucking sound with her tongue that had him turning toward her. "I don't understand why. Look what you have seen, experienced. You lived in a time I cannot fathom. You were a general in one of the world's greatest armies. For centuries, Rome ruled vast amounts of land."

"And fought bloody wars to ensure they ruled that land," he reminded her.

"Aye," she agreed. "Is that what eats away at you?

That you helped to destroy so much for Rome's quest of dominance?"

"I'd like to say, aye, but that would be a lie. Rome's brilliance could blind a man to her horrors. Rome was only as good as her emperor, as is evident by the few great ones who ruled."

She smiled suddenly. "So, you're proud to be a Roman."

He chuckled. "I didn't say that. Rome did many great things, but she also did many terrible things. I was fortunate enough to live during some of her greatness, but I thank God every day that I left when I did."

She sighed, her breath ballooning around her. Her face was pensive as she thought over his words. Then she crossed her arms over her chest and said, "I'm curious by nature. It has gotten me into more trouble than I care to admit, but I find that I'm vastly curious about you."

"What would you like to know?" He was pleased to know she found him intriguing.

"Once you pledged to the Shields, did you ever return to your family?"

If a jug of wine had been available, he would have lifted it to his mouth and drained its entire contents.

Nicole saw the change in Val. His body became rigid and his beautiful pale green eyes that had held such warmth just a moment ago turned cold and unforgiving.

"Nay."

That one simple word said more than an hour's worth of conversation. "I'm sorry."

"Don't be."

She wanted to call him back as he turned away from her. If she had only kept her mouth shut and not begun snooping into his past they would still be talking. She wrapped her arms around herself as the cold finally penetrated her. She hadn't noticed it before, not with Val near.

In truth, she never noticed much but Val. It was a sad state of affairs she found herself in. Finally, she'd found an attractive, alluring, intriguing man. It just so happened he didn't want anything to do with her.

"You'll soon freeze if you don't move away from the entrance," Val called over his shoulder as he stretched his arms above his head, the firelight playing over his bare chest.

She walked toward him watching the play of his muscles as he moved. "Your wounds are looking better almost by the moment."

"Aye, Gabriel's herbs work wonders."

"I see. His herbs didn't come from here, did they?"

His pale green eyes moved to her. "I honestly don't know. He has his black bag with him at all times, and occasionally, I've seen him stop and gather a few things. However, the other Shields and I have long suspected that when he spent time in the Fae realm that he gathered most of his herbs there."

"Amazing. Did you ever see the Fae realm?"

"Once, and only briefly. I met the king and queen."

Nicole was well and truly enraptured now. She moved closer to the fire and sank to the ground as Val continued to stretch his arms and torso.

Her breath locked in her lungs as she studied his amazing body. She knew what his skin felt like beneath her palms, she knew what it felt like to be yanked against his hard muscles. And she wanted it again.

"Really? What were they like?"

He smiled and rotated his shoulders. "Unlike anything I could describe. They are similar to Aimery with their long flowing pale hair and mystical blue eyes, yet there is something more regal to them."

"They are royalty," she reminded him.

"True." He leaned to the side and gently worked the muscles that were healing.

"Did they wear the royal purple like our royalty?"

He shook his head, his eyes sparkling. "Nay. They wear white and silver."

"Sounds beautiful."

"It is, and so are they."

"What?" she asked.

"All Fae are beautiful. Don't tell me you didn't find yourself attracted to Aimery?" he questioned, a knowing look on his handsome face.

She laughed and brought her legs up to her chest, then wrapped her arms around them. "I'll only admit that I found him exceptionally handsome."

"Most women throw themselves at him."

"Truly?" she asked, aghast that any woman would act so brazenly.

"The Fae are very alluring to us. Its one of the reasons they stay hidden."

"So, did you throw yourself at the queen?"

He threw back his head and laughed, the sound rich and deep bringing a smile to her lips. "Nay," he said. "Theron would have gutted me."

"Is their realm much like ours?"

He picked up his sword and swung it in wide arcs around him. "I didn't get to see much of it, only being there for a short time to take my pledge, but I've heard Cole speak of being raised there."

"He was raised there?"

"Aye. He said the Fae realm has magic running thick and deep within it, dragons flying in the bright blue sky and untold treasures that could never be compared to our world."

"Now I really want to see it. Dragons? Unbelievable."

"That's what I said." He began to lunge and thrust with his sword, his skin beginning to gleam with exertion.

For long moments Nicole sat quietly as Val continued to work with his sword. When he set down the sword and reached for the halberd, she was amazed to find him very adept at working the magnificent weapon.

She had noticed the intricate knotwork on both Val's and Gabriel's weapons – weapons the Fae had crafted for them. She was on her feet and by his side when he suddenly winced.

"What is it?" she asked looking over his wounds to see if any bled.

"Halt."

Nicole's hands stilled when she heard the pain in his voice. She raised her gaze to his and found his jaw clenched and his eyes closed. "Tell me where you hurt. I can help."

His eyes flew open. "You want to know where I hurt?"

She nodded, unsure of the strange light in his eyes.

"Let me show you," he said just before his arm came around her and his mouth took hers.

CHAPTER TWENTY

Val knew he should stop, but the sweet, intoxicating taste of Nicole's lips was just what he needed. He had pushed himself too far in his training and pulled a muscle that wasn't fully healed, but it was the touch of her soft hands on his heated flesh that had sent him over the edge.

His tongue swept inside her mouth and he drank greedily from her, his desire reaching new heights. He knew it had been wrong for Gabriel to leave him alone with her, but Val had thought he had more control than he did.

He ended the kiss and stepped away from her. Her lips were swollen and her eyes filled with desire.

"Why is it when you kiss me my body craves more of your touch?" she asked.

Val groaned and took another step away from her. "Don't," he begged her.

"Would it be the same if I kissed another?"

The thought of her in another man's arms sent his blood to boiling. He wanted to lie to her and tell her only he could bring such desire to her body. "Possibly."

"Kiss me again."

"Nay," he said more forcefully than he intended. "I'm

supposed to guard you. Not bed you."

The hurt that flashed in her violet eyes was like a dagger plunged into his gut. "Forgive me. I'd appreciate if you didn't kiss me again."

He couldn't fault her for her icy attitude, not after the way he had treated her. How many times had he pushed her away only to kiss her in the next heartbeat? It was beyond cruel.

"Nicole," he said as she turned from him. She didn't stop and he didn't go after her.

Val sighed and ran his hand down his face.

"That wasn't so nice."

He spun around to find Aimery behind him. "Shite, Aimery," he murmured. "Just how much did you see?"

"More than enough."

Val set down his halberd and reached for the tunic Aimery held out for him. "Thank you," he said before slipping it over his head.

He ran his hands down the soft cream-colored material. Just as with the first time he had felt Fae cloth, he was amazed by it.

"And this," Aimery said.

Val nodded and reached for his leather jerkin. He threaded his arms through it and then sighed. Warmth surrounded him as soon as he put on the tunic. "Thank you."

"Anything else you or Nicole need?"

Val looked over and found Nicole sitting beside Laird, stroking his massive head. "A bath," he said suddenly thinking that Nicole might like to take one.

Aimery's blond brows rose. "A bath? I expected a lot of things, Val, but not a request for a bath."

He shrugged. "We're stuck in this cave until Gabriel and I find a way to kill the gryphon. I thought a bath might be nice."

"Oh, I think Nicole will more than enjoy it. I'll have one sent."

"My thanks," Val said.

"How long are you going to tempt yourself before you take what she offers?"

Val lowered his eyes and tried to pretend Aimery's words didn't sting. "I cannot take what she offers so freely."

"And why is that?"

"You know why," he said as he raised his gaze to Aimery.

Aimery nodded. "It was a long time ago. You've more than redeemed yourself."

"Not when I'm nearly in the same situation as before. I refuse to allow myself to be tempted when my duty is to keep her alive."

For a long moment, Aimery studied him. "How bad is your need for wine?"

Val cursed long and low as he turned away from the Fae commander and paced. "Leave it be."

"Nay," Aimery said. "You drug yourself out of that pit, Valentinus, and I'll not sit by and let you sink into it again."

Val stopped his pacing when Aimery used his Roman name. With a sigh, he turned back to him. "I'll be fine."

"How many times have you had the need since you pledged to the Shields?"

Val swallowed and lifted his chin. "This is the first time."

"And why do you think that is?"

He shrugged as his frustration mounted. "I don't know. If I had the answers I wouldn't be fighting the need for a drink."

"The answer is right before you. You simply cannot

see it."

Val hated when Aimery talked in riddles. "Give me the answer. I don't want to sink into that despair again."

"As I said, you have the answer."

"Damn you, Aimery." Val couldn't bring himself to ask again, not when he knew Aimery would refuse to tell him. He hadn't sunk as low as before, but that was partly due to the fact there wasn't any wine available.

Aimery's head cocked to the side. "How strong are you, Val? Can you resist more temptation?"

"If you're referring to Nicole, I'll continue to resist her."

"You haven't done so well so far. Every time she comes near you, you kiss her. How many more times will that happen before you finally take her?"

"I won't take her," he said between clenched teeth.

Aimery crossed his arms over his chest and sighed. "Taking what pleasure you can has always been something I've encouraged the Shields to do. She is willing, and you are more than attracted to her. You know better than she that the feelings between you two don't happen every day."

"I am a Shield," Val said, straining to keep his growing ire in control. "She is a Chosen one. There cannot be anything between us."

"Hugh, Roderick, and Cole have each found their mates in one of the Chosen. What makes you think you are different?"

"Because I don't deserve to find my mate."

Aimery blinked and let his arms fall to his side. "You think you are unworthy because of one mistake?"

"A mistake that took innocent lives," Val reminded him.

"I was there," Aimery said. "I saw exactly what happened. You aren't the only one to blame."

"I won't argue this anymore," Val said. "Leave it be."

"Don't be a fool," Aimery warned. "Everyone deserves to find love."

Val laughed. "Not everyone."

Thankfully, Aimery decided to leave then, ending their argument, but Val found he couldn't stop thinking of Aimery's words.

If there was one thing he had been many times in his life, it was a fool. Wasn't a person supposed to learn from their mistakes and wrong decisions?

He turned his head and found Nicole staring into the fire. He longed to go to her, to talk and laugh as they had earlier, but he knew that wasn't possible. Being near her was a temptation unto itself, and he couldn't afford to be tempted anymore that day.

After grabbing his cloak, he moved to the entrance and sat down on one of the smaller boulders as he began to polish and sharpen his sword and halberd.

With loving hands, he traced the intricate design on his weapons. He had never been prouder than the day he was gifted with his weapons. Not even the day he was promoted to general compared.

Aimery had given him back his confidence and a need to live again, and Val would be forever grateful to Aimery. The Shields had also given him a sense of belonging and pride.

As he thought of his brethren, he found himself longing for their camaraderie and laughter. He knew with all of them surrounding him, he would never think to turn to wine when memories of his sisters threatened.

But he didn't have them. He really didn't have Gabriel since he had issues of his own to deal with after discovering his was immortal. Nay, Val only had himself.

In all honesty, he was surprised Aimery didn't send him

a jug of wine just to entice him. Val couldn't help but smile at the memory of that long ago day when he had been sober for about a month and training heavily with the Shields. He had returned to his chamber and found a jug of wine on his bed.

Aimery had sent it to tempt Val, to show him that he was strong enough to get over the craving to drown his memories in wine.

Val had been strong then, but he wasn't as strong now. There was no way he could pass up wine. Not now. Not when his memories of his sisters haunted him as they had begun to do.

He pushed away his morbid thoughts and scanned the horizon. No sign of the gryphon. Since Aimery had protected the cave and the gryphon knew it, it was simply a waiting game now. The gryphon couldn't attack them as long as they were in the cave, and they couldn't attack the gryphon since he was immune to their weapons.

Val prayed Gabriel discovered something of value while at the village. If he didn't, there was no telling how long they would be in the cave.

He scratched his neck as his mind ran through various ways to draw the gryphon out, and even with Gabriel's immortality, Val couldn't come up with a plan that involved killing the gryphon without losing their own lives.

~ ~ ~

The gryphon watched the cave and the Shield, Val, as he sat at the entrance. He had listened intently to Val's thoughts and argument with Aimery, and that's when he devised the perfect plan to draw Nicole out of the cave.

Anger simmered just below the surface as he shifted and felt the blue stone against his chest. All his years of loyalty and service meant nothing now. All that mattered to the evil one was the death of Nicole.

But what the evil one didn't realize is that he remembered just who Nicole was.

His talons sunk into the thick snow as his memories ran through his mind. The evil had tried to erase all the memories when he had been converted to evil, but he had been stronger and held onto a few precious memories.

Those memories had returned with a vengeance as he looked into Nicole's eyes while he choked the life out of her. The realization of who she was had been like a spear through his heart.

He knew then that he couldn't kill her.

And he might have found some way to keep her alive before, but not now. Not with the cursed blue stone controlling him.

He rose to his feet and stretched his massive wings. There was no getting around killing Nicole now, and once the deed was done, his soul would forever be in the hands of Hell, tormented and tortured.

CHAPTER TWENTY-ONE

Gabriel couldn't help but worry about Nicole and Val. It was obvious to anyone who looked that Val wanted her, but what he couldn't understand was why Val turned her away.

Despite the words of encouragement he had given Nicole, Gabriel wondered if they would indeed work on Val, for the Roman could be stubborn at times, especially when he got something into his head.

Gabriel sighed and walked into the village. The clean up from the gryphon's destruction was still taking place. He spotted the pub and walked inside. If he were to find out about the blue stone, the best place to do it was in the pub after someone had had a few drinks.

As he closed the door behind him, he quickly surveyed the small room. Off to his left was a bar with a room behind it, probably the kitchen. To his right was a hearth and tables scattered throughout the room.

He found an empty table and walked toward it, nodding to a few individuals as he passed. Most people stared at him curiously, but others gave him a baleful look. He ignored the hostile stares and took his seat.

"Ye must be new here," said a feminine voice.

Gabriel looked up to find a pretty girl with flame red hair and laughing green eyes. He smiled and nodded. "Indeed I am. Any chance I can get something to drink?"

"Oh, aye," she said with a wink. "I'll bring it right out."

Her thick Scottish accent was easy on the ears, and Gabriel found himself wishing he had a few more hours to entertain himself with the buxom lass. He stretched his legs out in front of him as he leaned back in the chair.

In a matter of moments, she returned with a large mug and placed it in front of him. Gabriel handed her some coins. "Keep the rest for yourself," he said.

She looked down at her hand and gasped. "Thank ye, sir. Are you some lord?"

"Nay," Gabriel said with a laugh. "I'm just a traveler who likes good service."

"Do ye happen to have a name that goes along with such a...handsome face?" she asked as she eyed him appreciatively.

He let a finger graze the knuckles of her hand that rested on the table. "Gabriel."

"If ye need anything, Gabriel, let me know. I'm sure I can take care of it."

"Well, there is something you might be able to help me with," he said as he leaned close to her. "What do you know of the laird of the castle?"

Her brows furrowed. "The Laird? He's an old man who doesna receive visitors anymore. Ye wantin' to see him?"

Gabriel shrugged and took a sip of the ale. He nodded, surprised at the good taste. "In truth, I'm looking for something."

"Really?" she asked intrigued. "And what might that be, me fine man?"

The more Gabriel spoke with her, the more he found he liked her. "A very precious stone."

Her nose wrinkled at his words. "A stone? Are ye daft, then?"

He laughed, not caring that it drew glances from other customers. He motioned her closer and whispered, "It's about the size of a child's fist, and it is the most unusual blue you could imagine."

"If there was a stone like that in this village, everyone would know of it," she said as he leaned back. "I'm afraid you willna find it here."

"What about in the castle?"

She tapped a finger against her chin as she contemplated his words. "It could be, but I doubt it. The steward robbed the poor old laird blind. There isna much left in the castle."

Gabriel tossed her another coin. "You've been most helpful."

"Any time, love," she threw over her shoulder as she walked away, the sensual swing of her hips drawing his gaze.

~ ~ ~

Nicole had never been bored before in her life, but she found herself going daft with nothing to do. She couldn't even walk around her beautiful loch. Instead, she was stuck in a cave with a man that would rather sit near the cave entrance than be near her.

She admonished herself immediately. She knew Val was sitting there to keep watch for the gryphon, but the other part of her argued that the gryphon couldn't hurt them inside the cave so there was no reason for him to stand guard.

Then she found herself wondering at the hushed conversation he and Aimery had had. It was evident by Val's pacing and rigid stance that he was agitated about something. Aimery's unforgiving look didn't help matters either, but she realized that if it had something to do with her safety, they'd tell her immediately.

At least she hoped they would.

Laird whimpered, and she resumed the stroking of his fur. She had lost track of time in the cave, and could no longer tell if it had been a few moments or a few hours that she had sat by the fire feeding it limbs.

She was so ready for something to happen that she was about ready to walk out of the cave and see what the gryphon would do. There had been no sign of the creature when Gabriel had left, which she found odd. If the gryphon wanted her dead so badly, shouldn't he take whatever chance he got to weaken them?

That in turn made her wonder why the gryphon hadn't killed Gabriel and Val when he had attacked them. Granted, he wounded them severely, but as a creature of evil, shouldn't his main objective be to kill?

All these questions she wanted to ask Val, but she knew he didn't wish to be bothered. She could barely see him around the boulders in the cave.

She lay on the pallet of blankets to stretch out her back and thought about what her life might have been like had her realm not been destroyed and she been sent to Earth. Would her parents have loved her? Would she have been married with children of her own by now?

Or would she be as alone as she was now?

In some ways, she liked not knowing where she came from. It had been easier to think she had been an orphan who was raised by a mean witch.

Her stomach growled, and she realized they hadn't

eaten their morning meal. She hastily gathered some food and stood. As she walked to Val she could sense his anger and turmoil, and she longed to help him.

"Hungry?" she asked as she held out the bread, cheese, and oatcake.

"Thanks," he said and reached for the food.

When he didn't offer for her to join him, Nicole turned and made her way back to the fire where she ate alone. Again.

~ ~ ~

With nothing more to do than stare at the walls, Nicole slept, waking only to bring Val food for the noon meal and then returning to eat alone. When she woke a few hours later it was to find a large tub set toward the back of the cave.

She stood and walked toward it. As she neared, she saw what looked like steam wafting up from whatever was inside. When she reached the tub and found it full of hot water, she gasped with delight.

The tub was as high as her chest and so wide that it could easily fit two people inside. Her thoughts immediately turned to Val and she could well imagine their bodies gliding against each other in the water.

Her breasts swelled and her sex throbbed. She had turned into a wanton after meeting Val, but since there was a greater chance of her dying than living, she wanted to experience what it was like to be held in a man's arms.

By the sensual way he kissed, she could well imagine he was a good lover.

A shiver ran over her body as she recalled the possessive way he molded her body to his rock hard planes, the way his hands had skimmed over her skin, bringing delightful sensations with every touch.

Nicole mentally shook herself then cast a glance at Val. His head was still turned away from her, so she hurriedly undressed and climbed into the massive wooden tub.

She sighed as she sunk into the steaming water and leaned against the back. Contentment washed over her as she closed her eyes and dreamed of a life that wasn't ripped apart by evil creatures.

~ ~ ~

Val stood and stretched. He had sat near the entrance all day, and as the sky began to darken, he found he was chilled to the bone and in need of warming. He turned to walk toward the fire and Nicole and stopped in his tracks.

At the back of the cave stood a large wooden tub. With a naked Nicole inside.

His rod swelled painfully, yet he couldn't look away as she slowly raised one arm, the water running slowly down her heated flesh as she washed.

He didn't even know his feet had moved until he found himself standing before the tub, his eyes feasting on Nicole as she continued to bathe, unaware of his presence.

Her silky midnight hair was piled haphazardly atop her head with tendrils sticking to her face and shoulders from the steam of the water.

His breath caught in his throat as her hands moved to wash her breasts. He itched to feel their weight in his hands, to watch as her nipple hardened beneath the onslaught of his fingers, to massage the sensual mounds until she moaned with pleasure.

In response to his vision, his cock jumped and throbbed with need.

Suddenly, she turned and looked at him.   After

everything he had done to her, he fully expected her to scream and rant at him to turn away and leave.

But as he watched, she slowly stood and he feasted upon her full breasts and dusky nipples already hard and yearning for his touch.

He tried to swallow but found his mouth dry. His gaze moved from her luscious breasts to her inviting mouth. How he wanted to yank her against him and devour her.

When she held out her hand, Val had never come out of his clothes so fast. He didn't stop to think, couldn't think beyond his need for her that overshadowed everything.

CHAPTER TWENTY-TWO

Nicole's heart thudded painfully against her chest as her stomach flipped then fell like a stone to her feet when Val climbed into the water.

She never got her fill of looking at his stunning form from his wide shoulders and torso that narrowed to a "V" to his trim waist. His muscles bunched then moved as he reached for her. It never entered her mind to refuse him.

Gabriel's words played over and over in her mind as she looked into Val's smoldering green depths.

"Don't give up on him if you really want him, Nicole. Val wants you badly. Give him the incentive he needs to give in to his wants and desires."

She would give him the incentive. Nicole had never wanted anything as badly as she did Val — and she was going to make sure he knew it.

When he lowered his head and gently ran his lips along hers, she let her hands glide over the hard sinew of his chest to his neck where she threaded her fingers in his hair.

Her bare skin met his, and she shivered at the delicious feel of him. But it was his hardness pressing into her stomach that caused her blood to heat and her heart to pound.

Before she could reach down and touch him, he moved his chest against her, eliciting a moan as he gently scraped against her already aching nipples.

His kisses moved from her mouth to her neck as she tilted her head back and rubbed her body against his. One arm wrapped around her, anchoring her to him while his hand moved over her back and bottom, then up her side, grazing the underside of her swollen breast.

Just as she was about to beg him to touch her, his hand cupped her breast. She moaned and gasped as he first massaged her breast, then moved his fingers over her nipple.

"You're sensitive," he murmured, his eyes on her breasts.

She wanted to answer him, but his fingers had begun to gently tug on her nipple. Suddenly, he turned them until he had her pressed against the tub.

"There won't be any running away for either of us this time, Nicole." His eyes blazed with desire and all she could do was nod in agreement.

She was on fire for him, and he had just started his assault on her. Both hands cupped her breasts as he placed a kiss on the top of each one. He took a nipple between his thumb and forefinger and began to drive her insane with a coiling need of desire that tightened with every pinch and tease.

Her body was ablaze and her sex throbbed. She needed more of Val but didn't understand how.

When his head dipped and his hot, wet tongue laved her nipples, she cried out, wanting more. There was no time to think, only to feel.

Just when she wasn't sure she could take any more, his teeth grazed her nipple and she bucked beneath him. The contact of her hips meeting his torso sent a shiver of pleasure through her. She repeated the motion and found her pleasure deepening.

"Not yet," Val said and took hold of her hips to still her.

Before she could argue, he took her lips in a fierce kiss while his hands continued to caress over her body. She wrapped her legs around his waist and felt his hot, hard arousal press against her sex. She moaned when the tip of him ran over a sensitive spot.

Val chuckled. "Ah, your clitoris," he said huskily as he kissed her neck. "Shall we explore it more?"

She tried to answer him, but her voice refused to work as his fingers moved slowly, seductively... enticingly over her sex. Her blood pounded through her veins as he nudged her legs open further. The feel of the warm water against her was new and exciting as it touched her heated flesh.

She whimpered as his fingers ran over her curls and along the sides of her sex, tempting her, arousing her...but not touching the part of her that ached.

"Please," she begged.

His eyes crinkled in the corners and the fire popped, but still he didn't touch her. The more he teased, the hotter she became. The desire wound so tight she thought she might burst from it. She was mindless with need, delirious with the emotions assaulting her.

When his finger finally dipped inside of her, she gasped and stiffened at the delicious intrusion. When he began to move in and out of her, she closed her eyes and gave herself up to the sensual sensations.

She had thought when he finally did touch her, it would ease the ache inside of her, but how wrong she had been. Instead, it only intensified the desire until she thought of nothing else, wanted, craved nothing else.

Then his thumb ran over the spot he had called her clitoris. Her body shook with need and pumped against his hand at the contact. He twirled his thumb around the nub, bringing her to new heights as he continued to delve inside of her with his finger.

She felt him add a second finger and moaned at the friction. Though she hadn't been around men, she had seen couples that had gone into the woods together. She knew exactly what Val was going to do to her...and she couldn't wait.

Suddenly, his hand was gone and she felt the tip of his cock against her. She opened her eyes and saw him watching her.

"This is your last chance to leave," he said hoarsely.

"I'm not leaving." To prove her point, she moved her hips against his rod.

He closed his eyes and groaned. When he opened them, they were dark with desire. "When I put my cock in you, it's going to hurt, but just for a moment."

"Hurt?" She didn't know why it would hurt. The women she saw seemed to enjoy it greatly.

"It's your first time. I must pierce your maidenhead."

"Oh," she said and lowered her eyes. There was so much she didn't know, and she hated to appear foolish in front of him.

His finger lifted her chin until she gazed into his eyes. "It's a privilege for a man to be a woman's first, which is why it's very important that you're sure you want me to take you."

"I've never been more sure of anything," she said.

He kissed her hard. Her body had cooled during their talk, but Val's hand returned to her clit, quickly bringing her back to the point of no return.

This time, when he moved his hands and she felt the tip of him against her again, she smiled and wrapped her arms around his neck. He shifted until he was sitting and settled her over him. He took a nipple into his mouth as he guided the head of his arousal into her.

Nicole sighed as she felt his fullness fill her. It was unlike anything she had ever experienced, and she knew she was lucky to have Val showing her what it meant to be loved by a man, for he wasn't just any man, he was special.

Inch by agonizing inch he filled her until he suddenly stopped. With one arm wrapped around her waist, he moved his other hand between them and took her clit between his thumb and forefinger. He began to move her nub between his fingers as she bucked against him. Pleasure so intense she could do nothing but experience as it engulfed her.

Then she felt herself moving toward something, her ache becoming more and more intense, and just when she thought she might reach the pinnacle, Val pushed through her maidenhead.

Nicole's eyes flew open as she gasped at the sudden pain. Val held her tight while he rubbed his hands along her back.

"The worst of it is over," he murmured. "And the best is yet to come."

"I was just about to experience the 'best' part," she grumbled.

His chest rumbled beneath her ears. "I know."

"You didn't let me on purpose?" she asked and sat up to look at him. When she moved, she felt him inside of her. All the pain she had experienced but a moment ago vanished as a new sensation rocked deep inside of her. She opened her mouth in shock.

"Exactly," Val said and took her by the hips. "Now, I'll

show you what it means to be loved by a man."

Nicole took hold of his shoulders as he rocked her hips back and forth. It wasn't long before he removed his hands to play with her breasts again, and Nicole got to experiment with being in control.

The ache inside of her doubled as Val plucked and suckled her nipples until they were so tender his breath upon them drove her wild. She dropped her head back and moved her hips faster, her need driving her on.

With a hiss, Val lifted his head from her breasts and caught her gaze. He moved his hand between them and found her clitoris again.

He barely touched her when her world shattered, blinding her with pleasure. She cried out as her body convulsed around him, and only vaguely did she feel Val pump into her one last time and then growl his own release.

~ ~ ~

Val gently toweled Nicole off before pulling her after him as he moved to his pallet. With a little nudge she sat, and he followed her down. His body, already hard and wanting her again, wouldn't be denied.

He leaned toward her and kissed her forehead, her nose, and then her lips. With his fingertips, he skimmed her arms up to her shoulders, then slowly pushed her back until she lay staring up at him.

She gave him a warm smile, her violet eyes watching him curiously. He sat back on his heels and looked over her body. She had full breasts that were incredibly sensitive, as he had already discovered, a narrow waist and gently flared hips. A patch of black curls hid her sex, and though he hadn't seen it yet, he had felt the most intimate part of her. His eyes drifted lower to her long, lean legs, perfect for wrapping around his waist and driving him deeper into her.

He licked his lips and rested his hands on either side of her face as he poised above her.

"I want you," he said.

She gave him a knowing smile and ran her hands over his arms to his shoulders. "I see that," she said and glanced down at his throbbing cock.

"I don't know what you've done to me, but I can't get enough of you."

"Good," she whispered and pulled him down atop her. "Because I cannot get enough of you, either."

Val ran his lips over hers, tasting her, learning her. He hadn't lied. Something happened between them when he made love to her, something that had never happened before. A sense of peace had settled around him, but he wasn't fool enough to expect it to last.

He pushed such thoughts from his mind and concentrated on Nicole's body. Only a few times had he taken a virgin, and he had never been fulfilled. Until tonight. Nicole was passionate, strong, and beautiful.

Everything he had ever wanted in a woman.

After pausing to look deep into her stunning eyes, he slowly kissed his way down her neck to her shoulders and then her breasts. He loved that her breasts were so responsive. The least little touch or kiss could set her on fire.

He ran a finger along the underside of her breasts and saw her nipples harden before his eyes, and then he leaned down to take a peak into his mouth. He ran his tongue over the turgid tip before he suckled her.

She moaned and gripped his shoulders as she pushed her hips against him. He moved to the other breast and repeated the process, watching as her body came alive before him once more.

Her skin was flushed and glowed red in the firelight as her moans echoed around them. He kissed between her breasts and down her stomach to her hips. As his mouth moved from one hip to the next, he settled between her legs.

He looked up as he moved his hands to her sex and saw her eyes widen.

"Val?"

"Trust me," he whispered just before he parted her lips and gazed at her sex.

Already she pulsed with need, and it drove his desire higher. He wanted to drive into her right then but held himself back by sheer will alone.

He gave her a smile as he ran his finger along her sex, separating her folds and teasing her clit.

She moaned and closed her eyes as her hands fisted in the blankets. He dipped his head and ran his tongue where his finger had been. She cried out softly, bringing a smile to his lips.

Val loved the taste of her. She was as exotic as he knew she would be. He licked her again, this time stopping at her clit and moving his tongue first slowly, then faster over the bud.

It swelled and pouted for more. He settled his mouth over her nub and used his tongue to tease her mercilessly. With a slight shift, he moved his hand and pushed a finger inside of her.

She was so hot and wet that he knew he couldn't take much more before he had to be inside her. When he felt her body begin to stiffen, signaling she was about to peak, he moved over her and slid his cock into her tight sheath.

He groaned with pleasure. When he was able to open his eyes, he looked down to find her staring up at him.

With slow, easy movements, he began to thrust. She easily met his movements and wrapped her legs around his waist.

Sweat beaded his body as he gazed into her eyes. His climax was coming too soon, and he tried to slow, to hold off until Nicole peaked, but she wouldn't let him. Just as the orgasm hit Val, he felt Nicole clench around him.

With a growl, he spilled his seed as bliss wrapped around them, taking them to heights he'd never experienced.

Time had no meaning as his body floated on a tide of pleasure. When he was finally able to open his eyes, he saw the satisfied smile on Nicole's lips.

His body now completely sated, he pulled out of her and rolled to his side. He pushed tendrils of her hair away from her face as she turned her head toward him.

"Thank you," she whispered just before she fell asleep.

For a long time afterward, Val watched her. He was well and truly caught in her web.

And he prayed that by doing so he hadn't condemned her as he had his sisters.

~ ~ ~

Gabriel left the pub and wrapped his cloak around him as the bitter cold ate away at his warmth. He looked to the mountain, wondering if Nicole had gotten Val to submit to her.

He was worried about his friend. Val was always ready with a smile, eager for a fight, and good with women. Gabriel had already decided that if Nicole didn't get Val to succumb to her, he was going to seek Aimery's help. He had never done anything like it before, but something was obviously wrong with Val that was linked with his past.

Gabriel sighed. There was no use worrying about Val

now. He had something else he needed to do. He leaned against the pub and waited. The village was quiet, as most people had retreated to their homes in the growing darkness.

He found his gaze moving to the sky and wondered if the gryphon would attack the village again. It would be so much easier to find the person who held the blue stone and destroy it, but the more Gabriel probed the villagers, the more he realized there might not be a blue stone to destroy--just as Val had said.

The pub door opened and the serving wench from earlier stepped out. She threw him an inviting smile. "Are you sure you don't want to find me chamber?"

"I'd like nothing better than to see your chamber and you lying across your bed naked. Then, I'd make slow, sweet love to you until you couldn't move."

"Ah," she sighed dreamily. "Wouldn't that be a better night than tromping up to the uninviting castle?"

Gabriel nodded and held out his arm for her. "Shall we?"

"If we must," she said with a laugh.

He had been pleasantly surprised when the little vixen had offered to take him up to the castle. Her sister was a servant at the castle and could get them inside. Gabriel wasn't about to pass up the chance.

The trek to the castle was long and cold, but she kept the conversation going with talk of the village.

"I've lived here me entire life," she said. "I'm sure they are better places to live, but I'm happy here."

"That's all that matters. I've seen many places, and I have to admit, Scotland is very beautiful."

She beamed. "You know all the right things to say."

He laughed and shrugged. "Isn't that what we men are supposed to do?"

"Aye, but most don't."

"Then they obviously don't know the correct way to woo a beautiful woman."

"Careful, my love, I might just throw you on the ground and have my way with you."

Gabriel winked and patted her hand as they reached the castle. They walked around to the side and knocked on the door. It took a moment, but finally someone opened the door, the woman's red hair escaping through the white cap on her head.

"Esmee?" she asked. "What are ye doin' here?"

Esmee nodded toward Gabriel. "I've brought someone who wants to see the castle."

The sister sighed then stepped away so they could enter. "If the laird finds out, I'll be out of a job."

"He won't find out," Gabriel assured her. "I'd like to ask you a few questions. Do you have a moment?"

CHAPTER TWENTY-THREE

Val woke to feel soft curves against him and a full breast in his hand. Images of the night before flashed in his mind, and he opened his eyes to find Nicole curled against him.

With a soft sigh, she rolled onto her back and turned her head toward him. "Good morn'," she said sleepily.

"Good morn'," he replied.

"I'm surprised you're still here."

He frowned. "Where else would I be?"

"I meant asleep with me."

"I was just about to get up," he said and slid out from the covers.

He noticed that her eyes followed him as he moved to his clothes. There was no denying his wanting her again this morning as his rod stood thick and hard.

She smiled and rolled onto her side. "You sure you want to stand guard so soon?"

Val chuckled. "As much as I'd love to climb back under the covers with you, I must do my duty."

"Thank you."

Val fastened his pants and raised his gaze. "For what?"

"For last night."

"I'm the one that should be thanking you. You gifted me with something precious."

She grinned, and Val pulled on his tunic and jerkin then reached for his boots. Once he was clothed, he fastened on his sword and daggers.

"I expect Gabriel soon. I noticed that Aimery had the tub refilled with more water, so take another bath while you can."

He turned away from her before he gave in to his desires and took her again. Already, he regretted making love to her. He had to stay focused and he couldn't do that when his rod was constantly begging to be buried in her tight sheath.

As he approached the entrance, the hair on the back of his neck rose. As he passed his halberd, he palmed it and slowly walked to the entrance. And that's when he saw it.

The gryphon.

The beast stood outside the entrance casually looking in as if it weren't there to kill them.

"You know you can't enter here," Val said.

The gryphon flicked its tail. "Aye. And you know if you come outside I'll kill you."

"So. A stalemate."

He could have sworn the gryphon smiled, which was impossible with his beak. "In a manner," the gryphon said softly.

Val immediately became wary. The gryphon had a plan to draw them out. "Tell me. Why didn't you kill me the other day?"

"I wanted you to suffer, to know that you and your weapons cannot kill me."

"As with all the other creatures, we will find a way to kill you," Val stated more confidently than he felt.

"Maybe. Maybe not. The evil one has something special planned for the wench. And he won't be denied."

Val gripped his halberd tighter and shrugged. "He's been denied before."

"True," the creature said and shifted his forelegs. "However, you need this wench to complete the Chosen so my master cannot reign. He knew this and took certain...precautions...to make sure neither the Shields nor the Fae succeeds."

"So you bound Nicole to this time. We've encountered obstacles before. We've succeeded without having to use underhanded tactics. Good always prevails over evil."

The gryphon snapped his beak closed. "I'm afraid this time evil will win. Prepare yourselves."

And with that, the gryphon flew away.

Val took a deep breath and turned to lean against the cave wall.

"What are we going to do?" Nicole asked as she walked toward him with a blanket wrapped around her.

Val jerked upright. "I thought you were bathing."

"I heard you talking."

Val raked a hand through his hair. "I don't know what we're going to do. I pray Gabriel discovered something at the village."

"And if he didn't?"

He raised his gaze to her troubled one. "We'll get through this, Nicole. I wasn't lying when I said we had faced difficult situations before. Good has always won."

"I trust you with my life, Val."

He inwardly cringed. "Aimery wouldn't have sent us if we couldn't do the job." He moved toward her and took her by the shoulders. "All will be well. Go soak in the warm Fae water Aimery brought for you."

With a smile, she turned and slowly walked toward the

tub. Val waited until she was immersed in the water before he turned back to the entrance and began searching for Gabriel.

~ ~ ~

Aimery rested his elbows on the table and dropped his head into his hands. He searched through numerous texts, and still found nothing to help him battle the evil's bond on Nicole.

"I've never seen you like this, my friend."

Aimery's head jerked up to find Theron leaning against the door. "For countless millennia we've held the greatest powers of all the realms, but never once have we tried to dominate. We've held the balance."

Theron pushed off the door and walked soundlessly across the blue and white tiled floor. "You still haven't found anything?"

"Nay," Aimery said with a sigh.

"You've got the entire royal library at your disposal and many Fae at your call. Set them to looking."

"I have." Aimery found himself wearier than ever. "There has never been a time when an evil's power was greater than ours. Equal, aye, but never greater."

"Of course an evil's power couldn't be greater. If that ever happened, the balance of power would shift and evil would reign."

Aimery leaned back in his chair. "I felt the power, Theron. I don't know how the evil one did it, but not only could I not shift Nicole to Stone Crest, I couldn't shift a Shield to Scotland."

"How are Val and Gabriel?"

"As well as can be. Val is becoming irritable. He wants a fight to end this, but without the blue stone, they must simply wait the gryphon out."

Theron walked around the chamber silently contemplating the situation. He glanced at Aimery and said, "Have you found anything on black gryphons?"

"Only a small section," Aimery said as he moved books around on the table until he found a large ornate text with gold lettering. He opened the heavy tome and began shifting through pages. "Here it is," he said and ran his fingers over the words. "It's not necessarily about the gryphon, but I thought it might help us discover how a gryphon had turned evil."

Theron came to stand beside him and looked over the text. "Go on," he urged.

"Documented in the Early Time was an instance where a phoenix, one of the purest creatures ever to breath, had turned evil. Though there was no record as to how he turned, once it was slain, the onlookers were amazed to find the phoenix wasn't an animal at all, but a man."

"A man," Theron repeated and slowly straightened. He looked at Aimery. "Do you think this gryphon is really a man?

Aimery shrugged. "I have no idea, but it's a possibility."

"Does the text say that the phoenix was a shape shifter?"

"Nay."

Theron suddenly stiffened. "What realm did this occur with the phoenix?"

Aimery looked over the text again. "Felox. Does that mean something?"

"Nay. That realm is too far away for us to have felt a soul lured to the dark side of evil."

"Shouldn't we have felt it if it occurred on Earth?"

Theron nodded solemnly. "Either the gryphon really is

a gryphon and not a man turned to the side of evil, or the evil one managed to block us from feeling the soul move to the dark side."

"I don't like either suggestion."

"Neither do I, my friend. Neither do I."

Aimery leaned back in his chair and steepled his fingers. He regretted the moment he split the Shields when they had first arrived at Stone Crest to battle the gargoyle. Each creature they had battled since then had grown in power and skill. Now, only two remained to battle the strongest of them all. And Aimery could do nothing but sit and watch.

"Don't even think it," Theron said.

Aimery chuckled. "You know me too well."

"I know that look," Theron corrected. "If we help the Shields more than we already are, we break the Code. That code is what keeps the balance."

"I know," Aimery said and rose to his feet. "I don't need a history lesson. I need a way to help Val and Gabriel. I cannot leave them to die."

"Nay, we can't." Theron scratched his jaw and walked to the door. "We need Nicole and the evil knows it. Do you have part of your army standing guard at Stone Crest with the other Chosen?"

"I do."

"Put them on high alert. If the evil one has the power I think he does, he may be toying with us regarding Nicole."

"So he can kill the others?"

Theron shrugged. "It's a possibility. One that we need to be prepared for."

"I have some of my best men there."

"Good. I'll search my private collection of books and see if I can find something that will help us."

Aimery gave Theron a nod as Theron walked from his

chamber, then he slowly sank into his chair. It had been a very long time since he had worried about the fate of the Fae.

He had to find out how the evil one managed to gather as much power as he did. Only one other man had managed to wield that kind of power. It was too bad Lugus had given that power up.

CHAPTER TWENTY-FOUR

Val was on his feet the moment he saw Laird speed past him out of the cave. There was only one reason for the wolfhound to act that way--Gabriel.

He walked to the edge of the cave and peered out to see Laird's gray form bounding down the mountain. He was nearly at the bottom when he stopped, his tail wagging so furiously Val thought it might fall off.

That's when he spotted Gabriel. Val kept watch on the sky in case the gryphon attacked. Every once in a while, he would glance to see Gabriel climbing the mountain with Laird at his heels.

"Good to see you," Gabriel said with a smile as he held out his arm.

Val clasped forearms with him and returned the smile. "I thought you might return early this morning."

"It was a long night," he said as he sat on one of the smaller boulders.

Val watched in amazement as Laird sat beside Gabriel and rested his great head on Gabriel's leg. Gabriel's hand automatically moved to the wolfhound and began to pet him.

"He missed you," Val said.

Gabriel smiled down at Laird. "I missed him, too. I see his wounds are nearly healed."

"After the way he raced down the mountain, I'd say you were correct."

Gabriel laughed and patted the wolfhound's flank. "So," he said turning his attention to Val. "What happened while I was away?"

There was no way Val was about to tell Gabriel of the incredible night he spent with Nicole, even though he knew that's exactly what Gabriel was asking.

"It was quiet."

"Really?" Gabriel asked, his dark brows lifted. He glanced to the back of the cave and whistled. "Is that a wooden tub?"

"Aye. I asked Aimery for it. I knew Nicole was bored and needed something to cheer her, even for a bit."

"Nice of you to think of a bath."

Val nearly rolled his eyes. "Don't think there's more to it than there is. I can still recall the bliss that was Rome's baths."

The sound of soft humming reached them then. Val turned toward the sound and listened.

"She hummed the night she tended you," Gabriel said.

Val looked at his friend. "It's a lovely tune."

"Aye. I've not heard the like before. I wonder if the song comes from her realm."

"Impossible for her to know that," Val said. "She was just an infant when she was sent here."

Gabriel ran a finger along his bow and shrugged. "I've thought a lot about that. Why would the requirement be that the ones sent be infants?"

"Why wouldn't they? People don't turn away helpless babies."

"True, but if they're too young to remember anything of their realm, how can they know what to do to defeat the evil one? Moreover, why didn't they defeat it on their own realm if they had the power to do so?"

Val ran a hand through his hair. "I've often thought of the last one, as well. If their realm truly did have the capability to end the evil one's reign, something must have happened to prevent them from fulfilling it."

"I couldn't possibly imagine what that could be."

"We're likely never to know."

Gabriel leaned forward and placed his elbows on his knees. "Do you think Aimery told us everything?"

"Why would he keep something like that from us?"

"I don't think he would. I was just curious. So, nothing happened."

"I said the night was quiet, it was this morning that I came to the entrance and found the gryphon waiting for me."

"What?" Gabriel asked, his eyes wide with disbelief.

Val nodded. "He stood right at the entrance."

"What did he say?"

"I think he was just here to taunt us. He said that his master had something special planned for Nicole, and he wouldn't be denied."

"Hmmm," Gabriel said and rubbed his chin. "I wonder what that 'something special' could be? What else did he say?"

"That the evil took special precautions to keep Nicole here and the other Shields away."

"Curious that he allowed us in, don't you think?"

Val nodded. "Most especially. It makes no sense to have allowed us in if other Shields are kept away."

"Not unless he has plans for us."

"That might be a possibility. When I asked the

gryphon why he didn't kill me when he had the chance, he said it was because he wanted us to know our weapons couldn't hurt him."

"Good always prevails," Gabriel stated.

"I told the gryphon that, as well. His response was that this time, evil would win."

"This looks grim, my friend."

Val hated to agree, but it was the truth. "Tell me you discovered something during your night in the village."

Gabriel grinned. "Not exactly what we were looking for, but I did uncover some more information regarding Nicole that might help us piece everything together."

"Should we call Aimery?"

Gabriel nodded. "Most definitely."

~ ~ ~

Nicole finished with her bath and slowly climbed out of the giant wooden tub. After such a short time, she was becoming spoiled by the size of the bath, which was a luxury for her.

Her muscles had been sore when she woke, and she knew it was due to the night of lovemaking with Val. He had been right, the water had helped ease the ache.

She glanced at the entrance and saw Gabriel had returned. She was happy to have him back, but was going to miss the time she and Val had spent together.

When she turned to reach for her gown, she found it had been replaced by another one. This one was made of the softest material, much like Val and Gabriel's tunics. It was a beautiful mix between a blue and light purple.

She hastily pulled on the new chemise that was softer than velvet. Next she reached for her stockings, except they weren't hers either, nor where they the thick wool ones she was used to. However, she trusted Aimery, so pulled on the stockings.

Finally, she was able to pull on the gown. It was unlike anything she had ever owned or thought about owning.

Once she was satisfied with the gown, she took the pins out of her hair and reached for her comb. After all the tangles had been driven from the long mass, Nicole decided to plait it to keep it out of her face.

She had just finished putting everything away when she heard something behind her and turned to find Val. "You were right about the warm water. I feel much better."

He returned her smile, but it didn't reach his eyes. "Gabriel has returned with news."

She nodded and looked over his shoulder to see Gabriel and Aimery walking toward them. Nicole glanced at Val, hoping he would give her some idea of what this was all about. Instead, he softly shook his head, silently asking her to wait.

Her stomach tightened into a painful knot at the intense look of both Val and Aimery. Only Gabriel's face held a smile, but that was for Laird. She licked her lips and waited for the worst.

Aimery was the first to speak. "The gown looks beautiful on you, Nicole."

She wasn't able to stop the nervous laugh nor the glance at Val, hoping he might comment, as well. "Thank you," she said to Aimery. "I appreciate the bath and most especially the gown. I've never owned anything so expensive."

"It matches your eyes."

Her gaze jerked to Val. A slow smile pulled at her lips. "Do you think so?"

He nodded and she beamed. When she looked at Aimery and Gabriel it was to find them watching Val intently.

"I gather Gabriel discovered something important," she said, unable to wait a moment longer.

Gabriel nodded. "We might want to sit. This is going to take awhile."

He began by telling them of meeting Esmee at the pub and how she offered to take him to the castle. "Now, once inside, I didn't think the servants would want to speak to me."

"But you were wrong," Val said.

"Very," Gabriel admitted. "Esmee's sister showed me around the lower floors. Apparently, the old laird doesn't leave his chambers."

"What keeps him in them?" Val asked. "Is he ill?"

"Nay," Aimery said. His eyes were shut as if he were deep in thought. His eyes snapped open, and he turned to Gabriel.

"What did you see?" Gabriel asked.

"Finish, and I'll tell you."

Gabriel nodded. "The castle had been stripped of everything valuable on the lower floors. Only a handful of servants run the castle."

"A castle that size?" Val asked. "They should have a couple dozen servants."

"My thoughts as well, but it seems the old laird is a bit eccentric and will only allow six women in the castle."

Nicole frowned. "Women. Why just women?"

"That was my question. Seems the old man doesn't trust men."

"I wonder why that is."

"Because it was men who made the pact with the Great Evil," Aimery said.

A chill raced down Nicole's spine. "Laird MacNamara wasn't part of it?"

Aimery shook his head. "He was against it and was punished for his actions."

"Punished how?"

"I will tell you all once Gabriel is finished," Aimery said.

All eyes turned to Gabriel. He took a quick drink from the waterskin and continued.

"The laird doesn't have the blue stone," Gabriel said. "But the stories the servants told me and what I saw in the castle made me think he might be connected to the Great Evil in some way."

Val leaned forward. "What stories did you hear?"

"The old laird screaming in the middle of the night for someone to save him. He told the servants he is tormented nightly."

"By what?" Nicole asked, and then regretted it immediately.

Gabriel shrugged. "They didn't know, nor would the laird tell them. He just asks that they stay in the castle and never allow strangers in."

"Yet they let you."

He smiled. "It's my charm."

Nicole rolled her eyes and joined in the laughter. Once they quieted down, they looked to Aimery.

"The laird isn't jesting. He is being tormented nightly by beings you don't wish to know about. The Great Evil cursed him when the laird tried to dissuade the villagers from accepting his bribe."

Val sighed and shifted his weight from one hip to the other. "What kind of bribe?"

"The Great Evil arrived with a baby - Nicole to be exact. He asked that she be kept alive and separate from others. And in exchange, he would bless the village. When it came time for him to come for her, he would make sure their village prospered forever."

Nicole felt as if a horse had kicked her. "Why me?"

One side of Aimery's mouth lifted. "I think he came across you by accident, but realized immediately who, and what, you were. He knew in order for him to continue with his plans, he needed to keep you away from the other Chosen."

"You mean until it was time for him to kill her," Val said then turned to look at Nicole.

CHAPTER TWENTY-FIVE

The gryphon's sharp eyes surveyed the dark chamber. Not even the many candelabra could dispel the gloom that surrounded the place.

It was just a flutter of the air around him that alerted him that the evil had arrived. Only dimly could he recall his master's true form. For many years, he had been able to focus his powers and take on the form of a human, but it only lasted a few hours.

"Well?" the evil one said as his life essence swept by him.

The gryphon swiveled his head as he followed the sound of the voice. "Val will take the bait when it's presented. A fierce battle rages within him."

"Ah, good," the evil one said and laughed. "I thought the return of his nightmares might push him into doing the unthinkable--leaving Nicole unprotected."

"He hasn't given in to the temptation yet."

"He will. He just needs to be pushed a little more."

The gryphon swished his tail. "How do you plan to do that? We cannot enter the cave."

His master laughed again, this time it was filled with

malice. "Aimery gave me the perfect solution. No man battling such self-doubt as Val does over his sisters' deaths will be strong enough to withstand the enticement I shall give him."

"Even though he and Nicole have shared their bodies?"

"That makes no difference," he hissed.

The gryphon stiffened an instant before the impact of his master's ire hit him. He only stumbled back a few paces and then hastily righted himself.

"You planted the seed of doubt," his master continued, his voice now edged with anger. "See to it that you continue to taunt him. Our plan won't fail this time."

He didn't wait for his master to finish, but stood and left the chamber. He walked the long tunnel slowly climbing until he saw the sunlight.

With a soft sigh, he closed his eyes and remembered a time when he used to dance in the sunlight, his mother's laughter floating around him. Those had been happy times. But happy times had faded to darkness and darkness to evil.

He wondered how long it would have taken for him to recall his memories if he hadn't seen Nicole. But wonderings of that kind never did anyone any good.

~ ~ ~

Val stared at Nicole, unsure of the strong feelings running rampant through him. He couldn't shake the feeling that the Great Evil was up to something, a trick of some kind.

"What is it?" Gabriel asked.

Val pulled his gaze from Nicole's questioning one and looked to Gabriel. "Just a feeling."

"Of what?"

Val shrugged. "I'm not sure how to explain it. There

were times when we were at war that the only way to survive was to listen to your instincts."

"As Hugh has always done," Aimery said.

"Exactly. Hugh used his for everything, but with mine, they always centered around treachery."

Aimery inhaled deeply. "Then I suggest you listen to it."

"What is it saying?" Gabriel asked, his brow furrowed.

"That's just it," Val said. "I'm not sure. However, I can't dispel the idea that the evil has set some kind of trap."

Aimery quickly rose to his feet. "You may be right. Guard yourselves well. Against everything."

Val noted that Aimery aimed the last part at him. It was too bad that he had already given in to a forbidden temptation—Nicole. Even now, when he saw her trembling slightly, her gaze boring into the fire, he wanted to pull her into his arms and love her worry away.

But that would be the worst kind of folly. He had to stay vigilant, and that meant keeping his body under control where Nicole was concerned.

Which was going to be harder than giving up the wine.

"Val."

He looked up and found Aimery and Gabriel waiting for him. With one last glance at Nicole, he rose and followed them.

Aimery waited until they reached the cave entrance before he said, "The evil will most likely attack with our greatest weaknesses."

"I expect that," Gabriel said.

"Are you truly prepared?" Aimery asked, then turned to look at Val. "Each of you came to the Shields with a past. Val, you know your past, and it haunts you to this day. There are many ways the evil can attack you."

Val clenched his jaw. "I'm only a man, Aimery, but I'll

do my best."

"I can't expect more than that," Aimery said softly. Then he turned to Gabriel. "I'm relieved that you've found something of your past."

"But you're worried the evil had something to do with it," Gabriel finished. "I have the same thoughts. There isn't anything that can be done about it now."

"You still haven't remembered anything of your past?" Gabriel shook his head.

Aimery sighed and looked to the sky. "There is no telling how the evil will come at you, Gabriel. Both of you are strong, capable men that have served the Shields well for many years, but everyone has a weakness."

"Even you?" Val asked.

When Aimery's unusual blue eyes locked with his, Val saw something in their depths, something he was sure Aimery had wanted to keep well hidden.

"Aye. Even me," he said softly. "Guard yourselves, but more importantly, guard Nicole. She's our last hope."

In a blink, he was gone. Val looked to Gabriel to find his fellow Shield deep in thought.

"Are you worried," he asked.

Gabriel shrugged. "Only a fool would answer nay." He turned his gaze to Val, his silver eyes guarded well. "And you?"

"Aye," Val answered readily. "I'm petrified, but not of what will happen to me. I'm afraid that I won't be there to protect Nicole."

"Is that what happened to your sisters?"

Val swallowed and looked away. He had never told anyone of his sisters and he wasn't sure he was ready. "Something like that," he finally answered.

"I didn't mean to pry."

With a deep sigh, he sat and reached for his halberd.

"You didn't."

He ran his hand over the long handle and sharp blade. The weight of the weapon was light, but with accuracy, it was deadly.

"Why did you choose the halberd?"

Both he and Gabriel jumped at Nicole's sweet voice. He stood and motioned for her to take his seat then he wrapped her cloak around her.

"What makes you think I chose the halberd?" he asked.

She lifted one shoulder and glanced at Gabriel's bow. "Both of you wear swords, but Gabriel will reach for his bow and you your halberd before the sword. Why?"

Gabriel picked up his bow and pulled back on the string as he sighted down his arm. "My strength was the bow. I'm decent with a sword but deadly with a bow."

Val nodded. "It's the truth. I've never seen anyone so accurate with a bow as Gabriel."

She smiled at Gabriel as he sat and returned his bow to his quiver of arrows against the cave wall. Then, she turned her violet gaze to Val. "And you?"

Val shrugged. "I like the halberd."

"I've seen you use it. You're very good."

Gabriel grunted. "He's better than good at it, he's excellent. But then again, Val was gifted with being able to pick up any weapon and use it with lethal precision."

"Really?" she said, awe in her voice.

Val hated that the admiration in her tone excited him. "Gabriel exaggerates."

"Nay, my friend," Gabriel said. "You just don't want her to know the truth."

"And that is?" Nicole asked.

Val turned away from them and pretended that his halberd needed examining. He had never been one to talk about himself, and it made him uncomfortable when others did it.

"When we were brought to the Shields, each of us was trained by the Fae, and each of us excelled at one weapon. Hugh's weapon was the crossbow, Roderick's a flail, Cole's a war axe, and mine the bow. However, each time Val picked up a weapon, he excelled at it. He chose the halberd because none of us could handle it."

"Aye, so now you know," Val said more harshly than he intended.

"I've never known anyone with that kind of skill," Nicole said. "It must come in handy when you are in battle."

Val shrugged and set aside his halberd. "Sometimes."

"Sometimes my arse," Gabriel said with a chuckle. "As I said earlier, I'm decent with a sword, we all are, but if I lost my bow, which is my strength, I'm at a disadvantage. Whereas, if Val lost his halberd, he could easily find another weapon to use."

"Fascinating," she said, her chin in her hands as she looked at Gabriel.

Val turned back to them. "Enough about me. We need to talk of what could very well happen in the coming days."

He made the mistake then of looking at Nicole's lips. The memory of her kisses sent blood shooting to his rod. He licked his lips, the fire in his blood raging, demanded to feel Nicole's soft body against his, to bury himself deep within her tight sheath.

Finding ecstasy as he had never felt before.

He watched as she slowly stood and faced him, her violet eyes darkening as she saw the need in his. Their bodies were attuned as if they had been lovers for years instead of just hours.

Her lips parted, a soft sigh escaping. He nearly came

undone. Never had he had to exert such control over his body as he did when it came to Nicole. If only they were in another time, another place where he would be free to take her as he wished, as often as he wanted.

Instead, they were bound to a village that had damned themselves by bargaining with evil.

Gabriel saw the desire between Nicole and Val and knew they needed privacy. He nearly laughed aloud when he saw Val's hands fisted at his side and his jaw clenched. He was fighting his need for Nicole, but Gabriel knew that Val's need would win in the end.

He thought to tell them he was leaving and then decided against it. They needed more wood for the fire anyway. He gave a pat to his leg and waited for Laird to reach him before he exited the cave.

CHAPTER TWENTY-SIX

Nicole trembled, not from the cold, but from the desire pumping through her. Her sex throbbed with a need only Val could quench. Her breath came faster as her breasts swelled and her nipples hardened.

"Nicole," he whispered and reached for her.

She didn't hesitate in going to him, and when her body came in contact with his, she nearly groaned from the pleasure of it. His hands parted her cloak and slid around her as his mouth found hers.

His lips teased hers with light kisses and nips at the corners of her mouth, and each time she licked his lips, he would pull away.

She wanted, nay, she *needed* his touch. When she didn't think she could take anymore, his hands crushed her against him and his lips met hers. His velvety hot tongue stroked hers, bringing her need so high she thought she might burst from it.

Suddenly he wrenched his mouth from hers and looked down at her. She tried to calm her racing heart and ragged breathing, but all she wanted to do was strip him of his clothes and feel his rod thrust inside of her.

"How is it that I can't get enough of you?" he asked softly.

She numbly shook her head and ran her hands over his thick chest. "I don't know, and I don't care to find out. Just as long as you want me is enough."

Her eyes closed and her head tilted back as his lips found her neck.

"By the gods, you smell wonderful," he murmured.

Nicole shivered as his hot breath tickled her skin. "Stop teasing me," she begged, "and fill me."

A low growl reached her ears. "I can't," he said simply and pulled away from her.

Nicole felt his loss immediately. "Why?" she asked, not understanding how he could want her so desperately and not take her.

"I can't take the chance that I'll be so enthralled with my want of you that I allow you to die."

"That won't happen."

"How do you know?" he demanded. His eyes blazed with fury and determination.

She realized at that moment that whatever had happened between them last night might never happen again. With her body on fire with need, Nicole brushed past him and walked to the fire.

It was then she noticed that Laird and Gabriel were gone. She had completely forgotten about Gabriel standing beside them, but apparently Gabriel had been gentleman enough to leave without notice.

She should be embarrassed at her brazen behavior, but she had realized what Val meant. How could she expect him to make love to her and guard her when she couldn't even notice Gabriel's leaving after one kiss?

And she had been angry with Val when all he was doing was trying to protect her. She'd like to think he was protecting her because he cared about her, but the truth was, she was the survival of Earth and the Realm of the Fae.

Neither her nor Val's feelings mattered at this point. Survival did.

~ ~ ~

Val wanted to follow Nicole back to the fire, strip her of her clothes and make sweet, slow love to her. Yet, he would stay by the entrance and hope the draft from Scotland's harsh winter would cool his resolve.

To help turn his mind from his raging desire, he began to contemplate how the Great Evil could trick or trap him. His one great weakness was his past.

You have another one if you would just admit it.

Aye, he did have another weakness. Nicole. She had started off as any other mission, but somewhere along the way she had turned into much more than that. She had become someone he cared about.

And that worried the hell out of him.

He closed his eyes and prayed for guidance. After so many years with the Shields, he never thought to be in a situation similar to the one that made him leave Rome.

Everyone thought him strong and able, but deep inside, he was nothing more than a man running from his past and seeking a place where his memories would no longer haunt him.

He wasn't the gifted warrior general the other Shields thought him to be. He was a weak link that could very well break the Shields and end the balance of good and evil. The weight of just what kind of man he was weighed heavily on his shoulders.

How he wished the gryphon had killed him that day

instead of toying with him. He didn't think he could bear Nicole's look when she discovered his true nature.

He licked his dry lips and tried to swallow. The hunger for a taste of wine was stronger than it had ever been. Val began to shake.

With deep, even breaths he tried to bring himself under control. But one haunting question kept running through his mind – if there were a jug of wine in front of him, would he be able to turn it away?

He was afraid the answer would be nay.

Each day his thirst for the wine grew. If they didn't kill the gryphon soon, he knew he would succumb to his nemesis and fall prey to the oblivion the wine would give him.

If he finished this mission, he would leave the Shields. He wasn't the warrior the Shields needed. They needed someone they could depend on--not an inebriated ex-general who wasn't man enough to face his demons.

"Is everything all right?" Gabriel asked as he walked into the cave.

"Aye," Val answered. "Where did you go?"

Gabriel's brows lifted, then he looked down at the armful of wood he held. "I went to milk a cow," he said and knocked the snow from his boots. "Care to tell me why you aren't with Nicole by the fire?"

"You didn't have to leave."

"I did. You were about to tear each other's clothes off. Now tell me what's going on with you?"

Val raised his gaze to Gabriel. "Everything is fine. What happened between me and Nicole cannot happen again."

Gabriel shrugged and began to stack the wood. "I don't know what's gotten into you, my friend, but I know the desire between the two of you doesn't happen every day. You should grab hold of her with both hands and never let go."

"She deserves someone better than me."

"What?" Gabriel said as he straightened. "Have you gone daft? You are one of the best men I know, Valentinus Romulus."

Val was humbled by Gabriel's words and gave him a brief nod of thanks. Though he couldn't accept any of the praise.

"Tell me," Gabriel said as he removed his cloak and draped it across one of the boulders. "Has the evil already gotten into your head?"

Val sighed. "Could be."

"Maybe it's time we shared all our secrets. We've been brethren for too long not to be honest with each other. We have to watch each other's backs, and I can't do that if I don't know how the evil might affect you."

"I don't want you to know my past."

Gabriel harrumphed. "Nothing you say will convince me you aren't a great warrior, dedicated Shield, and loyal friend. I know you, Val, regardless of what you did in your past."

Val closed his eyes and ran a hand down his face. "I don't really know where to begin."

"How about from the beginning?" Gabriel offered as he found a seat on a boulder and waited.

Maybe Gabriel was right, Val thought inwardly. Maybe it was time he told someone what had happened. He looked to Gabriel and found his friend quietly waiting for him to begin.

"Very few men reach the status of general, and even fewer reach it at the age that I did. Once I achieved that honor, I knew my father, a powerful Senator, would be proud."

"And was he?" Gabriel asked.

Val shrugged. "I'm not sure. I would like to think he was, but after my mother's death, what little time he had spent at home ceased altogether. He was too busy with Rome's politics."

Gabriel nodded sympathetically. "What father wouldn't be proud of a son who was a general of one of the world's greatest armies?"

A smile pulled at Val's lips. "In truth, after I told him, it didn't matter to me if he was proud or not. I had achieved what I wanted. And with the title and responsibility came notoriety."

"Ah," Gabriel said and rubbed his hands together. "Then the fun began."

"Aye. More women than you could imagine, expensive gifts, invitations to private parties, and a wine goblet that was never left empty." He stopped and looked down at his clasped hands.

This is where the telling became difficult. He leaned forward until his elbows rested on his knees. He kept his head lowered and tried not to hear his sisters' screams or see their brutalized bodies.

"Val?"

Gabriel's voice jerked him out of his memories. He silently shook himself and continued. "Both of my sisters had married well. They convinced their husbands to move to a province of Rome, not far from the great city herself, but away from the evils."

"Why?" Gabriel asked. "I'd have thought being raised in Rome they wouldn't want to leave."

"They didn't. Until they had children of their own. Then they saw the darker side of Rome, the side Romans like to pretend doesn't exist. Their husbands were good men, and to please their wives, they moved. I gave them my word I would check on them regularly.

"The province where they moved had some trouble years before, but once Rome quieted the troublemakers, it settled into a nice city."

Val squeezed his eyes closed then rose to his feet and faced the cave entrance.

"I gather there was trouble," Gabriel said.

Val nodded. "I was a few months away from taking my men to the border of Germania when we got word that there might be trouble in the province. I didn't put much credit in the report since it came from a man that had been known to lie. Still, I vowed to my sisters I would keep their children safe."

"Not many men would have done that, especially considering they moved from Rome."

He shrugged. "They were all the family I had."

"What happened?"

"I let my cock rule me, and I went off with a woman instead of following through and determining for myself if the report was true or not. I was awoken in the middle of the night to take some men to the province after a skirmish broke out."

He stared at the shimmering water of the loch, but he didn't see it. Instead, he saw fire. "By the time I got there, the city was in flames. My sisters lived next to each other at the edge of town. They had been locked inside and the house set afire. I could hear them screaming as I rode up, could hear their children crying."

Val swallowed and blinked back tears he had never shed. "I tried to break through the door to reach them, but the flames were too great. The only thing I managed to do was burn my hand," he said and lifted his left hand. He gazed down at the flesh on the back of his hand.

"It wasn't your fault," Gabriel said softly.

Val turned to him, the anger he had always felt bubbling to the surface. "It was my duty to protect them. I gave them my word. Instead, I went off with a woman."

Gabriel leaned back and crossed his arms over his chest. "What happened afterward?"

"You mean after I found who was responsible and killed them?"

"Aye."

Val sighed. "I became a drunk. It was the only way I could stop hearing their screams. The wine made me forget, if only for a moment."

"You may not remember, but I was with Aimery when he brought you to the Fae palace."

"So you saw me at my worst."

"What I saw," Gabriel said as he stood, "was a man with a great load of guilt wearing him down. You may have promised your sisters you would keep them safe, but that should have fallen to their husbands. Don't blame yourself for their deaths, Val, blame the husbands for leaving Rome."

CHAPTER TWENTY-SEVEN

Nicole's eyes burned with unshed tears. As soon as she heard the mumbled sound of Val's voice, she moved closer until she could hear. Now she wished she had stayed near the fire.

Her heart cried out for the pain Val carried with him, and if she knew him at all, he would carry the weight of his family's deaths with him until the day he died.

She happened to agree with Gabriel, but she knew Val didn't see it that way. He only saw that he had failed to protect someone. And she realized the reason he had begun to act the way he did toward her was because he was comparing her to his sisters.

Slowly, she walked back the fire and sat before the flames, hugging her legs to her chest. She heard footsteps and looked up to find Gabriel and Laird. Her eyes followed Gabriel as he sat and patted the spot next to him. The wolfhound lie beside him and put his head on Gabriel's leg, his large dark eyes lifted to Gabriel's face.

"What do you think?"

Her gazed jerked to his. "About what?"

"Don't pretend. I know you heard."

She sighed and shrugged. "I now understand his guilt and why he pushes me away."

"Is that all?"

"I wish I could help take away his pain."

Gabriel leaned forward, the fire glittering off his silver eyes. "Maybe you can."

"It won't work," she said before he could begin. "Now that I understand what motivates him, I won't thrust myself on him."

"But you must," Gabriel argued. "You're the only hope he has of letting go of the past. The evil will begin his tricks, and I fear for Val. His pain is too deep, his guilt too heavy for something not to happen."

"What do you want me to do?"

"Stay with him. Get him to talk about anything. Just make sure he is never alone."

"That will work both ways," she said as she shifted her legs and folded them to her side. "If I'm with him, he can keep watch over me as well."

"Exactly."

"What about you?"

He sat back and scratched behind Laird's ears. "For the most part, I will be with both of you."

"And the other times?"

"Someone has to keep watch."

Her brows rose as she stared at him. "Val shares that responsibility with you."

He chuckled. "True, but I planned to make sure he has the early shift so both of you will have some time alone."

"I know what you're trying to do, but it won't work."

"We'll see," Gabriel said. "We all must depend on each other to come out of this alive."

"I still don't know if seducing him is the right thing to do."

Gabriel inhaled deeply, his nostrils flaring slightly. He sat quietly for a moment as if he contemplated her words. When he spoke, his voice was soft, but honest. "I've known Val for many years. In that time, I've seen him bed plenty of women but never have I seen him look at one as he looks at you. Whether you want to admit it or not, there is something special between the two of you."

His words spread a warmth through her that chased away her chill. "I've nothing to base my feelings on. You and Gabriel are the first men I've been around other than Donald who is old enough to be my grandfather."

"Our leader, Hugh, would ask what your gut tells you."

Nicole blinked and thought about Val's gentle caress on her skin, how her body came alive with just a look from him, how she yearned to feel his arms around her, and how she was content to just have him near.

"My gut tells me that my feelings for Val run deep."

"Is it love?"

Love. Something she knew nothing about. "I don't know," she said. "I don't even know what love is."

He licked his lips and crossed his feet at the ankles. "Love is as complicated as it is simple. Love also has many different forms. For example, the love a mother and child share. That love is different from the love between a man and a woman."

"How?"

"Well," he said and sighed. "When a man and a woman fall in love, it isn't just their bodies they share, but also their hearts and souls. When two people find each other that are meant to be, it's as if you find the other half of yourself."

"You feel complete?" she offered.

Gabriel grinned. "Exactly. You haven't been out in the world and seen what happens when two people are married that aren't meant to be. Their lives are hard, and whatever tender feelings they might have shown their true mate, turns to bitter anger toward their spouse."

Nicole scrunched up her face. "Maybe I should be happy that I haven't seen that."

"You're fortunate not to have seen it, but at the same time, by not seeing the bad marriages, you won't know the right mate when he finds you."

Nicole tucked hair that had come loose from her braid behind her ear. "So how do you know when you've found the right mate or love?"

"It will feel right to you. Another way to determine if a person is your mate is how you would feel if you would never see them again or were made to go with another."

"I can't imagine myself with anyone but Val, and I don't even want to think about a time when he isn't with me."

Gabriel smiled sadly. "If you think he might be your mate, there will come a time where you will have to tell him of your feelings."

She wondered at the sadness that suddenly surrounded Gabriel. Then she realized what it must be. "Where you ever in love?"

His gaze lowered. "I sometimes feel as though a part of me is missing, as though I might have had that kind of love, but I let it go."

"I'm sorry."

He blinked and raised his head, once again the Gabriel she knew. "Don't be. A man without a past doesn't deserve love.

"How can you say that?" she asked, appalled that he would even think that about himself.

"Think about it, Nicole. No one, not even Aimery, knows what I've done in my past. I could have been a good, decent man, or I could have been the most evil of men."

"You weren't," she said. "You are a good man."

One side of his mouth lifted in a smile.

~ ~ ~

The Great Evil summoned his powers around him. It was time to begin. He had allowed his most treasured and loyal creature, the gryphon, to terminate Nicole, but he had failed.

For a moment, he had wondered if Dane recalled his memories, because if he had, he would have fought the return of the blue stone to control him. Nay, Dane hadn't remembered anything of his past or his family, which was for the best. He had lost so many of his beautiful creatures to the Shields that he couldn't stand the thought of having to kill Dane.

He was so close to having the return of his own body that he could practically taste it. He had been a wandering soul for so long that he almost forgot what it felt like to have water touch his skin, cold numb his fingers, heat scorch his body, or the feel of a woman as he eased the ache of his loins.

It wouldn't be long now until he felt all those things once again. All he needed to do was kill Nicole, because the last remaining member of the Chosen didn't even know what she was, and neither the Fae nor the Shields would ever find her.

Nicole was their last chance, and once she was out of the way, it was his time. For too long good had won over evil. It was time for evil to reign.

First, he needed to test Gabriel.

And tempt Val.

CHAPTER TWENTY-EIGHT

Val was amazed to find he felt better after talking with Gabriel. Though he disagreed with Gabriel about whose fault it was for his sisters' deaths, he also realized his brothers-in-law should have either stayed in Rome or found a better province.

He couldn't change the past, but he could make damn sure it didn't repeat itself with Nicole.

Just the thought of Nicole dead sent a chill down his spine. He refused to delve deeper into his feelings. At least not until they destroyed the gryphon and got her to the safety of Stone Crest and the other Chosen.

He looked out over the frozen expanse of Scotland, the serene beauty of the loch, mountains and forest broken only by the greed that resided in the village. That greed had nearly killed Nicole.

Val jerked as if he had been stabbed and turned toward the fire to see Nicole and Gabriel deep in conversation. He rushed toward them, unable to believe they hadn't thought of the village before now.

He passed the first huge boulder protruding from the cave wall and noticed something lying atop it. He leaned closer and saw it was a waterskin. Someone must have set it here by accident, so he reached for it, but as soon as it was in his hand, he had the uncontrollable desire to drain its contents.

With his hands shaking, he made himself drop it. Instantly, Gabriel was at his side.

"What is it?"

Val shook his head, unsure how to explain what had happened. He watched as Gabriel lifted the waterskin, uncork the top and take a drink.

"It's just water," he said and turned to the fire.

Val was so shaken that he needed to be alone. He turned back to the entrance and slowly sank onto a small boulder, his heart pounding a slow, sick beat in his chest. For an instant, he thought he smelled the unmistakable aroma of wine, and his mouth had salivated for a taste.

But Gabriel said it was water. Val watched him drink it and knew it was nothing but water because Gabriel would never deceive him. He closed his eyes and tried to think of anything but wine. He knew it was talk of his sisters' deaths and his turning to drink that brought back all the old longings.

He had pulled himself out of the drunken stupor once, and he didn't want to go down that bumpy road again. Hades would freeze over before he picked up another goblet of wine, no matter how bad the temptation was.

A glance outside showed that snow began to fall again. He watched one large flake drift from the sky, unable to shake the sensation that something awful was about to happen. He wished he had some clue as to what it could be. It was obvious that it was directed at Nicole, Gabriel, or him, and if he had to guess, he thought it might be Nicole.

He found his sharpening stone and reached for his

halberd. He needed to be ready for whatever came.

Something he'd been thinking tried to resurface, but then he glanced at the waterskin. Was it wine within?

~ ~ ~

Aimery watched Val from the forest. He hadn't left the Shields since he and Theron had spoken, and he wouldn't leave until the gryphon was dead.

Val's emotions were high, and by his jerky movements, something had happened. He closed his eyes and focused on Val, and that's when he felt it - Val's need for wine. Aimery opened his eyes and cursed long and low. He thought the evil would try and tempt Val with one of his weaknesses, he just hadn't expected it so soon.

But Val had come through the test.

Aimery turned and searched the forest. He wasn't alone. Someone - or something - was out there watching the cave, as well. Was it the gryphon? Or was it the Great Evil himself?

He didn't think the evil was foolish enough to venture from his hiding hole in an off chance that he might run into a Fae. Though his powers were great at the moment, if the evil ever encountered a powerful enough Fae, he might not survive.

And Aimery was powerful enough to want to test the bastard.

Too many innocents had been lost in the evil's quest for power and dominance. Aimery couldn't stand for any more lives to be taken. He would gladly give up his own to end it all.

And then he smelled it. Evil.

He turned and looked behind him to see the dark gryphon slowly walking toward him, his great black wings tucked against his side, his lion's tail swishing behind him, and his eagle eyes trained on him.

Aimery narrowed his gaze. The gryphon shouldn't be able to see him since he was cloaked, but the creature could surely smell him just as Aimery smelled his evil.

"Where are you?" the gryphon called. "You must greatly fear the lives of your men to keep watch, Fae."

"You say that word as if it's shoddy."

"You didn't answer my question. Do you fear for your men's lives? Do you think they can't win against the growing power of the Great Evil?"

Aimery clasped his hands behind his back. "My Shields have killed every creature your master has sent. I don't fear for them."

"Then why are you here?"

"You couldn't possibly understand."

The gryphon chuckled and sat back on his hind legs. "You think because I'm evil I don't feel compassion?" He tsked. "You should never underestimate your opponent."

"Oh, I don't underestimate you," Aimery said. "However, I do know exactly what you are and how you think."

"You know nothing," the beast all but hissed. His feathers ruffled and his tail flicked wildly.

Aimery silently circled the massive creature. He couldn't help his amazement in seeing one of the purest creatures ever to live be turned to the dark side. His magic cloaking him allowed him to get close to the gryphon, closer than most he would imagine.

"How do I look to your eyes?" The gryphon was once again calm, his tail tucked against him.

Aimery stopped and raised his gaze to find the gryphon staring at him. He knew the beast couldn't see him, could only feel and smell his presence. "Have you ever met one of your brethren?"

The gryphon laughed dryly and clicked his beak together. "You mean the *pure* ones? Nay, I haven't, and I pray I never do."

"Why? Because you're afraid of what they might do to you?"

"They couldn't do anything to me if they tried. I hold more power in one wing than an entire herd of gryphons. Afraid? I think not, Fae."

Aimery removed his cloaking spell and showed himself to the creature. "Tell me something."

"A curious Fae. How odd," the gryphon stated, his tone heavy with sarcasm. "Ask your question, Fae commander."

Aimery smiled and moved to stand in front of the creature. So the gryphon knew who he was. Interesting. "Why did you turn to the dark side?"

The gryphon looked away and sighed. "That's a complicated answer, one that I can't share."

Aimery hadn't expected the creature to tell him, still he found himself disappointed.

"However," the gryphon continued, his tone low and cautious, "I can tell you that I wasn't always as you see me."

That was a bit of information Aimery never expected. "What were you?"

The gryphon shook his head. "You aren't asking the right questions. You are supposed to be one of the most powerful species in the universe, yet you can't discover my origins. What does that tell you?"

"That evil has gotten very good at keeping their movements hidden."

"And become more powerful," the gryphon added.

Aimery nodded. "That as well. The Fae know this now and won't allow it to continue."

Sadness seemed to overcome the creature. "I'm afraid you're too late. It'll take more than your Fae power to stop what is coming."

Aimery refused to believe the gryphon, yet part of him realized that there might be some truth to the creature's words. "There has always been balance."

"True," the gryphon said with a nod of his large head. "Has no one ever wondered what would happen if someone tilted the balance of power?"

Anger began to simmer inside Aimery as he realized the gryphon had been toying with him. "There has always been balance, and there will always be balance. It is evil's destiny to continue to try and gain power, and it is good's destiny to outwit the evil and keep the balance. That is the way things are."

"If only it were that simple."

"What are you hinting at?" demanded Aimery.

"I cannot say."

"Cannot or will not?"

The gryphon shrugged. "You pick."

Aimery gnashed his teeth and glanced at the cave.

"They will die," the gryphon said. "Or at least one of them will."

He had no doubt the gryphon referred to Nicole. It would take much more than the creature to kill his Shields.

"Stay and watch," the gryphon said as he rose and turned to walk away. "It may prove entertaining," he threw over his shoulder.

Aimery glanced at the retreating creature and focused his attention on the cave. Something was wrong, but he couldn't place his finger on exactly what it was.

He wanted to check on his men, but he needed to report to Theron and Rufina on his conversation with the gryphon. Maybe it was time the Fae stopped following the rules set down when time began. If the evil had gained as much power as he suspected, it was either let the evil rule, or do what needed to be done.

Right then and there he decided to do whatever it took to keep his men alive and keep the power balanced.

~ ~ ~

Gabriel stretched and rose to his feet. He had taken the second watch, and just as he expected, no evil approached the cave. How he wished he could speak to the creature as Val had. He couldn't explain his need, he just knew that if he did, he might discover something.

The fact that the discovery he thought to make had nothing to do with Nicole and everything to do with his past frightened him like nothing else could.

He had asked Val to share his secrets, yet he himself hadn't shared any. Yet how could he? He didn't really know anything. It was all speculation on his part. Speculation and gut instinct, he reminded himself.

With a sigh, he looked over his shoulder to find Val sleeping near Nicole. If everything worked out as he hoped, a few days of sleeping beside each other should cause Val to see what was right before him.

Before it was too late.

CHAPTER TWENTY-NINE

The awesome heat of the fire scorched him before he even jumped from his horse, but Val's only thought was to get to his sisters and their families. Smoke billowed from the windows so thick that Val could barely make out the structure.

"Augustina! Luciana!" Val screamed as he banged on the door.

A clinking sound caught his attention, and he looked down to find the door handle chained and locked. A sick feeling of doom overtook him. He tried to swallow but found his mouth dry as he began to choke.

"General!" one of his men yelled. "We should ride after the raiders."

But Val ignored him. The screams of his sisters and their children drowned out everything. He had to save them.

He kicked the door, hoping to splinter the wood, but the damn thing held. Next, he slammed his shoulder into it and bit back a groan. He was running out of time. Already the littlest of the children had stopped crying.

Val refused to think that it was because she had died. Instead, he moved to one of the windows and tried to push the shutters open. The outside of his left hand touched the heated wood, immediately blistering the skin.

He grabbed his hand with a curse and looked helplessly at the house.

"Val, please help us!" he heard Augustina cry out faintly.

Then he heard nothing but the crackling of the fire.

Val sat up with sweat covering him and his breathing harsh and ragged. He looked around the cave, realizing only then that the nightmares had returned. He lowered his gaze to his hand expecting to see a fresh burn and not the old scar that met his gaze. The dream had been so vivid. Never had he experienced anything like it.

A piece of wood cracked and splintered in the fire sending sparks flying into the air. He shivered as the sweat dried in the cool air. His mouth was dry and his hands shook.

He needed a drink desperately and he thanked the gods nothing was near because he didn't think he was strong enough to turn it away from it. Nay, his dream had brought back so many painful memories.

"Val?"

He closed his eyes as he heard Nicole's sweet voice. She was like an anchor, one that he needed to hold onto with both hands.

Before he changed his mind, he turned toward her and covered her body with his.

"What is it?" she asked as she wrapped her arms around him.

"Nothing."

"You had a dream," she said softly.

Val didn't deny it. Somehow she always knew what truly bothered him.

Her hands ran through his hair kneading his head and neck. "The past is the past. Let it go."

"I can't."

"You must."

Val looked deep into her beautiful violet eyes. "Help me let go."

"All you had to do was ask," she said with a smile, then gently pulled his head down and kissed him.

Val's dark emotions evaporated the instant Nicole's lips touched his. He didn't question how or why, just took what comfort he could find in her kiss.

He plunged his hands into her long, black tresses and gloried in its thickness and softness. His mouth moved across her cheek to her jaw and down her delicious throat. His tongue flicked across a sensitive spot on her neck and heard her moan. A primal male smile pulled at his lips. He knew just how to touch her to send her spiraling out of control.

And if he were honest, he would admit she had the same power over him.

His cock was already bulging with need, and it didn't help that Nicole rubbed her hips seductively against his. He groaned as he savored the feel of her hands roaming over his back and shoulders. When she pushed at his leather jerkin, Val shifted to shed his jerkin and tunic.

The smile on her lips as she eyed his naked torso only made his desire burn brighter.

"You're magnificent." She sat up and began to kiss and touch his chest and abdomen.

Val closed his eyes and dropped his head back as he gave himself up to Nicole's touch. His skin burned as her fingers left a scorching trail down his torso. He clenched his hands at his sides as his emotions whirled around him. He didn't know what was right and what was wrong anymore. And he was tired of caring.

All he wanted to do was feel, and with Nicole in his

arms, he was doing just that.

Her hot tongue licked his nipple, sending a chill across his skin. Val opened his eyes and looked down to see Nicole watching him intently.

"You little vixen," he murmured just before he reached up and cupped her face in his hands and took her mouth in an intense kiss.

He needed her right then. She must have sensed his urgency for she began to pull up her skirts as he unfastened his pants. When his rod sprang free, Val looked up to find her lying on her back waiting for him.

"I need you too desperately to go slow."

"Stop talking," she said and reached for him.

Val had never known a woman so in tune with his emotions that she knew what he wanted before he did. He didn't question his fortune, just accepted it and took what pleasure he could.

Nicole's fingers threaded through his hair as she pulled his head toward her. He ran his lips across hers as his rod brushed against her sex.

He heard her sharp intake of breath and smiled. When his rod found her slick opening, he licked her lips before sliding his tongue into her mouth. Then he pushed deep inside of her. A sigh left him as he buried himself to the hilt, and he felt Nicole stiffen beneath him. She buried her head in his neck and wrapped her arms tightly around him.

"It's never enough," she whispered.

He raised his head and looked at her. "What?"

"You." Her violet eyes were sad as she looked at him. "I can never get enough of you."

He knew there was more she wanted to say, but he didn't press her. Instead, he moved within her and heard her gasp. She needed a respite as much as he did, and he intended to give her that.

His arousal begged for release, but he held back. He continued his leisurely movements as he pulled out until only the tip of him remained, then he slowly filled Nicole until he touched her womb. Again and again he repeated the movement until sweat glistened his body and Nicole's soft moans turned to cries of pleasure.

Only then did he thrust deeper and faster. Soon he felt his climax building and he knew he wouldn't be able to stop it, but nor did he want to reach his release before Nicole.

He shifted his weight to one arm and reached between their bodies until he found her clitoris. Her back arched as he ran his thumb across the little nub.

"Val," she cried out softly as her body convulsed around his.

He buried his face in her neck and plunged within her warmth, seeking not only fulfillment, but also peace. As his orgasm claimed him, he pumped his seed deep within her.

There, within the pleasure, was the serenity only Nicole could give him. He held on as long as he could until the last vestiges left them.

No words were spoken, not because Val didn't have anything to say. He was afraid to say them. Instead, he rolled to his back and brought Nicole against him. He stared at the ceiling of the cave as the fire danced upon the stones until he heard Nicole's breathing even into sleep. Only then did he allow himself to think about the feelings churning within him.

He kissed the top of her head and wrapped his arms tighter around her. The mission should have been simple. Kill the creature and save the girl. Now he found himself feeling things for Nicole that should never have happened.

To make matters worse, he couldn't take the chance and tell her. If he thought the water earlier was wine, Val knew the evil was playing with his mind. And if that was the case, then Val couldn't trust anything, not even the woman in his arms.

If he survived this, only then would he look at the strange feelings inside of him. Until that time, he would have to tread carefully. Since the evil played havoc with his mind, there was no telling what it was doing to Nicole and Gabriel.

He sighed and wished for an end to the madness.

~ ~ ~

The gryphon found a comfortable spot and lay down. He still wasn't sure what had prompted him to seek out Aimery. Once upon a time he would have made sure to stay as far away from the Fae as he could. Then again, once upon a time, things hadn't been so convoluted. And there hadn't been Nicole.

He shook his head but couldn't erase the image of her violet eyes. It was her eyes that had triggered the memories. He sighed forlornly. Being the right hand of evil no longer held the appeal it once had.

To this day, he still didn't know why he had so easily turned to the dark side. He had been scared, yes, but he had been armed with knowledge, coin, and a weapon. It had been enough to find him settled.

But he had been weak. In truth, he always had been. The only time he had shown anything other than weakness was when he released Nicole from certain death.

He wondered if the time came again, would he have the strength he wanted, or would the coward would show his true colors once again. The gryphon reached up and touched the blue stone hidden beneath his feathers over his heart.

With the stone, it didn't matter what he wanted, because once one wore the blue stone, the only person's will that mattered was his master's.

He opened his eyes to look to the cave. Even from the great distance, he could sense the feelings of Nicole and Val. It was easy to discern Nicole's feelings. She was falling in love with the Roman.

But Val was a different story. The general kept a tight clamp on his emotions and hid them from everyone, including himself. It was just as the evil wanted.

The gryphon then turned his attention to Gabriel. The Shield thought he had no past or memories, but that wasn't the case. The gryphon knew for a fact Gabriel had a past, and it was a past that was fast catching up with the warrior.

All too soon each of the three in the cave would face death. He had tried to warn Aimery that at least one would die, he just hadn't bothered to tell Aimery that it would be Nicole and Val.

The balance of power had slowly been shifting to the dark side for several decades. It had been in such tiny amounts that the Fae had never picked up on them. And once the balance shifted, it would be near impossible to get it back.

The beautiful land of Scotland would be laid to waste with the creatures his master would release. All that was good and pure would be wiped out, leaving only darkness and hate.

"Such a waste," he mumbled.

And it wasn't just this realm that would be taken over. The Realm of the Fae would be destroyed, as well. And with it, all the magic the Fae drew their power from. Yet it wouldn't stop there. Each realm would be affected in some way, shape or form.

And to his utter shame, he was going to be an intricate

part of evil's rise to power.

"*'Tis time.*"

The gryphon jerked at his master's voice in his head. Slowly, he stood and took one more look around the quiet beauty of the loch. His gaze stopped on what was once Nicole's cottage.

With slow, measured steps he began walking toward the cave.

CHAPTER THIRTY

Val came awake slowly. No more dreams had plagued his sleep, but it hadn't been a restful night. He had woken every hour or so and checked to make sure Nicole was still with him. It wasn't enough that she was next to him with her head on his chest. He had to actually see her.

He watched as she sighed in her sleep. Her creamy skin glowed in the dimming firelight, and her long tresses cascaded over his arm like a dark waterfall. Gently, he ran a finger down the side of her face.

Her beauty was unlike anything he had ever seen, but it wasn't just her outward beauty he spoke of. Her heart was more generous and giving than any he had ever encountered in all his travels.

She would make a wonderful wife and mother. His heart clutched painfully when he thought about her with another man. He didn't delude himself into thinking he could settle down as Hugh, Roderick, and Cole had done.

He slowly moved from underneath Nicole and stood. He wished with all his heart that things could be different. She gave him the peace he thought to never find.

Reluctantly, he pulled on his tunic and jerkin and

walked to the entrance.   Gabriel turned his head at his approach.

"Sleep well?" he asked.

Val grunted in response. He wasn't in the mood for a conversation, and by the haggard look on Gabriel's face, neither was he. "The sun isn't up yet. Take a few hours sleep. I'll keep guard."

"Nay," Gabriel said as he rose and stretched.   "I couldn't sleep if I tried. I think I'll go and look for some more firewood."

"Be careful," Val cautioned. "It has been too quiet."

Gabriel nodded and slung his quiver of arrows over his shoulder. "I agree. I think I'll take a walk around the loch as well, and see if I find any tracks."

"I don't know.   Remember what Aimery said yesterday."

"I can't wait around here much longer," Gabriel said testily. He ran a hand through his hair and reached for his bow. "I'll be fine, and if it makes you feel better, I won't go around the loch. I'll just scout the area."

"Thank you."

Val watched Gabriel and Laird make their way down the mountain and to the forest. He then turned his eyes to the sky. Sunlight was just beginning to shift the sky from black to a light gray. He wished Gabriel had waited until it was lighter to venture out.

"Thirsty?"

Val whirled around at the voice that sounded behind him, but there was nothing there. No evil could enter the cave, but he had a feeling the evil wasn't in the cave. It was inside his head.

He tried to ignore the growing hunger for wine, but it became increasingly more difficult to do. His craving for the wine, even in his most pitiful state, had never been this intense.

Sweat covered his body. His mouth became dry and he tried to swallow, but couldn't. He hurried to the waterskin Gabriel had drunk out of the night before and lifted it to his lips. It wasn't until the third swallow that he realized it wasn't water.

It was wine.

~ ~ ~

Gabriel patted Laird on the head and took a deep breath. The cold air burned his lungs, but it was just what he needed to help wake him.

Suddenly, Laird tensed and Gabriel quickly notched an arrow and waited. Then, Laird bolted to the left. Gabriel laughed when he saw the rabbit. He decided to let Laird have some fun before he called him back.

He put away his arrow and slung his bow over his shoulder as he began to search for more wood. He was venturing farther and farther from the cave in order to find any wood, and he hoped he didn't have too many more days searching through the snow and then waiting for the wood to dry out so they could burn it.

The hair on the back of his neck suddenly prickled. He looked around him but saw nothing. He was glad he listened to Val and stayed close to the cave, but now he had the desire to return immediately.

Something was close. Something that was there to harm.

The fact he couldn't smell the evil made him clench the bow tighter. Of all the creatures he'd hunted and killed, nothing had been as elusive or more difficult to hunt than the gryphon.

He whistled to Laird and began to make his way back

with long strides to the mountain. As he exited the forest, he glanced at the cave but didn't see Val guarding the entrance. He wasn't worried though. He knew Val was in the cave with Nicole.

A smile pulled at his lips at the memory of seeing Nicole sleeping on Val's chest that morning. Those two were meant to be together, and he was going to do whatever it took to make Val realize that.

A sound behind him in the forest caught his attention. He turned around to find Aimery. Gabriel cursed and removed his hand from the dagger at his waist.

"I wish you wouldn't sneak up on me," he said to the Fae commander.

Aimery just smiled. "But it's so much fun."

Gabriel was about to respond when Laird bounded from the forest, his teeth bared and growling low in his throat. He looked from the wolfhound to Aimery.

"What's wrong with your dog?" Aimery asked.

Gabriel shrugged. "I'm not sure. He's never acted like this around you before. Maybe the evil has gotten to him."

"If so, then we need to kill him."

Gabriel narrowed his eyes. He'd never questioned Aimery before, but there was no way he was allowing the Fae to lay a finger on the dog. "You aren't going to touch him. Laird is my responsibility. I'll take care of him."

"See that you do."

Gabriel began to worry why Aimery was acting so strangely, but then again, their realm was about to be destroyed by evil. It could all be getting to the Fae. "Laird," he called.

The wolfhound circled Aimery and slowly made his way to Gabriel. He stroked the animal's back and felt his muscles quivering. Sorrow filled him as he realized the evil had gotten to Laird and the animal would indeed have to be put down. He enjoyed having the wolfhound with him and would miss him greatly.

Gabriel reached for his dagger when Aimery's voice stopped him.

"Use mine. It's more powerful," the Fae said.

Gabriel nodded and held out his hand for the weapon. As soon as the weapon touched his hand he felt a sting as something raced through him. His eyes widened, unable to move as Laird attacked Aimery. Laird knocked him to the ground and Gabriel struggled to keep his eyes open.

He tried to call out to Val, but it was too late. Whatever had gone through his body halted his speech. As his eyes closed, he watched as the image of Aimery disintegrated.

~ ~ ~

When Nicole woke she felt disoriented and out of place. She rolled onto her back and rubbed her eyes as she tried to get her bearings. Memories of her night with Val filled her mind, and she smiled.

He had come to her. By his troubled eyes, he had needed her, but she promised herself she wouldn't push him. Then, to her surprise, he had turned to her in his time of need.

A smile was still on her lips as she stood and added more wood to the fire. She wished she had awoken when Val did, but it had been nice to sleep with him, something she hoped to repeat that night.

She grabbed some food and a waterskin and walked to the entrance. She was sure that neither Val nor Gabriel had eaten since they both often waited for her. Her steps were light and her mood happy as she made her way toward her warriors.

Her warriors. She laughed at how she had begun to think of Val and Gabriel. The smile on her lips faded as she saw Val's boots sticking out from one of the large boulders. She raced around the boulder and dropped the food and water when she found Val unconscious.

"Gabriel! Come quick," she called as she fell to her knees and ran her hands over Val's body. She didn't find any wounds, but it was obvious something was wrong.

"Gabriel!" she called again and looked over her shoulder to find the cave empty. "Oh, dear God," she mumbled as she turned back to Val.

She tried everything she could to wake him, but he wouldn't respond. Tears blinded her as she struggled to think of what to do. She knew she needed to find Gabriel, but she couldn't leave the cave. Yet she couldn't leave Val like he was either.

All of a sudden she stopped and listened. Was that someone calling her name? She rose to her feet and walked to the entrance, careful not to get too close. Her eyes scanned the area but found no one.

"Nicole!"

She looked down the mountain. It had sounded like a child calling to her. Just as she was about to give up again, she saw a patch of red hair as the girl climbed up the mountain.

"Nicole," she called again.

She didn't know whether to answer the child or not. No one was supposed to know she was here, and this could be a trick.

Several long moments went by as the girl climbed the rest of the way to the cave. "There you are," she said between huffs of breaths. "I've been calling to you. Why haven't you answered?"

Nicole watched the concern in the child's blue eyes. It

seemed genuine. "I don't know you."

"Aye, you do," she said. "I'm Francis, the miller's daughter. My father made me hide every time you came into the shop."

Nicole smiled then, relieved to know it wasn't a trick. "What's wrong? How did you know where I was?"

"Gabriel sent me."

"Gabriel?"

The girl nodded her red head. "Aye, he sent me to get you so you could bring his black bag."

Nicole shook her head as she tried to understand what the girl said. "Gabriel wants me to leave the cave? To bring his black bag?"

Again the girl nodded. "He said you'd know what bag he was talking about."

Of course Nicole knew, and if Gabriel wanted his herbs, that meant someone was hurt. "Are you sure he wanted me to bring it, and not someone else? Val perhaps?"

"Nay. He asked for you."

Nicole looked over her shoulder at Val and wondered what to do. Gabriel would never purposefully put her in danger, but there was something she couldn't put her finger on. Something was off.

"Nicole, please," the girl begged. "Donald is verra sick."

Her head jerked back to the girl. "Donald?" Nicole looked at Val. There were no visible wounds and his breathing was even. He seemed to be just sleeping. If she went to help Donald she could talk to Gabriel and get him to hurry back to check on Val. Without another word, she raced back to the fire and grabbed Gabriel's black bag, then ran to the entrance. "Let's go."

She followed the girl down the mountain, glancing at

the sky every now and then to make sure the gryphon wasn't about to attack her.

As she passed her house, she saw the girl looking at it. "What happened?"

Nicole shrugged and walked faster. "I don't know."

She didn't know what prompted her to think about Aimery or why she silently called to him, but she knew she would feel better if the Fae commander could check on Val and see what was wrong with him. She still didn't like the fact she had left him, though she comforted herself with the fact he had been breathing and didn't have any wounds.

It wasn't until she entered the village and saw the people lining the streets that she knew she had been tricked. She turned to the little girl, who ran to her father, an evil smile on her face.

Nicole turned on her heel to race back to the cave, but a line of men blocked her way. She turned and scanned the crowd and found two men holding Donald, blood dripping down his face from a wound on his head.

"I'm sorry, lass," he said.

She smiled sadly and raised her chin. She would not die a coward.

CHAPTER THIRTY-ONE

Nicole scanned the many faces of the people who crowded around her. For years they wouldn't look her in the eye for fear of turning evil, yet now they stared at her with malice and anger.

By their sneers and laughter, Nicole knew her end would not be painless or quick.

"Move," a man snarled behind her as he poked her in the back with something sharp.

She hid her wince and began to walk slowly through the village. It was ironic that she had begged Margda to allow her to come to the village, and now all she wanted to do was run away and never see it again.

Her hands trembled, so she hid them in her skirts. She didn't want to show an ounce of fear to the villagers. To do so would make her death even more painful.

The hair on the back of her neck began to rise and she knew the gryphon was near. Would he be the one to kill her? Or did the evil have something else in mind?

She stopped looking at the villagers and stared at the ground ahead of her as she walked through the main street of the village. Their taunts and mocking laughter no longer affected her. She ignored them and concentrated on putting one foot in front of the other.

It wasn't until she saw the large wooden structure in front of her that she realized just how painful a death she would endure.

~ ~ ~

Esmee watched Nicole from between the two men standing in front of her. A quick glance around showed that everyone's attention was on Nicole. Esmee took the chance and leaned back against the inn.

Then slowly she edged toward the alley. She took a deep breath and slipped into the dim alley and waited for someone to come after her. When no alarm was raised, she turned and ran to the back of the inn where there was a seldom-used trail that led to the loch.

She prayed Gabriel was still there. As her strides lengthened, she fisted her skirts in her hands and hiked them over her knees. Her breath burned her throat and chest, but she didn't slow. She had to reach Gabriel before it was too late.

Her toe tripped on a root hidden by snow just as she passed the ruins of Nicole's cottage. She fell to her hands and knees. With her heart beating wildly and urgency pushing her onward, Esmee climbed to her feet then stilled.

An unearthly sound reached her ears. It was the same sound she had heard the night their village had been attacked. Slowly, she raised her eyes to the dawning sky and saw the large, black shape that flew threw the air.

"The gryphon," she murmured.

She didn't waste any more time as she lifted her skirts again and raced toward the mountain. Many times she slipped on the loose rocks, ice, and snow as she clawed her way to the top.

When she finally reached the cave entrance her entire body quivered with fatigue. Her eyes searched the darkened cave as she looked for any signs of Gabriel or his friend Val. But nothing moved. She saw a flicker of light toward the back of the cave signaling that there was a fire.

"Gabriel?" she called out hesitantly.

No one answered, so she took a tentative step inside the cave. "Gabriel, it's Esmee. Nicole is in trouble and needs help."

She was about to turn and leave when she spotted someone lying in the shadows. Thinking it was Gabriel, she ran to him. As she leaned down she found another man. She shook him, and when he didn't wake, she set about trying to find a wound. When she didn't find that, she knew she had to locate Gabriel.

And quickly.

~ ~ ~

Gabriel groaned as he rolled to his side. His entire body ached as if he had been thrashed soundly. He shivered and tried unsuccessfully to find warmth. As he opened his eyes, he recalled speaking to Aimery and Laird's unexpected behavior.

But then Aimery hadn't vanished as he usually had. He had disintegrated. Which meant it hadn't been Aimery at all.

Gabriel's hand sank into the snow as he pushed himself onto his knees. It was only because of the unique and magical material that his clothes were made from that prevented the snow from soaking them. It took him a couple of tries to get on his feet, and even then he wasn't too steady.

Whatever it was that had acted like Aimery had used dark magic to put him down. Gabriel shook his head to try and clear away the fog that clouded his mind. He had to get to Nicole and Val before it was too late.

As he started up the mountain, he felt something at his heels and looked back to see Laird.

"I thought I'd lost you," Gabriel said as he scratched the wolfhound's neck. "Glad to know you're still with me."

Gabriel looked up at the cave and thought he saw movement. A glance at the rising sun showed he had been unconscious far longer than he would have liked. It was Laird nipping at his heels that got him moving faster. Whatever it was, Laird felt some urgency that Gabriel did not.

When he neared the entrance to the cave he saw Esmee standing there. "What are you doing here?"

"I've come ta get ye," she said.

He noted strands of her flaming hair plastered to her face and her breath ragged. "What is it?"

"'Tis Nicole. And your friend."

Gabriel's heart plummeted to his feet. "Val? What's wrong with Val?"

"I doona know," she said shrilly.

He saw she was becoming hysterical and increased his rate of climbing instead of asking her more questions. When he stood in front of her he saw how she shook and fear filled her green eyes. "Where is Val?"

She pointed over her shoulder. Gabriel ran to his friend and leaned close listening for a heartbeat. That's when he smelled the alcohol on Val's breath. Anger coursed through him as Gabriel sat back on his heels and looked down at the man he had placed his trust in.

He slapped Val. Hard.

~ ~ ~

Val struggled through the haze that surrounded him. Something hit the side of his face and he groaned in response. Another slap made him roll to his side to avoid more hits. He heard grumbling beside him and recognized Gabriel's angry voice.

It took all of Val's control just to be able to push up onto his hands and knees. His head reeled, his arms and legs felt weighed down, and his mouth was as dry as the desert.

He was drunk.

Val cursed as he sat back on his heels and tried to stop the world from spinning.

"I expected more from you."

He inwardly winced at Gabriel's icy tone. He opened his mouth to speak, but found that the throbbing in his head dimmed everything else.

"Dammit, Val," Gabriel roared. "How could you get sotted?"

"Enough." Val tried to yell, but it came out only as a squeak, and even then it hurt his ears. With the help of the boulder beside him, Val managed to stand, then leaned heavily on the massive rock.

He opened his eyes and found Gabriel glaring at him. "You condemn me before you hear my side?"

"I don't need to hear your side," he growled. "I can smell you from here."

"Gabriel, please."

Val blinked and slowly turned his head to look at the woman beside Gabriel. "Who are you?"

She gave him a small smile. "I'm Esmee from the village."

He grunted. "So, while I'm here battling the evil by

myself, you run to the village to have some fun."

"I didn't go to the village," Gabriel said as he took a menacing step toward him.

Val pushed off the boulder and steadied himself on his feet. He felt as weak as a newborn kitten, but at least the effects of the wine were wearing off. "Then where were you?"

"Unconscious on the side of the mountain," Gabriel said and turned away. "I was tricked into thinking I spoke to Aimery. Only Laird knew the difference."

"There's more pressing-" Esmee tried to get in.

Val ran a hand down his face as he struggled to comprehend all that was happening. He glanced at Esmee but talked over her. "If the Great Evil attacked both of us at the same time..."

He stopped and looked around the cave. "Nicole," he called and stumbled toward the fire. "Nicole!"

"She's not here," Esmee said softly. "She is the reason I came looking for Gabriel."

Val closed his eyes and felt something pierce his heart. "Tell me they don't have her."

"I wish I could."

Slowly Val turned and faced Esmee. "Tell me where she is?"

"The village. She was tricked, as well. They plan to kill her."

"I must save her," he said and brushed past Gabriel to his halberd.

But as soon as he reached for his halberd, Gabriel's hand took hold of his arm. Val turned to look at his brethren.

"Wait," Gabriel said.

Val jerked out of his grip. "For what? They're going to kill her."

"You need to sober up," Gabriel said between clenched teeth. He took a deep breath, and in a more even tone said, "And we need to determine just how the evil got to all of us before we go running into the village."

Val knew he was right, he just didn't want to take the time away from saving Nicole. He sighed and released his halberd. "All right."

"Good," Gabriel said and crossed his arms over his chest. "Now tell me what happened?"

Val gritted his teeth together and opted for the shortened version. "The evil got in my head, I reached for the waterskin that you drank from the previous night, and it wasn't until I had downed half the contents that I realized it wasn't water but wine."

He watched as Gabriel bent down and retrieved the waterskin. With his eyes trained on Val, he bent and sniffed the bag. "It's water."

Val laughed and reached for his halberd. "If you actually think that I somehow managed to get wine without leaving this damned cave, then you are sadly mistaken, and I'm not going to sit here and argue about it when Nicole's life is on the line."

"We need to have a plan."

Val narrowed his gaze on Gabriel. "Tell me, are you really Gabriel? Has the evil somehow gotten to you that you'll do whatever it takes to stop me?"

Since he was itching for a fight, he was glad when Gabriel dropped his arms and stepped toward him.

"All right, ye two blasted idiots," Esmee said. "Can ye see what's happening? The evil has managed to come between ye. If ye think ye can save Nicole, then ye have to band together."

Val glanced down at the woman and realized she was right, but he still wanted to hear from Gabriel that he was the same man he was before they had come to Scotland.

Instead, Gabriel brushed past him and stood at the cave entrance.

"He has my bow," Gabriel said after a moment.

Val cursed. "We can't do this without Aimery."

"Then it's a good thing Nicole called for me when she did," said a voice from behind them.

CHAPTER THIRTY-TWO

Val had never been so happy to see Aimery before. "You know what has happened?"

Aimery nodded. "Here's another bow," he said as he held out the weapon to Gabriel and then smiled at Esmee.

"My thanks," Gabriel said as he took the bow.

"You're going to have a tough time of it," Aimery said. "The village has surrounded Nicole."

"Which means innocents will die."

Val grunted. "They aren't innocents. They chose the path of evil."

"True," Gabriel agreed.

"Rules have been broken," Aimery said softly. "Because of this, the Fae army is here just in case you can't kill the gryphon. The balance of power has been shifting for some time now."

"How did the Fae not realize this?"

Aimery sighed. "It was done by tiny increments that never caught our notice. And now it may be too late. Theron has taken Rufina somewhere safe to protect her and her unborn child. The Fae realm is on alert, as well."

"How I wish the other Shields were here," Gabriel said.

Val silently agreed. "What do they plan on doing to Nicole?"

"Burn her," Esmee said softly.

Val could wait no longer. He spun on his heel and grabbed his halberd. There were little effects from the wine still left in him, and by the time he reached the village, it would be purged from his system.

"Val," Aimery said. "Don't blame yourself."

He looked at the Fae. "Who else do I blame? I gave in to temptation."

"Nay. You thought you were drinking water. That isn't the same thing. It was a trick."

"None of it matters if Nicole dies," Val reminded him and headed from the cave.

Aimery watched Val exit the cave and turned to Esmee. "You don't seem too concerned that I just appeared in the cave."

She shrugged and smiled. "I've seen more than I'd have liked to living in this village. I'm just glad to know the Fae are real and are involved."

He waited until she followed Val before he looked at Gabriel. "What bothers you?"

"I can't explain it. Something feels...off."

"It's the evil in the air."

"It's more than that," Gabriel argued. "He appeared to me as you, and I couldn't tell the difference."

Aimery released a long breath. "If the magic is strong enough, anyone can be convinced, Gabriel."

The Shield's silver eyes blazed. "Aren't you the least bit concerned that he didn't kill me?"

Aimery was highly concerned, but he wasn't about to tell Gabriel that. "Nay. Apparently, the evil has plans for you and Val. Or both of you would've been killed days ago."

But Gabriel knew it was more than that. Val had been in the cave where evil was prohibited to go. He had been alone and the evil right before him. The evil should have killed him, not knocked him unconscious.

The more Gabriel learned of this evil, the more he feared it was somehow connected to his past. Whether he had been on the side of good or evil was still in question, and he hoped he discovered the truth before any one else did.

~ ~ ~

Nicole focused on the mountains in the distance as her hands and feet were tied to the wooden stakes that formed a large cross. Her blood had turned to ice in her veins, freezing her more assuredly than the cold ever could.

Most of the villagers held torches as they waited for the time when they could light the bundles of wood that surrounded her. Nicole refused to look closer at their expressions of glee. It hurt her too deeply, and caused her to shake even more.

She thought of her beautiful loch and the waters that had always calmed and soothed her. It had been a majestic place to see every day despite Margda's cruel hand and the viciousness of the villagers. She was going to miss the loch and the mountains. Though she might not have been born of this realm, she had come to love it.

"Time to die," someone whispered in her ear as he viciously yanked the rope that bound her wrist, cutting into her skin until she bled.

But the pain was going to be nothing compared to being burned alive.

Her arms were stretched out across the plank of wood that was parallel to the ground, and her feet were bound tightly to the pole at the base of the platform. She was a sacrifice.

Death stared her in the face, and there was no escaping it. She just wished she had been able to tell Val she loved him when she'd had the chance. She'd known it was love in his arms the night before.

His gentle touch, passionate kisses, and erotic claiming of her body and soul would last for many lifetimes to come. He had touched her as no other person could. She would have liked to have known what their future could have been had they met in another time and place.

She berated herself for leaving the cave. She should never have been tricked, and she couldn't help but worry over Val. She hadn't found a wound, but that didn't mean the evil hadn't gotten to him some other way.

And where was Gabriel? Had the evil gotten to him as well? It was the only explanation she could come up with for them leaving her alone.

She hoped when she called to Aimery that he heard her this time, but since he hadn't appeared, she wasn't so sure. At least if he was there, he could see to Val and Gabriel. Nothing could be done for her now. The evil had indeed won, and all because she left the cave as Val and Gabriel had warned her not to do.

"Forgive me, Val," she whispered into the cold wind that had sprung up.

Her eyes rose to the sky where she saw dark clouds rolling in ominously. Any other time she would say it was a storm, but she knew it was the evil that approached. A dark spot in the sky drew her attention, but she didn't have to look twice to know it was the gryphon.

"The time has come," a man said and stepped before her. He spit on her before he turned to the villagers. "For years we've protected and raised the evil that stands bound behind me. Now, it is time for her to die. And with her death, prosperity for this village until the end of time!"

A loud cheer went up at the end of his short speech.

Nicole was amazed at the idiocy of the villagers. Did they really think she was the evil? Fear made her heart jump into her throat as she saw the people coming closer with the torches.

One woman pointed her gnarled finger at Nicole and scrunched up her old, haggard face. "She must die!"

"Please, listen!" Nicole shouted, but the villagers were too crazed to pay attention. They were yelling for her death, and there would be no stopping them now.

The wind began to howl as it whipped viciously about them. Nicole turned her head to the side as strands of her hair were pulled from her plait and stung her face. Her skirts bunched about her legs and the trees groaned in protest as they were slung from side to side.

And then just as suddenly as the wind appeared, it stopped. In the midst of the villagers, facing Nicole, stood a lone figure in a long, black hooded cloak that hid his face. She knew without having to be told it was the Great Evil Val had come to fight. The man who had rescued her and brought her to this village, only to bring about her death.

"Why?" she asked him.

He moved toward her as if his feet never touched the ground, and his voice, when he spoke, was hollow and cold. "Because with your death, not only will I have all the power I've always sought, but I can once more have my body."

She peered into the dark hood, but saw only darkness, the icy claws of malevolence sinking into her. It was as if he didn't have a face. Or even a form.

"I don't," he said. "I'm merely a spirit existing because my magic is as great as it is."

"Why didn't you kill me as a baby? Why wait?"

"I had to," he said. "The Fae had to see their power slipping from them, they needed to know their mighty magic can do nothing to stop me."

Nicole blinked back her tears. "You'll never win. The Shields and the Fae will defeat you in the end."

"Not this time, my dear. After today, the Shields will never be the same, and without them, the Fae cannot win."

Nicole shook her head. "You have me, leave the Shields alone. They are no match for your power."

"True," he said, a smile in his voice. "However, they do have something that could very well alter the outcome if I hadn't seen to it beforehand."

"Why are you telling me this?"

"I want you to know just how hopeless the situation is, Nicole," he whispered as he moved closer. "No one will come for you. No one will save you. You are nothing. You mean nothing."

She looked away, hating how his words cut her. "I know."

"Good. Then don't fight your destiny."

Nicole's hands began to go numb as the cold penetrated her. Strangely though, her skin covered by the unique gown Aimery had given her was warm.

She leaned her head back against the thick wooden post and closed her eyes. She thought of her loch during the spring, and envisioned herself and Val swimming in the cool waters, then making slow, sweet love beneath the tall pines that lined the water's edge.

A smile pulled at her lips as she recalled his light green eyes and the way they darkened just before he kissed her. She imagined running her fingers through his silky shoulder-length golden brown hair or over his bulging muscles.

The shouts of the villagers had grown louder and

closer. Nicole didn't have to open her eyes to know that they were about to bring about her death.

"Val," she whispered.

CHAPTER THIRTY-THREE

Val stopped in his tracks when he saw the crowd that surrounded Nicole. She was strapped to a large cross while the villagers moved closer to her with torches in their hands. He didn't like the catch in his throat or the way his heart clenched painfully at seeing her so helpless.

All his anxieties of not being able to save her rushed to the surface. He tried to catch Nicole's gaze, but she had her eyes closed. Val glanced to his left as Gabriel came up beside him.

"This isn't good," he said.

Val gripped his halberd tighter. "Nay."

"All right, General. What do you want to do?"

"We've the element of surprise. Let's use it to our advantage."

"Two against fifty," Gabriel murmured. "Not good odds."

"Recount," Esmee said as she walked to the other side of Val.

Val smiled as he caught sight of the bow in her hand. "Can you use that?"

She glanced at his halberd. "Can you use that?"

He looked over at Gabriel who shrugged. "Three is

better than two."

"All right, Esmee, you loop around to the right behind the buildings. Gabriel, you go left. I'm going to head down the center of the village. Right now, I want to get Nicole free. I'll need both of you to cover me."

Both Gabriel and Esmee nodded before they branched off. Val stared at Nicole, willing her to open her eyes and see him, to know that he had come for her.

With his halberd in both hands, Val began to creep toward the villagers. Their attention was on Nicole, so they never saw him. When he was a few strides away, he whistled and got a man's attention. As soon as the man turned, Val swung his halberd and knocked him in the jaw.

The villagers were chanting Nicole's death too loudly to hear the man cry out as he fell unconscious to the ground. Val smiled and began to clear a path - slowly but surely - to Nicole.

It wasn't until he reached the front that he saw the cloaked figure standing in front of Nicole. Suddenly, the figure turned, and he knew it was the evil.

The figure hissed and raised an arm toward him. The villagers grew quiet, the stillness deafening. Val kept his gaze on the cloaked figure and waited. When nothing happened, he glanced at Nicole to find her watching him.

"Now," the figure bellowed.

Before Val could move, men threw torches onto the bundles of wood at Nicole's feet. He watched in horror as they caught fire. He tried to move toward her, but the villagers grabbed at him, halting any progress he made.

With a hiss of frustration, Val swung his halberd and knocked the villagers away, but as soon as he was free, more attacked him. He heard a vicious whoosh by his ear and watched as a man fell to his knees, an arrow sticking from his throat.

Val never stopped fighting as he slowly moved toward Nicole. Every so often he would hear Gabriel and Esmee release arrows, but the villagers kept coming at him.

It was when he heard Nicole's screams that he knew he was going to lose her. He yanked his gaze to her to see the fire licking at her feet. It was like his sisters all over again, and he refused to allow that to happen again.

He threw back his head and bellowed his rage as he tossed two men off him and raced toward Nicole, ramming his shoulders and halberd into anyone who got in his way. He jumped onto the platform and reached for her ropes.

"You came," she said through her tears.

"I gave you my word."

His fingers fumbled with the knots, and before he could release her, he was jerked backward, his halberd flying from his hands. He landed on his back with a bone-jarring thud. Bright lights flashed before his eyes, and he couldn't catch his breath.

Val concentrated on taking a deep breath and was rewarded as air filled his lungs. He rolled onto his hands and knees, ignoring the pain that lanced through his back.

A loud thump jarred the ground, and Val raised his head to see the gryphon standing before him as the villagers fled in fear. He glanced at Nicole over his shoulder and saw resignation fill her beautiful violet eyes. Her long black tresses whipped about her face as the wind began to quicken and smoke filled the air.

"You should've stayed in your drunken stupor," the creature said as he walked toward Val.

Val turned back to the gryphon and climbed to his feet. "Are you too afraid to face me without resorting to tricks?"

The gryphon laughed and folded his wings against his great black body. "Afraid of *you*? I think not."

No sooner had the words left his mouth than a volley

of arrows pierced him. The gryphon reared back on his hind legs and pawed at the air as he roared in pain.

Val used the diversion to unsheathe his sword and watched in amazement as the gryphon pulled out the arrows and tossed them to the ground. As Val looked on, the wounds inflicted by Gabriel and Esmee rapidly healed.

He had expected this, but he hoped for a little more suffering from the creature. Val barely had time to spare Nicole a glance before the gryphon charged him. He stood with feet apart, knees bent, and his balance on the balls of his feet. He gripped his sword in his right hand and waited until the last possible moment before he dove to the side.

Val didn't come away unscathed. The gryphon's talons raked down his legs, leaving three gaping wounds. He ignored his now throbbing legs and rolled to his feet to see the flames about to reach Nicole.

Fear wound its icy manacles around him and threatened to drag him down. He opened his mouth and took deep breaths, and then took a step toward her.

No sooner had he taken that step than something wrapped around his neck and squeezed painfully. Val clawed at the talons as his air was slowly and ruthlessly cut off.

"How does it feel?" the creature asked? "Does it pain you to know that once again you'll have failed the ones you love?"

Val closed his eyes against the gryphon's words, but not before he saw the stark terror in Nicole's gaze. He knew he would die. He had just wanted to free Nicole before his time came.

He kicked back and connected with the gryphon. The beast grunted and loosened his hold for a moment. Val gulped in a tiny amount of air and opened his eyes to search out Gabriel. He managed to spot his fellow Shield in the chaos as the villagers ran about screaming. With the blackness beginning to encroach on his vision, he had precious little time in which to give Gabriel a signal. Val managed the barest of nods and prayed that Gabriel realized what it meant.

"I've no choice but to kill you," the gryphon said in Val's ear.

And then to his amazement, the gryphon eased his grip again. "There must have been good in you at one time," Val said through the pain in his throat. "Find it again and help us."

For a long moment, there wasn't an answer, and then the gryphon said, "I'm afraid that part of me is dead."

As the gryphon's grip tightened once again, Val saw Gabriel notch three arrows and let them fly. The arrows hit the creature, and he instantly released Val.

Val hit the ground and rolled. As he climbed to his feet, he reached for the dagger at the back of his waist. He looked over his shoulder to see the gryphon already healed and his black eyes trained on him.

With time of the essence, Val jumped over the roaring fire and embedded the dagger beside Nicole's hand. He briefly met her gaze before he jumped down and raced for his halberd.

Nicole looked to her right and spotted the dagger protruding from the wood near her hand. She didn't hesitate to loop the rope over the blade and begin to saw through her bonds. Her heart thudded in fear, but not for herself - for Val.

She watched in awe as he sheathed his sword and reached for his halberd, and then proceeded to use it to knock away villagers that tried to attack him. The villagers were no match for Val, but the gryphon that lurked behind them was.

It had taken everything she had not to call out to Val when the gryphon had choked him. As strong as Val was, and as gifted as he was with weapons, none of that could compare to the gryphon's dark power.

She felt the rope around her wrist slacken and she renewed her efforts. She tried not to pay attention to the ever-approaching fire that licked at the hem of her gown, which somehow miraculously refused to catch fire. The heat from the flames had sweat running down her face and neck.

Suddenly, the rope gave way and her arm dropped. She reached up and tugged the dagger from the wood and moved to release her other hand when her arm was wrenched back against the wood.

Tears stung her eyes as pain erupted in her arm, and she nearly dropped the dagger. She looked around to see who had stopped her. The cloaked figure stood off to her right, his robes billowing around him as if the wind couldn't stand his presence. She could all but see his power directed at her.

The flames swiftly rose and scorched the hem of her dress, but it still didn't catch fire. Nicole cried out as the flames rose higher and higher. Then, as rapidly as they had grown, they were doused. And that's when she spotted Aimery.

"Stay out of it," he yelled to the evil.

The evil turned his hooded head to Aimery. "Never."

"You know the rules," Aimery said and advanced on him. "You can't interfere."

"Neither can you."

"I'm merely balancing the power," Aimery said and raised his hands. "I'll continue to do so as long as you interfere."

The evil laughter reverberated around the village

making Nicole's skin crawl. "A Fae who has finally had enough. Does your king know of your intentions?"

Nicole moved her gaze to Aimery and waited for him to answer. When he didn't, she again heard the evil's laughter.

"Since you know the laws so well, then you'll know what will happen to you now that you have broken one."

Aimery shrugged, his long, flaxen hair blowing behind him as the wind picked up again. "It is a chance I'm willing to take."

"Then you're as foolish as I had hoped you were."

Nicole's arm that the evil had pinned back against the wood was freed, and she hurried to cut through the ropes on her other hand.

She threw a glance at Aimery and the evil to see them advancing on the other. She had no idea what would happen if they began to fight, and she greatly feared what the outcome would be.

And then, just as Aimery raised his hand to attack, the evil disappeared and the wind died. With both hands now freed, Nicole reached down to free her legs. The village began to quiet as the people found their homes and hid.

Nicole cut through the ropes binding her ankles. With the dagger still in hand, she lifted her skirts and jumped over the smoldering wood. She landed heavily and steadied herself as she searched the area.

Her gaze sought Val's as he and the gryphon fought. She stood rooted to the spot as Val used the tip of his halberd to cut open the creature's chest.

The creature roared and swung his large front paw at him. She sucked in a breath as Val jumped back just before a talon could cut open his torso.

Val needed help, and she knew there was one person who could aid him as no one could – Gabriel. Nicole's eyes searched until she caught sight of him. He stood to her right, an arrow notched and sighted, yet he didn't release it.

Nicole waited with bated breath for Gabriel to help, yet he did nothing more than stand there. "Gabriel!" she yelled. When that didn't get his attention, she turned and ran toward him.

"Gabriel, help him!" she shouted again and again.

She pushed her way through a throng of frightened villagers and raced toward Gabriel. She didn't know what was stopping him, but she knew if he didn't help Val soon, Val could die.

"Gabriel," she said when she reached him. "What is wrong with you? Why aren't you helping Val?"

Nicole glanced at Val and watched as the gryphon tried to peck at him with his sharp beak.

"Gabriel, please," she begged.

When it became obvious that Gabriel wasn't going to help, Nicole lifted her skirts and clutched the dagger as she ran toward Val.

She was just about to reach him when she stumbled over a dead body and fell to the ground. She watched in horror as the dagger tumbled from her hand to land several paces away. Tears stung her eyes as she struggled to her hands and knees with her legs caught in her skirts, and crawled to the weapon.

When it was once again in her hand, she looked to Val to find the gryphon standing over him.

"Nay," she screamed as she found her feet. Her only thought was to save Val as she ran toward the gryphon. She knew what the consequences were when she buried the dagger in the gryphon's back.

She just hadn't expected to feel so much fear when he roared and turned to face her.

CHAPTER THIRTY-FOUR

"Nicole?" the gryphon asked, his eyes filled with sorrow. "Why?"

Nicole swallowed and backed away. "Just get it over with," she said and let the tears fall. She didn't look at Val. She couldn't bear to see the love of her life watch her cower in fear.

The gryphon reached around and pulled the dagger from his back, then stepped toward her. "I never expected this of you. You must care for him a great deal."

"I love him."

The gryphon closed his eyes and sighed. "I wish things were different."

No sooner had the words left his mouth then his entire demeanor changed. Gone was the compassionate creature she had seen but a moment ago, and in its place was the monster she had glimpsed the night he tried to kill her.

The scream died as his large claw wrapped around her throat. She gripped his claw and stared him in the eye.

"Leave Val alone once this is over," she said with her last breaths.

His claw tightened as he closed his eyes, the resignation in them surprising her.

~ ~ ~

Val dragged himself off the ground and made his tired, aching body grip his halberd. One eye was swollen shut after a vicious knock from the creature, and blood poured into his other eye from a cut at his temple.

He swiped at the blood running into his eye and lifted his arm to throw the halberd when suddenly the gryphon turned toward him.

Val saw the acceptance in Nicole's eyes and his heart cried out. He turned to the creature to find his dark gaze on him.

"There isn't much time," the gryphon said as though he were in a lot of pain.

Val's forehead furrowed as he waited to see if it was a trick.

"He's controlling me," the gryphon ground out and then grimaced. "I can't hold him off much longer."

To Val's surprise, the gryphon then moved aside the feathers over his chest, and that's when Val saw it. The blue stone.

He moved to plunge his halberd into the gryphon's chest and through the blue stone, but hesitated. "Why?"

The gryphon groaned. "Just do it."

Without another thought, Val reared back and hurled his halberd at the gryphon. It sunk into the creature's chest and through the blue stone. Bright light shot out in all directions as the gryphon let out a loud roar and released Nicole.

Val covered his eyes and waited for the light to disappear. When it was gone, he opened his eyes to find not the gryphon upon the ground, but a man with Val's halberd sticking from his chest.

He rushed to the man and knelt beside him when he saw he was still alive. "You were turned."

"Aye," the man said, his voice faint and his breathing labored.

"Aimery. Gabriel. I need help!" Val yelled.

The man shook his head. "Nay. Let me go. I need to atone for my sins."

Val felt something beside him and looked up to see Nicole. He took her hand as she fell to her knees, her gaze never leaving the man's.

"I'm sorry," the man said. "If it hadn't been for your eyes, I would've killed you that first time."

"My eyes?" Nicole repeated.

A faint smile touched the man's mouth. "Our mother's eyes, Nicole. It was the only way I recognized you."

Val's heart ached when he heard Nicole gasp and reach for the man's hand. "I thought only infants were sent here."

He laughed and then choked as blood dripped from the corner of his mouth. "Our parents ruled our realm. They refused to keep me there to die, so they sent me after the infants had left to look for Nicole and help raise her. I failed."

"Nay," Nicole said and took his hand in hers. "You found me."

"Almost too late," he said. "You brought back all the memories my master tried to erase."

"What is your name?" she asked.

"Dane."

"Thank you, Dane," she said and leaned down to kiss his cheek.

When she straightened, Dane's eyes were lifeless. Val

reached over and took Nicole in his arms as she cried silent tears. He looked over her shoulder to find Aimery and Gabriel watching.

"I'm sorry," Val whispered in her ear. "If I had known..."

"There was nothing you could have done," she said as she leaned back and wiped her eyes. "In order to end all of this, you had to do what you did."

"There might have been another way."

She put a finger to his lips. "It's all right."

He kissed her finger then rose to his feet and held out his hand to assist her. Aimery walked toward them, a cloak over his arm.

"We'll make sure he has a proper burial befitting someone who gave their life for love," Aimery said. He pulled Val's halberd from Dane's chest and tossed the cloak over Dane's nude body.

No sooner had the cloak touched Dane's body, then he disappeared along with the cloak.

"Thank you," Aimery said as he turned to Val and Gabriel. "You both did well. The spell has been broken, and we can now take Nicole to the safety of Stone Crest."

Val sighed in relief, but he noted Gabriel acting strangely. "Gabriel? Everything all right?"

"Everything is fine," Gabriel said and turned to Esmee as she walked up.

"You did well," Val said and wrapped an arm around Nicole. "Let's get out of here."

All four moved to follow Aimery, only to stop after a few steps when an old man blocked their way.

Val moved his hand to the hilt of his sword the same time Gabriel reached for an arrow, but Aimery's raised hand stopped them.

"You're free now," he said to the old man.

The old man shook his head, his long, white hair moving slightly with the motion. "I'll never be free."

And then, before their eyes, the old man's age began to diminish until the man standing before them was a young, vibrant man.

"The spell is broken," Aimery said with a grin. "The evil is gone from this place."

"He's left his mark here, Aimery," the man said softly, though great authority carried in his voice. "That'll never go away. I may once again have my youth, but the horrors will forever plague me."

"I'll have one of my men stationed here."

The man nodded and turned on his heel.

"Who was that?" Gabriel asked.

Aimery looked over his shoulder at them. "The laird."

"I always wondered what he looked like," Esmee said, her eyes following him. She smiled and turned to the group. "Your journey continues, but mine stops here."

"Thank you for everything," Val said.

Esmee smiled and moved toward Gabriel. She stood on tiptoe and kissed his cheek. For long moments, she stared into Gabriel's silver eyes before she turned to Nicole. "I'm sorry for the way you were treated before."

Nicole smiled and took Esmee's hands in hers. "You've more than made up for all of it. I'm just sorry that the village has turned out this way."

Esmee shrugged. "With the laird once again himself, I think the village will revert back to what it once was. Good luck to all of you," she said and walked away.

Val looked at Gabriel. "Are you sorry to see her go?"

Gabriel grinned. "I confess, I'd have liked to have one night with her, but duty calls."

Val wasn't fooled by Gabriel's cheerful tone. There was something in his friend's silver gaze that was troubled.

What it was Val had no idea.

He took Nicole's hand and pulled her to a stop as Aimery and Gabriel walked on. When her violet eyes turned to him and he saw the questions swirling there, he found himself nervous. He didn't know how to bring up that he had heard what she said to her brother. Hearing that she loved him had broken through all the barriers he erected so long ago.

Val took a deep breath and faced her. "There is much I want to say."

"Then say whatever it is you'd like," she said and smiled brightly.

"There are many horrors in my past, things I don't know if I'll ever be able to leave behind."

"If you mean your sisters' deaths, I know," Nicole said softly, the smile gone. "I overheard you telling Gabriel."

Val blinked and nearly sighed out loud. "I'm relieved. It took so much just to tell Gabriel that I didn't know if I'd be able to speak of it again. But I would have. For you."

A soft smile pulled at her full lips. "Really?"

"Aye. I may not deserve you, but I can't let you go. I've lost count of the many years I kept my heart guarded, but somehow you broke through and made me feel again."

"Say the words, Val. I need the words."

He chuckled as he pulled her into his arms and lowered his mouth to her lips. "I love you, Nicole."

"And I love you."

A chuckle sounded behind Val. "If you two are finished, can we now leave for Stone Crest?"

Val turned and found Gabriel behind him with his arms crossed and Aimery a few feet away with a big smile on his face.

"Are you ready?" Val asked Nicole.

"With you by my side? Always."

"Then let us go. I'm eager to see the rest of the Shields," he said to Aimery. He leaned down and whispered in Nicole's ear, "Not to mention a nice bedchamber with some quiet time for us."

She laughed and smiled up at him just as Aimery opened the portal.

EPILOGUE

"You can open your eyes now."

Nicole sighed when she heard Val's voice in her ear. She had never traveled through time before, and was a bit worried, but Val assured her all would be well.

She slowly opened her eyes to find herself staring at a beautiful castle with a thick forest surrounding it. "Is this Stone Crest?"

"Aye," Aimery said as he moved to stand beside her. "This is where you'll stay until the evil is destroyed."

"And there are others like me here?"

Val wrapped an arm around her. "Aye, love."

Her heart warmed at his words. She was wondering how long it would take them to reach the castle when she spotted horses thundering at them.

"I think Hugh spotted us," Gabriel drawled from behind them.

Nicole stood back as six horses came to a stop before them. A large man with dark hair and kind brown eyes leapt off his horse and approached Val and Gabriel first. They clasped forearms and slapped each other on the back.

The other two men in turn approached Val and Gabriel welcoming them before the three men moved to stand beside the women on horseback.

Val took her hand and walked her before the couples. "Nicole, I'd like to present the leader of the Shields, Hugh, and his wife Mina."

She returned the couple's smiles before she looked at Val. These were his people, his family. And she was now a part of it all.

"You'll be happy here," he whispered.

"I know."

His brow furrowed. "You do?"

"Of course. You're here."

He let out a laugh and lifted her in his arms before he claimed her mouth in a hot, demanding kiss. It never entered Nicole's mind to be embarrassed that there were onlookers, because whenever she was in Val's arms, she forgot everything but him.

Gabriel folded his arms over his chest as Cole came to stand beside him. "Another of us has found happiness."

"You're next," Cole teased.

"Not me."

Cole swung his gaze from Val and Nicole with Laird trailing beside them and stared hard at Gabriel. "Why do you say that? You deserve happiness just like the rest of us did."

"Do I? How can you be so sure?"

"How can you not be?"

Gabriel shrugged, not willing to answer. The mood was light with the arrival of Nicole, another Chosen, and the fact that Val had found love. He wasn't going to dampen things for them.

But the time was approaching, and there was nothing he could do about it.

Read on for a preview of the next SHIELD romance from Donna Grant,
A Warrior's Heart...

CHAPTER ONE

England, 1123
Stone Crest Castle

If Jayna had known what she would become, she would have plunged the dagger into Gabriel's heart when she'd had the chance. That decision had cost her her soul.

And she paid for it every day.

She didn't like what she had become, but her mother had told her that in order to survive, one had to adjust. Jayna had certainly adjusted.

As she stared at the imposing mass of rocks that was Stone Crest Castle, she thought about the people within its thick walls. A shiver raced over her skin, but it wasn't due to the icy night air.

She had finally found Gabriel.

And it was time he paid for his crimes.

Jayna smiled with anticipation, her heart pounding with excitement. She'd waited so long for this moment that she almost couldn't believe it had arrived. Yet it had, and she was going to carry out all the ways she'd thought of to make Gabriel pay.

She pulled the hood of her cloak up to cover her head and face. Getting into the castle wasn't going to be easy, but she was certainly up to the challenge. After all, she had waited nearly an eternity to see the look on Gabriel's face when she confronted him.

"Gloating already?"

Jayna stiffened when the familiar wash of air moved around her. He might not have a form, but he was the most powerful being in any of the realms.

"I know I shouldn't," she answered as she kept her eyes on the castle.

A tsking sound came from behind her then a warmth enveloped her. "My dear, Jayna, did I teach you nothing?"

She smiled a true smile and breathed deeply. "You taught me to survive, and for that I owe you everything."

"Do you think I kept you alive just so you could mete out your revenge against Gabriel?"

For the first time in centuries, Jayna felt a gnawing sense of worry. "I assumed so, aye."

"That was part of it, my dear," he whispered in her ear. "Once I regain my form, I'm going to need a queen. Someone who knows how to rule with beauty, grace, and the iron fist of vengeance. In other words, Jayna, I need you."

Jayna didn't know what to say. For too many years all she had cared about was finding Gabriel and killing him. Never had she thought about a husband or family. It had always been about Gabriel.

As if reading her mind, he asked, "Just what had you planned on doing once you killed Gabriel?"

"I don't know. I've never thought about it."

"I think the time has come for you to think about many things. My mission is nearly complete. For the first time since time began, evil will dominate the realms. No longer will good triumph and evil be punished. It will be our time. Think about it."

And just as suddenly as he had appeared, he vanished. Jayna pushed aside his words. She needed to focus on Gabriel, on finding him and sinking her blade deep into his heart as he had done to her so very, very long ago.

A DARK GUARDIAN

The first book in the *Shield* series

Dear Reader,

Have you ever wanted to travel through time with weapons crafted by the Fae themselves? To experience adventure so thrilling and dangerous you don't know if you will live to see tomorrow? Now my men and I are faced with fighting creatures only thought to live in legend but which have been brought to Earth by evil bent on annihilating all the realms. That is my life – and I love it.

At least I did until I found myself staring into the angelic, innocent face of Lady Mina of Stone Crest. In all the time I have led the Shields I've trusted my instinct to keep us alive, yet now I don't know what to believe. Everything points to Mina as the evil summoning the creatures, but she proclaims her innocence.

I should be able to see through her lies, if she is indeed lying, but my attraction to her blinds me to even that. The last time I found myself so lured to a woman, it nearly cost me the lives of my men. I cannot allow that to happen again. I *won't* allow that to happen again.

Yet every time she looks at me, begging me with those blue-green eyes to believe her, I find myself sinking further under her spell. Her mouth is a temptation mortal men will never know and her love will either bring me the peace I thought I'd never find – or the death I've managed, thus far, to avoid.

Hugh the Righteous

A KIND OF MAGIC
The second book in the *Shield* series

Greetings Dear Reader,

I was born an immortal prince on the realm of Thales. I lived the life of grandeur, revered and respected, but my one true love was fighting. I was given a special gift in my battle abilities and soon became known as Thales' finest warrior. But all that changed the day my brother died and an evil descended upon my realm. With Thales on the verge of ruin, I bound myself to The Shields to protect the realms from the evil that ravages them. But I have a dark secret that I must atone for. Then and only then can I return to Thales and face my family. My special battle skills and my immortality help to keep my goals in front of me. They have always been clear...

Until Elle.

Elle makes me long for things I cannot have. Her innate goodness makes me want to grasp what she offers with both hands, but I know that we can never have what she seeks. Elle bears a mark that signals her one of a chosen few who were sent to Earth as infants. She and the others who bear the mark must be found and kept hidden from the ancient evil that seeks them, for they hold the key to the evil's ruination.

The only way to keep Elle safe is to keep her by my side, but can I resist the temptation to take her love?

Roderick of Thales

A DARK SEDUCTION

The third book in the Shield series

Dear Friend,

Most would give all they had to be raised in the Realm of the Fae. I had no choice. I was too young to remember anything of my own realm, save for snatches of memories no more than my imagination. But if it hadn't been for the Fae who found me wandering between realms after mine was destroyed, I would be dead now. It was the Fae who raised me and trained me in weaponry and battle skills until I became a warrior to be feared. When hat same evil that destroyed my realm threatened Earth and the Fae, I was the first to volunteer for the Shields

With my immortality the only link I have to my past, I take what comfort I can in he arms of women. I want nothing more than one night with them, one night to forget that I can't remember my family, one night to take what pleasure I can. It isn't until I find Shannon that I begin to think of more than just one night in her arms.

Shannon has been brought back in time from Chicago to 1244 England because the evil knows what she is – one of the Chosen. Somehow the evil has found the Chosen before the Shields. His plan is to kill Shannon, but I won't allow that. My duty is to protect her at all costs.

I've never known fear until now – until Shannon

Cole the Warrior

A WARRIOR'S HEART
The fifth book in the *Shield* series

Regards Reader,

There are those who would love to rid themselves of painful memories, to forget nasty pasts and mistakes. They say its hell to live with those memories. I say its hell to live without them. I have no memories of my past, my friends, or my family.

I owe my life to the Fae who discovered me bleeding and nearly dead at their doorway. They saved me and offered me a new life, regardless of my pat. So I've served the Fae and the Shields since that day. My special knowledge of herbs and healing has been needed to save the Shields countless times. They are my brethren, my family, yet I am alone.

No matter what I search or what questions I ask, I discover nothing to open a doorway in my mind of locked memories. Until I catch a glimpse of a woman who seems as familiar to me as breathing.

Jayna.

Though she claims to not know me, our bodies know each other. I agonize over what she keeps hidden in the depths of her haunted hazel eyes. I fear the dark thoughts that lurk in my heart and wonder at any black deeds in my past. If what I dread comes to pass, death won't come swift enough.

Above all, I must keep Jayna safe. She's the only one what has quieted my soul and shown me serenity.

Gabriel the Hollow

Thank you for reading **A Forbidden Temptation**. I hope you enjoyed it! If you liked this book — or any of my other releases — please consider rating the book at the online retailer of your choice. Your ratings and reviews help other readers find new favorites, and of course there is no better or more appreciated support for an author than word of mouth recommendations from happy readers. Thanks again for your interest in my books!

Donna Grant

www.DonnaGrant.com

**Never miss a new book
From Donna Grant!**

Sign up for Donna's email newsletter at
www.DonnaGrant.com

**Be the first to get notified of new releases and be
eligible for special subscribers-only exclusive content
and giveaways. Sign up today!**

ABOUT THE AUTHOR

New York Times and *USA Today* bestselling author Donna Grant has been praised for her "totally addictive" and "unique and sensual" stories. She's written more than thirty novels spanning multiple genres of romance including the bestselling Dark King stories, *Dark Craving, Night's Awakening*, and *Dawn's Desire* featuring immortal Highlanders who are dark, dangerous, and irresistible. She lives with her husband, two children, a dog, and four cats in Texas.

Connect online at:

www.DonnaGrant.com

www.facebook.com/AuthorDonnaGrant

www.twitter.com/donna_grant

www.goodreads.com/donna_grant/

CPSIA information can be obtained at www.ICGtesting.com
Printed in the USA
LVOW11s1037130616

492367LV00006B/218/P